TAKAKUSH

GENUS MAGICA BOOK ONE

RAINE REITER

To my father, who believed when I didn't.

———————

Special thanks:
Kitsap Writers Critique Group (Kristina, Jerry, Archie, Michelle, Paul, Carrie, Megan, Evan, Ira, Karel and others), Bremerton Writer's Meetup (Marie, Katie, Mason, Laura, Ferrel, Nikki and others), and Silverdale Writer's Round Table (Laura, Rebecca, Dave, and others).
To my editors (Paul Marquiz, Joel Bahr, and Amanda Rutter), cover designer (Kim Dingwall) and Lithuanian translator (Ruta Lojkaite).
Love and thanks to my family (especially Mom, Midge, Eileen, Cheryl Jean, and the late Francis Frasier) and friends (Kate, Gail, Penny, Shana, Mary, Sarah and others).

———————

Lastly, to the memory of the late Steve Tobias. I'm sorry you never wrote your books.

DAY ZERO

MEDŽIOKLĖ

CHAPTER ONE

REGANA - HOME

Regana stood between the two worlds, watching her sleeping body. *When did I become so old?*

The wrinkled face, spun-sugar mop, and gnarled fingers in Real-Time bore little resemblance to her divine avatar in the Penumbra. *Marks of time mean nothing.* She chuckled.

Lithe and nimble as a sprite, Regana kicked off from the boundary and floated through the *between*, sorting threads of possibility as she passed.

"Goddess of the Crossroads, why draw me here?" She waited for an answer.

Thick fibers of probability whirled and pulsed with light around her, while others faded into implausibility and blinked out.

Soon, her temper frayed. Braiding destinies and untangling misfortunes amused Regana, but her fatigued human body in Real-Time called for rest. "Show me the blasted job and let me get out," Regana said. "Lady of thresholds, doors, and portals, your priestess readies to serve you." Her cry echoed through the Penumbra. "What must I do?"

A scarlet rope, thick as an anaconda, whipped out

of the tangle and garroted her waist. Hot, near burning, it reeked of dark magic and death.

"See." The voice hit her like a hammer, and a kaleidoscope of images overwhelmed her mind's eye. "Be present," ordered her goddess.

GALAHAD - MCCLEARY, WA

Across the field, wind stirred the chimes, bells, and bamboo noisemakers hanging from the eaves of the main house.

Galahad dozed in the pasture with an ancient horse blanket covering him.

Frost on the grass and pasture fence resembled snowfall. A freezing fog surged along the paddock, encircling his legs.

He woke. Something was different, unfamiliar. It wasn't fear, it was curiosity.

With drowsy eyes, he surveyed the tree line. His nostrils flared, sampling the air. *There.* Hiding beneath the aroma of evergreens, a sickly-sweet stench. A predator.

The old warrior's heart sped as he readied for a fight. At sixteen hands, he was massive and courageous. Last spring, he ran off a pack of coyotes come to snatch a newborn kid.

Galahad snorted and shook his mane. The frigid air transformed his breath into plumes of steam. He pawed the earth, kicking up divots of soil.

The wind ceased. The chimes quieted.

It struck Galahad, mounting him from behind and wrapping its limbs around Galahad's belly. The horse arched his back as incisors sank into his neck.

Claws raked his abdomen and up his flanks, scoring slashes through the blanket into his hide. The metallic tang of his blood joined the beast's stench.

Galahad's hind legs kicked into his attacker's midsection, but it only embedded its fangs deeper. Blood spurted from the wound.

The embrace tightened. He bucked, rearing and struggling for footing. The attacker threw Galahad to the ground and remounted.

The stallion screamed.

Teeth ripped flesh from Galahad's throat, severing his jugular. His sight darkened, and his blood melted the frosted grass. Passing through and away, the horse saw the blackness clinging to his murderer.

The malignant thread released, and Regana's vision ended. In the mundane world, her eyelids flew open, her heart hammering in her chest.

"Blood-red magic rings the waxing moon." Her voice croaked with the remains of sleep. "Medžioklė begins."

ANIMAL ATTACK KILLS LIVESTOCK NEAR STATE CAPITOL

McCleary, Wash. (AP)-Washington Department of Fish and Wildlife officials reported a twelve-year-old horse was killed by an unknown predator.

Sgt. Odin (Boone) Anderson confirmed the injuries were consistent with a bear or cougar attack. Until they capture the animal, he recommends residents exercise care with children, family pets, and livestock.

The officer said animal attacks near Olympia, the state capitol, are rare.

DAY ONE

WEDNESDAY

CHAPTER TWO

BOONE - OUTSIDE MCCLEARY

Trees creaked in a light wind, and a distant raven cawed.

Sergeant Boone Anderson of the Washington Department of Fish and Wildlife took each step with care. A broken twig might announce his presence. The dog at his side halted at his gesture, and the man squatted, inspecting the earth.

The trail spoke to him. *Short claw marks, so not a cougar.* Boone stuck his shades into the neck of his shirt. He pushed back his ball cap and leaned into the prints.

A black bear's arc and toe separation, so not a grizzly. Of course, that's unlikely.

He discovered scat a mile back, confirming the animal's normal diet: roots, berries, and insects. But there was considerable meat, likely small wildlife, garbage, or missing family pets.

Somebody's gonna shoot this boy if we don't relocate him today. Boone checked the Casio Pathfinder on his wrist. *Rain stopped before daybreak. These tracks are a few hours old.*

The black and white dog's gaze riveted on his master, awaiting a signal.

"You love this, don't ya, buddy?" Boone grinned and patted the dog's head. "You ready to get us a bear, Ohto?"

The Karelian Bear Dog's broad, pointed ears perked, and a quiver ran through his compact body.

Boone adjusted his armored vest. With marijuana legalized, he didn't bust criminal growers anymore and seldom needed body armor.

Beads of sweat cascaded down his spine. *I shouldn't have worn this thing.* Boone shrugged his shoulders. *It's not worth the risk. Those trainees are great kids but inexperienced and armed.*

For the fifth time this morning, Boone reviewed his plan. *First, locate the bear, corral it, and drive it to the capture team. Dan darts him, and the trainees load the animal for transport. Easy.*

With a pat, he checked the Remington 700P slung over his shoulder. "I guess we're fixed."

Boone made eye contact with his dog. An unspoken command passed between them, and they crept forward. Ohto strained to the limit of the leash tethered at Boone's waist.

That bear's been spotted ranging these woods and the subdivision. "That guy is here somewhere." He glanced at Ohto.

At the base of a giant cedar, Ohto stood at attention. The tip of his curved tail brushed his back. His snout sniffed the air. He whimpered. *The quarry is near.*

Boone and Ohto slipped through a gap in the underbrush, reaching an alley bordering the subdivision's back fence.

They froze.

A hundred yards down the bank, a black bear snuffled around some garbage cans. He swatted a bin with his paw. It rattled and teetered but didn't topple.

Boone whispered into the radio. "Doc, prepare for

a patient: two years old, four-foot-long, and maybe ninety kilos."

"Check that," squawked the receiver.

Downwind and undetected, Boone and Ohto crept into range. He aimed and fired.

The rubber bullet *spanked* the bear in the butt. He recoiled, overturning the trash can.

"Get him, boy." He triggered the leash's release, and Ohto bolted, sprinting along the fence line with Boone following.

Near the end of the barrier, Ohto sped ahead and passed the intruder, cutting him off. The animal skidded to a halt, confused. With a lunge, the dog nipped at the bear's behind, then jumped out of range.

The bruin whirled to his flank and struck out with three-inch claws. He missed. Ohto circled for the next assault.

A snap of the dog's jaws pinched his thigh, bringing the bear around a quarter turn. Another sneak attack rotated the creature off right, toward the service road. Tiring of the game, the bear bolted.

"Our new friend is on his way," Boone rasped into his walkie. "ETA two minutes."

Boone and Ohto harried the animal toward the waiting team. They reached the clearing. Without instruction, Ohto raced ahead once more. Barking and circling, he kept the animal in place.

Fearful, the bear puffed and clacked his teeth. His vision remained fixed on the dog, preparing for the next attack.

Dan Sitton, the forty-year-old wildlife veterinarian, stood near his pickup with the two trainees fanned out, Tanika Hudson to the left, and Manuel Mendoza to the right. Boone caught the doctor's eye.

Okay, doc. Aim and fire. Boone nodded.

Pffft. A dart shot out of the barrel of the Pneu-Dart G2 X-Caliber rifle. It embedded in the bear's hindquarters. His roar reverberated through the meadow.

The animal growled, took a couple shuddering steps, stumbled, and collapsed on his side. An intense spasm ran the length of his body, but the next was gentler, until he relaxed into sleep.

Ohto watched the bear for signs of aggression. With a slap to his leg, Boone called the dog to him.

"Clean shot, doc."

"So, I'm almost as good as you, Anderson?"

"I wouldn't go that far," Boone smiled.

The doctor knelt, checking the bear's vital signs.

Fist raised, Boone put Ohto in a sit/stay, and the dog dropped to his rump.

"You need help there?" He sauntered to the vet.

"I never say no," said Doc Sitton.

The two men repositioned the animal and straightened his limbs.

Hudson offered the carry sack. Boone took it from her shaking hands.

"Is this your first relocation, officer?"

"Yes, sir. This is the closest I've ever been to a live bear." The petite brunette spread a tarp parallel to the body and adjusted the carry-handles at each corner.

"He's stable," the vet said. "Let's move him to the trailer."

Boone nodded, and the trainees assumed their places, and in one motion, rolled the bear onto the canvas.

"A single man can lift a two to three-hundred-pound dead weight using a pulley," Boone instructed. "But, today, we do it the old-fashioned way. Everyone grabs a corner. Ready? Lift."

Pallbearer style, the team carried the bear to an aluminum tunnel mounted on a trailer.

Dan Sitton gave the young bear's butt an affectionate pat. "Better cut back on the grub, fatty. Open the trap, Officer Mendoza." Dr. Sitton gestured with a nod of his head.

"Yes, sir." Still holding his end of the tarp, the trainee fumbled with the catch until the door sprang open with a *clank*.

Boone nodded to his team. "On the count of three: one, two, three."

As they practiced in training, the bear slipped into the culvert trap.

The doctor leaned in for another vitals check. "He's tolerating the meds well."

Through the mesh, Boone watched the bear's breathing. His chest rising and falling at a steady pace.

"How did this bear end up around here?" the female trainee, Tanika Hudson, asked.

"This yearling is fresh out of his mother's den," said the vet. "He probably struck out on his own recently and is looking for territory."

"As a rule, I prefer luring an animal into the trap," Boone said, "but there was no time. He was so close to all those families." Sympathy for the large animal tugged at Boone. "And if he becomes tame, he's another dead bear."

"Where are we moving him, sir?" asked Hudson.

"Not far. A lengthy trip runs the risk of complications," Boone said.

Hudson nodded, noting every word and action.

"Capture myopathy." Mendoza puffed out his chest. "Don't want a fatal buildup of lactic acid." He smirked. "This is my third, you know."

The vet rolled his eyes, then turned back to his patient.

"The Mount Olympia Forest Reserve will make a good home for our boy," Boone said.

"Please, bring my medical bag, officer," the doctor said.

Hudson raced off. Minutes later, she returned with the med-kit.

Dr Sitton administered injections of cortisone, muscle relaxants, and saline.

"Let's get on the road, people." Boone pitched the carry bag to Mendoza, who caught it with one hand.

"You two ride with the doc," he said.

"Sure thing, sarge," said Hudson, her smile bright and confident.

"Great job out there, guys." Boone winked.

"Thanks," Mendoza said, a smile covering his broad face.

"Let's be off, young'uns," said Sitton from the cab of his vehicle, motor running.

Mendoza and Hudson sprinted to the truck, and moments later, it disappeared down the road.

A few feet away, Ohto focused on a raven watching from a high branch.

Boone opened the driver's side door and whistled. The dog's ears swiveled, but he refused to come, still fixated on the bird.

At the second whistle, Ohto turned. With two elongated strides, he pushed off from his haunches into a ten-foot leap. The cab rocked as the dog landed in the front seat.

"Show off."

The dog greeted his partner with a lazy grin. His pink tongue lolled out of the side of his mouth.

Boone hid his smile as he slid behind the wheel and started the engine.

VARNAS - CAPITOL FOREST WEST

The raven, Varnas, contemplated shadowing the man and his wolf. He cawed and hopped along the branch.

No. No. Later. Later. My lady's vessel comes. Serve. Protect. Varnas ruffled his feathers.

Last night, he sensed forging sorcery nearby. It

smelt of dark magic with a tang of blood. He made a quick reconnaissance, but the source remained elusive. Disappointed, he roosted for the night and renewed his powers.

Before dawn, the raven returned to his survey of the wilderness but failed to pinpoint the discordance.

As the sun peeked over the horizon, something captured his interest. This man had magic. He read the land and became one with his wolf. Their capture of Lokiukas, the forest prince, had been entertaining.

No dark magic there.

With a two-footed hop, Varnas took flight. His legs pumped in opposition to his wings. Oily feathers gleamed in the rising sun, and he defied gravity with each beat.

Varnas turned into the wind; catching a thermal he set out to circle the mountain. Slow flaps alternated with great expanses of soaring and gliding. Like a hawk seeking prey, the bird's eyes searched the land for magic sign.

Scout, guardian, and messenger, Varnas served twenty generations of priestesses and would serve twenty more before he earned rest and reward.

Huge. Varnas' wingspan reached five-feet. The Salish recognized him as the trickster, and other cultures a herald or omen. But he was Varnas, the pranašas, the familiar servant and protector to the lady Mediena and her vessel.

Men had denuded swatches of Larch Mountain, but hundred-year-old cedar and fir covered most of the Capitol Forest, many trees with a diameter of two to three feet.

From above, the thick canopy hid many secrets, but not from the sharp eyes of Varnas.

On his second pass, a distinctive warp in the land's aura caught his eye. Wings tucked to his sides, he dove headfirst toward the ground, achieving a hundred miles per hour.

Fff-woop. Varnas extended his wings, transitioning into a smooth, downward spiral.

His strong claws outstretched, he lowered his fan-shaped tail and touched down in a twenty-foot clearing.

Skeletal saplings, silent witnesses to clear-cut and wildfire, haunted this place, and a fine gray ash smothered any fresh life. A miasma rolled along the ground and hung in the trees. Humans couldn't see it. Varnas could.

This place is fertile ground for evil.

Charred logs and long dead cinders hunkered at the center of the clearing. An after-shadow of the ritual circled the fire pit but was faint and unreadable. Using his beak, Varnas searched among the ashes, uncovering a few shards of bone but nothing more.

Prruk-prruk-prruk. The pranašas furled his neck feathers and stomped his feet.

I must warn my mistress of the blood magic. How? How? The vessel's thought bond remains incomplete, and the goddess can only reach her with ceremony.

The bird shook and settled his feathers. *No, no, no. Nothing to do now, Varnas. Look. Wait.*

He took wing to higher ground on a scrub fir's limb and waited for the wind to change.

Mediena, my deivė leads her vessel home. Prepare the way.

Anticipating the airstream, Varnas launched. Like sails, the current filled his wings, and he rose. The bird wheeled into the dawn to his rendezvous with the human he protected.

CHAPTER THREE

ELENA - SWAN HOUSE

Only the idle of Elena's MINI Cooper disturbed the sleeping street. She rolled down the drive and parked in front of a three-story Victorian.

Out front, a sign read 'Swan House Inn and Retreat.' To Elena Lukas, this was home.

Ornate gingerbread, balusters, and spandrels decorate the eaves, gables, and a covered veranda wrapping around two-thirds of the main floor.

No lights blazed in the bay windows or the turret where her young sister slept.

No one's up. She relaxed into the bucket seat.

Her weeklong journey across the country kept Elena distracted. Now at her destination, a backdraft of memories assaulted her tired mind.

Only three weeks ago.

Like body blows, one image after another struck Elena. Colin standing in the dormer, hands clasped behind his back. Him pulling away from her touch. His mid-Atlantic accent, flat and emotionless. "I'm leaving." A slamming door, silence, and her collapsing into their empty bed.

"Stop." Her fist slammed the wheel.

I left Boston, my friends, and the job I loved to escape this stupid thinking. She tamped her threatening tears.

"No more crying, dammit. Three thousand miles is far enough," she said, forcing a smile. Her keys dropped into the burgundy handbag on the passenger seat. "I'm ready to face them," she said, but her voice sounded uncertain. *Am I?*

Elena gripped on the door handle.

A girl of fifteen burst through the French doors, all long, tanned legs and arms. After a momentary pause on the veranda, she bolted down the steps.

"You're here," she said. "I can't believe it."

The teen wrenched open the driver's side door and threw herself on her sister.

Words exploded in a torrent. "I miss you so much, sis. Mama's impossible. School is a nightmare. And-"

"Take a breath, Gabby. You don't need to tell me everything at once."

"But I do. I'm bursting like a grocery store piñata." Gabby's green eyes glinted with tears.

"Kiddo, we have two weeks before my new job starts. We'll talk every moment of every day until the quarter begins." Elena brushed back her sister's ginger hair and lifted her chin. "I want to hear about the boys you like, and the classes you hate. Everything."

Gabby wrapped her arms around Elena's neck, laying her head on her older sister's shoulder.

Elena whispered, "Please, get me a cup of coffee first?"

She detached Gabby and gave her a nudge toward the car door. Gabby scrambled off her sister's lap.

Elena released the seat belt, and it retracted. "I'll pop the trunk, and you grab my overnight bag." Elena unfolded her long slender frame from the small automobile and stretched. The house looked great. "I like the green trim. It goes well with the white. Very elegant."

"They call it 'Colonial White,'" the girl said in mock seriousness. "And we had the driveway repaved, too." Her gesture resembled a courtier's bow.

Elena's brows knitted. *That's a huge expense for a troubled business.* "Gabs, how many guests do we have?"

"We have reservations for the weekend. Mama says it better pick up by this summer."

What the hell? Elena stared at her luggage spread out across the driveway and forced her tight shoulders to relax.

Gabby pulled another bag from the trunk and sat it with the others.

"Just grab the small flowered one, kid. I'll come back for the rest later." Elena, shaking her head, turned toward Swan House.

"Mediena, welcome home." A thick Baltic accent floated through the morning air. On the porch, a tiny woman waited. Dressed in black capris, an oversized striped tee, and ballet flats, a Parisian elegance surrounded her.

With a hand shielding her eye, Elena squinted against the rising sun. "Hello, Mama. I'm glad to be here." Any remaining ambivalence dissolved as she climbed the steps.

Mina Lukas stood on tiptoe and kissed her daughter on both cheeks. "You are welcome to this house, Deivė Mediena," she said in Lithuanian.

The woman's trim figure and pixie cut lent her a youthfulness, and only the hint of crow's feet implied her true age.

"Not Mediena, please. I haven't committed to serve her, so my name remains Elena," she said, her eyes averted.

"As you wish." A Mona Lisa aspect settled on her mother's face.

Arm-in-arm, they passed through the doors into

the entry.

A creamy damask papered the foyer walls, and an oriental runner added warmth and a touch of sound-proofing to the mahogany floor.

Mina's eyes twinkled as she watched her younger daughter dragged Elena's bags, four at once, up the stairs, bumping along the way.

Elena lifted her head. "Gabs, I'm staying in the carriage house. Please leave everything here." Her thumb and index finger pinched the bridge of her nose.

"Okay, okay." Gabby wiped moisture from her freckled forehead.

"Your grandmother is waiting for you, *Elena*." Mina gave her name extra emphasis.

"Um huh," Elena said. *I'm not ready for any of Nana Regana's drama.*

"Coffee first, yes?" Her mother gestured toward the dining room. "You must tell us about your trip."

A long mahogany bench seat ran the length of a bank of conservatory windows. A formal buffet bordered the back wall. One grand and several small tables waited for patrons to gather.

Elena crossed to the sideboard, picked up two cups and saucers, and carried them over to a marble tabletop balanced on heavy spindled legs of dark mahogany. At the center, a cream pitcher and sugar bowl in a matching china pattern lay on an inlaid wooden tray.

Elena took a deep breath, drawing in the aroma of cinnamon, clove, and furniture polish. *I love this room.* She sighed and smiled.

"Will you grab the coffee pot, Gabs?" she said.

Gabby grabbed a glass cafetiere off the buffet and thrust the plunger, expressing the coffee. The girl sniffed. "It smells nice but tastes yucky." She wrinkled her nose. "Tea is trending. Coffee is so over."

Mina smiled but said nothing.

"Bring it over here?" Elena said. "I need caffeine, stat."

"I'm coming, Professor Bossy Pants."

The carafe hit the table with a thump. Glaring, Gabby returned to her tea bag scavenger hunt.

Elena shrugged to her mother, who shook her head.

Mina picked up the pot and tipped it. The rich black beverage poured from the spout until it reached the rim. She handed it to her older daughter.

Elena took a drink, swallowed, and sighed.

Her mother patted her hand.

Gabby joined them at the table, taking the chair opposite her sister. Cellophane crinkling, she unwrapped a lavender package with Organic Licorice printed on it, then dunked the teabag in the hand-thrown mug she brought with her.

Watching her sister, a reassuring sense of home filled Elena. The smell of lavender sachets and crisp Egyptian cotton sheets fresh from the clothesline danced in her thoughts.

"I am so knackered," Elena said.

"I can help," Gabby said, peering through the lashes of her lowered lids. "I could take your bags to the guesthouse for you. But I'd have to... um... drive your car?" The girl glanced at her sister, then to her mug of tea.

"Maybe," Elena elongated each syllable.

Gabby slumped into the opposite chair, dumped too many spoons of sugar in her drink, and gave it a brutal stir.

After an uncomfortable pause, Elena tossed the keys to Gabby.

"Be gentle with my baby."

A grin flowered on Gabby's face, and she raised her right-hand Scout fashion. "I pr—"

"Silence, Gabija," a gravelly voice spoke from the shadow of the butler's pantry.

Startled, Elena and Mina turned.

"Grandmother?" said Elena. *This can't be. Grand-mother Regana never leaves her room downstairs.*

"Mediena. Come. Tai prasideda."

MINA - SWAN HOUSE

While Elena held an audience with her grandmother, Mina retired to her office to get some work done. Opening the laptop, she checked the Swan House email account for any bookings. There was one overnight reservation for the end of the month, three general inquiries, and an advertisement for herbal Viagra, but nothing else. A colorful desk calendar sat on the blotter.

Although Mina was not sentimental, she'd chosen it herself. Each month featured an architectural wonder of Europe: the Powder Tower of Prague, Budapest's Fisherman's Bastion, and the Hofburg Palace in Vienna. Once she'd lived in each of these cities and witnessed many of those magnificent structures' construction.

May showed the historic central district of Kraków, Poland. She smiled at a childhood memory, strolling the fabric market at first light holding her mother's hand.

Mina shook her head, drawing herself back into the present, then glided her finger along the days of the week.

Today, she planned to man the children's ward book trolley. She taught yoga at the senior center on Thursday morning, then served lunch at the homeless shelter in the afternoon.

Mina quickly transferred the appointments to her phone's calendar. When she finished, she said, "I'm not too busy."

Mina set aside her calendar and tackled her stack of bills.

CHAPTER FOUR

GABBY - SWAN HOUSE DRIVEWAY

Gabby revved the motor, inching forward. The clutch ground as she rode it down the drive. She killed the engine twice and only nudged the garage door before slamming on the brakes.

The MINI sputtered and died. *Perfect. This moment belongs on my timeline.*

Gabby took a barrage of selfies and uploaded the best six to Instagram. "Next stop, the DMV and that learner's permit," read the caption. Within two minutes, her posting racked up thirty-two likes and six comments.

The MINI's old. Elena needs a new car. She opened the trunk and removed the first two suitcases. *On my sixteenth birthday, I can have it, and I'll drive cute guys to school every day.*

Gabby future-tripped through each scenario until she'd carried every suitcase up the steep staircase to the chauffeur's quarters.

A jumble of luggage littered the bedroom's Jacobean floral carpet. *I'm sorry about Elena's wedding and all, but there is no way I'll end up living in this dump when I'm a grownup.* Gabby thrust her jaw forward. *No matter what.*

The carriage clock in the living room chimed.

I'm gonna live somewhere foreign and exotic like Morocco or California. No serving the goddess of home and hearth crap for this girl.

Another chime.

Gabby froze. "Yikes, school."

She scampered out the door. The locked door closed with a slam, and she thundered down the stairs. On the breezeway leading back to the main house, she ignored the daffodils, tulips, and blossoming cherry trees lining the walk.

Reaching the kitchen door, she heard it.

Myak. Mmmm-yak.

Fists on hips, Gabby scanned the yard attempting to triangulate on the sound. "Hello? Is someone there?"

Meee-row.

She tipped her head as far back as it could go without toppling backward. *What is in that tree?*

A budding silver maple dominated this plot of lawn. Dew on each blade of grass sparkled, dampening her high-tops.

Rrrr-Row.

Gabby's gaze traveled up the lichen-covered trunk. An enormous black cat perched in the spring foliage.

"Who are you? Here, kitty, kitty," Gabby said. "Come down."

The feline studied her. With a flick of its tail, it sprang and landed at her feet.

"Very impressive, handsome." She clapped her hands.

It rubbed its flank against her leg.

"What is your name? Where is your collar?"

The animal craned its neck until its nose touched her outstretched hand.

"Are you lost?"

The cat's purr increased several decibels.

"Where do you live?" Her hand slid along his back until, reaching the base of the tail, she scratched.

He arched his back to meet her.

"Do you have a home, kitty?"

Sphinx-like, the cat studied the her.

"I'll bet you'd like to live with me. Wouldn't you?"

Prrrt. Prrrt. The cat rubbed against her leg twice, spun, and strutted to the house.

ELENA - SWAN HOUSE

Elena reached the landing and called out, "I survived my ordeal." She checked around the corner to the parlor and across to the dining room. They were empty.

"Hello? Hel-lo? Where is everybody?"

"Back here," called Mina.

Her mother's voice drifted down the hall. Elena followed it and arrived at the bright morning room her mother used as an office.

Through the casement, a ray of sunlight struck Mina's white bobbed hair, creating a halo around her timeless face.

Elena's breath caught. *She's a Renaissance angel.* A transiting cloud obscured the sun, and Mina's halo faded.

"That is quite a stack of bills you have there," Elena said.

"It's been a difficult year," Mina said. "Last summer, I paid for the new roof, painted the exterior, and refinished the dining room floors."

"It looks very nice," Elena said. "And I'm guessing it's a good investment."

"It would have been, but then the state mandated we do asbestos removal. It took all my reserves. There has always been a delicate balance between staying afloat and going out of business."

Mina rubbed her eyes with her fingertips. "If the business remains soft, this may be a difficult year."

She sliced through the electric bill's envelope with her mother-of-pearl letter opener, unfolded the contents, and frowned at the payment due.

"I've paid the home insurance, internet, and water bills. The rest of these can wait." She added the light bill back into her *pay later* pile.

Elena sat in the guest chair at the side of the desk. "Do you need some help, Mama? I'm not rich, but I've put something aside."

"That is very generous, honey, but I have a few tricks in mind."

"You've got my attention now." Elena leaned forward.

"Have you ever watched the Travel Channel's *Shrewd Traveler with Tobias Stephens*?"

"The patrician guy with the attitude?" She wrinkled her nose.

"That's the one," Mina said. "On a whim, I registered the bed-and-breakfast with his website. I doubted Swan House would garner his attention. Olympia is not a popular travel destination. I was wrong." She opened the desk drawer, took out a letter, and held it up to Elena. "*The Shrewd Traveler* himself arrives later this week."

Elena took *The Shrewd Traveler Production's* letter and read it aloud.

"It is with great pleasure we inform you the Swan House was selected by Mr Tobias Stephens. Swan House will host his party during his upcoming junket to the Pacific Northwest," she read. "After his visit, Mr Stephens will review your establishment on shrewdtravel.com and share his thoughts with his two-million social media followers. A few locations may be chosen for filming and broadcast on The Travel Channel's *The Shrewd Traveler*.

His team arrives-"

Elena stopped reading. "This is major."

"A favorable review will bring in customers. He is very popular. But an unfavorable one- well, that isn't worth considering," Mina said. "I suspect he will be a challenging guest. Read the last paragraph." She dropped her gaze to the words on the page.

"Mr Stephens is allergic to dust, pollens, mildew, and animal dander. Please, launder linens with hypo-allergenic detergents. Surfaces and floor must be-" Elena whistled. "Yikes. I see what you mean." She handed the letter back to her mother.

"The kid off to school?" Elena asked.

"Yes, reluctantly," Mina said. "I meant to ask, how was your audience with your Nana? Why so urgent?"

"To be honest, I'm still not clear. Nana's message was cryptic and rambling. So, the usual."

The pencil dropped from Mina's fingers and rolled onto the floor. "She's ancient, and her time drifts."

"I'm sorry?" Elena picked up the implement and sat it on the desk.

"Nothing. What did your grandmother tell you?" Mina asked.

Elena mimicked her grandmother's cadence while waggling her index finger. "He is hungry as a cuckoo in another bird's nest." She shifted her weight in the wooden chair. "Most of the time, she refused to speak English, and my Lithuanian is very rusty, so it's diffi-cult to know for sure."

"She's been teaching our language to Gabija," said her mother. "I thought her rejection of English was part of the lessons, now I believe she's forgetting how to speak it."

Mina shuffled the bills into a tidy pile, set them aside, and opened an old-fashioned accounting jour-nal. "She's served the goddess of fate for too long. To your grandmother, the past, present, and future merge."

"Serving any goddess is a difficult path," Elena said. "I thought when I decided to marry Colin, I wouldn't have to face any of this. Now, I'm not sure what to do."

"True. Our way has benefits but also costs. You must take your time before you decide." Mina lowered her eyes. "So, it is certain. There will be no marriage?"

Elena touched the engagement ring on her finger. "I'm still wearing the ring, I don't know why. In my heart, I know it's over, at least on his side."

"I am glad to have you home, but not if it costs your happiness."

Elena's smile didn't show in her eyes. "I'm okay. Taking one step at a time."

Mina picked up the pencil and placed it alongside the ledger on the desk. "Your grandmother spends too much time in the Penumbra sorting futures. It's a chore to make her surface for meals and the other needs of her body." Mina leaned her chin on her palm and closed her eyes. "Any time now, Gabby's illumination begins, and we won't understand her gifts until they manifest."

"She's an emotional spirit," Elena said. "Gaining control of her talents will not be easy for her. Or for you."

Mina opened the book and made a notation in it. The scratching of her pencil on paper hung between them until Elena cleared her throat.

"I'm going up to the Capitol Forest," Elena said. "Nana gave me quite a list of plants to gather and made me promise to go today. She said the timing's important for the ritual."

Mina frowned. "You've only arrived and should rest before she sends you on her quest. Her deivė is selfish and cruel."

"It's all right. I'm getting my second wind." She shrugged her shoulders. "As Regana always tells us, we can sleep when we're dead."

"Who's dead?" Gabby stood in the doorway holding the largest black cat they'd ever seen.

BOONE — CAPITOL FOREST WEST

Two Department of Fish and Wildlife trucks bounced up a dirt road. They rattled and shook to the top of the rise, then coasted into the meadow.

The doctor slid out the driver's side, followed by the trainees. "This is an excellent home for him," he said. He extended his arms and rolled his shoulders.

From the second vehicle, Ohto leapt out behind Boone and ran to meet the vet by the trailer.

"Gather around, folks," Boone said. Mendoza and Hudson turned to face him. "When you choose a place to release, always make sure there is shelter, like these woods back here. Plenty to eat and drink. The department's released here before, and the animals stuck around," he told the trainees, then addressed Dr Sitton. "Will your patient be awake soon, doc?"

The wildlife vet opened the gate. "He's rousing."

Through drooping eyelids, the bear scrutinized the vet, but he didn't move.

The trainee officers leaned in, examining their captive.

"You're doing just fine, kid." Dan administered the reversal shot to the bear, scratched his ears, and withdrew from the trap.

Hudson secured the gate.

The two rookies hung back. Boone called, "Everyone understand what to do?"

They stood at attention, nodding.

"One more time from the top," Boone said. "Doc Sitton pulls the release. Manny, what do you do?"

"I'm the bullhorn and fireworks guy," said Mendoza, the husky officer with the crew cut.

"Tanika?"

"I have the rifle in case the mission goes sideways."

"What aren't you doing?" Boone winked.

"I will not shoot you or Ohto, sergeant," she grinned.

"Sounds like everyone's got it," he said.

They nodded.

"Doc, how long until your patient's fixed to move into his new home?" asked Boone.

"A half hour, maybe less." The vet pushed back his cuff and checked his watch. "High noon?"

"Take a break," Boone said. "There's a thermos of coffee and stale doughnuts in my pickup."

For twenty minutes, the bear moaned and worried the door.

"He's ready," said the vet.

"Everyone in place?" Boone caught each trainees' eyes. "Stay sharp."

The other two shared a nervous glance.

"Let's do this." At Boone's nod, the hatch sprang open.

But nothing happened.

"Looks like he needs a bit of encouragement, doc," Boone said.

The vet hammered on the conduit. "Okay, free-loader, you're evicted."

The bear erupted from the culvert like a clown shot from a cannon. He didn't stop. He didn't look back. With the bullhorn blaring and firecrackers exploding, the creature ran like the demons of Hell were on his tail.

The beast reached the tree line.

"Tell him to get, Ohto," Said Boone.

Unhooked, the dog loped away, and Boone followed.

The thick canopy above swathed the trail in darkness.

Boone's pupils constricted. Wearing dark glasses, he was near blind. He snatched off his shades and leaped over a fallen log, snagging his uniform on the underbrush. Dog and bear disappeared, their bellowing and baying fading.

When he could no longer hear the pursuit, he thought, *This is deep enough.*

"Our bird has flown," Boone told the radio. "We're heading back." It squawked an unintelligible response.

He whistled. No crashing brush signaled the dog's return. Boone whistled again. Nothing. Ohto's bark greeted the third whistle.

Curved tail wagging, the black and white dog galloped up to Boone, twirling and prancing.

"Pretty proud of yourself, eh, fella?"

Ohto dropped into a sit.

"I guess you've done a good job today," Boone told his dog. He pulled a treat from his flak vest pocket and tossed it.

Ohto caught it with a crunch.

"Let's head back." Boone smacked his thigh, and the dog fell into line. The celebration was over.

In the late morning sun, steam rose off the trail. A breeze ruffled leaves, producing patterns of dappled sunlight. Fiddleheads pushed through the rich earth as warblers and sparrows trilled overhead.

The fragrance of loam and cedar greeted his every breath. Here in the wild places far from the war fields of Iraq and Afghanistan, Boone could relax.

Why not head up into the backcountry?

His grin wilted. *Why not? Doc and the team will wait until I show up, that's why not.* The hint of a smile once again formed in the corners of his mouth. *I could dismiss everyone.*

"Let's get off early and hike to Lake Lena, okay, buddy?" With a doggy grin and tail in motion, Ohto turned and cantered away.

When they entered the clearing, Boone discovered a single truck waiting. In the bed, Dr Sitton relaxed with a hardback copy of *Call of the Wild*.

"Where's everyone?" he said, striding up to the pickup.

The vet shrugged. "All hands on deck."

Boone's brows knit. "Another attack?" His rifle slotted in the gun rack.

"Yep, a park visitor on the opposite side of the reserve, they found him an hour ago." The vet's snapped the novel shut.

"Couldn't be this boy then. Damn, I assumed we solved it."

Ohto leapt into the truck bed and settled his head on the vet's leg.

Boone stiffened. "Were they badly hurt?

"Pretty serious. put the old guy in the hospital. He was out there birdwatching, not bothering anybody." Dr. Sitton stroked Ohto. "Now, he might not make it. Headquarters wants you in the search area now."

CHAPTER FIVE

ELENA - CAPITOL FOREST EAST

Elena took a knee and studied the shiny leaves and bell-shaped blooms of the ground-cover. *In late summer, the pink flowers matured into red-orange berries.*

She brushed her dirty hands on her jeans as she rose, extracted a field notebook from her rear pocket, then printed, "Kinnikinnick — wide variety of uses." She noted the GPS coordinates beneath the words to make sure she could locate the specimen later.

Elena addressed her imaginary class: "Coast Salish people dried the leaves for smoking. Don't get excited, kids. It has no psychotropic properties. The berries *are* mighty tasty with salmon eggs, though."

The phantom students dismissed with a flick of her wrist, Elena returned to the notebook and wrote, *Oregon grape, skunk cabbage, and trillium all nearby.*

The single rap of a woodpecker came through the trees, a bachelor calling for a mate. No response materialized. Like Elena, he was alone.

Her phone displayed the time. *It's past one. If I run, it'll take twenty to thirty minutes to return to the trailhead. I'd better start home.*

Elena stowed her equipment in her pack, slung it on her back, and took off at a slow jog.

Breaks in the canopy peppered the forest floor. Stripes of darkness and light alternated across the wood plank trail.

Considering the morning overcast, today changed into the perfect spring day.

She loped along, and soon, sweat accumulated on her skin. In the first large patch of sunlight, Elena stopped and unzipped her emerald green goose-down jacket. She stuffed the garment into a tiny nylon bag and placed it in her knapsack.

Wild birds rioted in the branches overhead. Elena turned her face into the sun, closed her eyes, and stretched out her senses, opening to the spirits of nature.

Her goddess whispered, "I am here."

Elena smiled and began the prayer. "I offer myself to you, Mediena, protector of the forest. I am your vessel. Be with me, be in me."

A bubble of joy rose from her core. The world burst into a spectrum of vibration and color when the dievė neared her.

Elena remained the college professor, but was also Mediena — ancient, wise, and powerful. Her soul emerged with the eternal.

A nearby mother tree called across the mycelium network to the young ones she mentored. The god-dess walks. Each connected birch and fir acknowl-edged and welcomed them with a release of resin.

In that moment, Elena was one with the insect for-aging beneath her feet. But she was also the mother squirrel nursing babies in the nest above, as well as a chevron of mallards flying over the canopy. They were bound for a pond two miles from-

Wait. What's that?

An alien presence brushed them. The spirit of the goddess probed.

The other flinched and stiffened.

Nausea and otherness filled Elena.

The darkness turned on her.

Elena's eyes flew open, her heart racing.

Clouds engulfed the sun, the wind kicked up, and the trees creaked and moaned.

"I see you," a voice rasped. It was close.

Elena's soul latched onto her body, and she gasped. A dull pain throbbed at her temples, and the bitter taste of fear filled her mouth.

The goddess was no longer with her.

Hold still. She listened. *Silence. No, less than silence. Life holds its breath.*

In the underbrush, a single twig cracked. Elena spun to confront the danger. Her lizard-brain screamed, "Run."

Wait. Listen.

Haltingly, like the mixing of a soundtrack, the forest noises reemerged. First, the shriek of a hawk, a lone gust of wind, and an owl's call. Sounds from each source returned in succession until it was just another day.

Did I imagine it? "Don't turn all Blair Witch." Her voice quavered.

Cool water from the canteen quenched her parched throat. She wiped her mouth with the back of her hand.

The sun's rays beat the clouds into submission, and light and warmth filled the clearing. But everything was different. Somewhere, it still watched.

Elena stood with feet planted. *This is my domain, and no waft of hostility drives me away.* Moving into a strong stance, she said with greater confidence than she felt, "I need to leave, but don't get comfortable. I will return." After a final glance over her shoulder, Elena dashed away.

BOONE - CAPITOL FOREST EAST

Boone's truck bounced along D-1530, a secondary road leading to the Fall Creek trailhead, arriving at his search quadrant shortly after two in the afternoon.

Taking his radio microphone in hand, Boone said, "Wildlife six in position. Dropped Doc at the Bordeaux Gate. Beginning my canvas. Out."

Boone snapped his fingers. "Let's move, Ohto."

The dog bounded out of the cab, panting.

They followed Monroe Creek overland in the direction of Fuzzy Top. Boone's eyes remained fixed on the ground, looking for sign.

The ground's wet from rain this morning, so there should be tracks. "Where are they?" Boone scratched his head.

Ohto lifted his nose and swiveled his neck from one side to the other, sniffing. After repeating the movement twice, the dog cocked his head.

"Can't find 'em either, Ohto?"

Ohto's drooping tail wagged.

"Let's keep looking, fella."

They set off north on a deer path.

Douglas fir encased in yellow-green moss lined the approach. Sword, bracken, and maiden ferns grew in abundance. Every couple hundred yards, a fallen log barred the way, forcing them to crawl over or slip beneath. It was slow going.

At three, they came to the Green Line Trail, a mud bog in the rainy season and a dusty rut by the end of summer. The spring growth had returned, but the churned earth stood out in relief. *Those damn ATVs are loving this wilderness to death.*

"We don't like those gas guzzlers, don't we, boy?" He reached to scratch Ohto's ears, but he was gone.

His dog should be at heel. "Ohto? Where did you go?" Boone whistled, and the leaves beyond rustled.

A six-foot salal hedge leaned in, menacing his route.

He squinted through the leathery jade-green leaves and sticky blossoms and spotted his partner. Ohto nosed around an evergreen copse.

"What you got, fella?" Shrubbery still obscured much of Boone's view. He pushed into the brush and called again.

The dog didn't respond, continuing to snuffle the earth.

"Don't make me come in there."

Pawing the ground, Ohto whined.

"Damnit." Boone pulled the brim of his hat over his brow and secured his rifle. He waded into the thicket, pushing the branches aside with both hands. A sapling snapped back, hitting his cheek and knocking off his sunglasses.

He touched his face and sucked in a breath. Dark blood smeared his fingers.

Boone struggled to retrieve his shades and stored them in his uniform's breast pocket. Sticky flowers stuck to his gear. With considerable effort and numerous expletives, he finally arrived at the clearing.

"Ohto, leave it." Boone stomped toward his dog.

Eye averted, feigning disinterest, the dog retreated from his prize.

"Good, leave it."

The acrid scent of an animal's mark burned his nose. Boone stared at the source of the dog's fascination: a mangled log, once the host of seedlings, moss, and fungi. *New life born from death.* Boone snorted. *Now, that's morbid.*

This nurse log and her brood met a grisly end. An explosion of shredded wood, plant matter, and debris littered the clearing.

"What the hell did this?" Boone scratched his chin. "Ohto?"

The dog, staring at a western red cedar, growled low.

"What d'you find now, pal?"

It stank. Boone examined the stringy gray bark like a crime scene investigator.

At eye level, a hank of coarse dark hair clung to the bark. *The roots are still attached. Good.* Boone pulled a plastic evidence bag and tweezers from his vest, gathered the sample, and stored it in his pocket.

Boone pushed back his cap and stepped backward. About twelve feet from the base, three parallel scratches scarred the wood. Red pitch bled from the deep gashes.

Nothing in these woods, hell, no animal in this state can touch those marks. Boone's abdomen muscles clenched.

The bear dog jumped to attention, and his growl became a snarl.

Thump, thump, thump. Something bounded along the pathway in their direction.

"Quiet, Ohto," he whispered. *If it's the bear that attacked the old man, I'll let it pass and catch him unawares.*

Boone held his breath and waited. The crashing sound approached his location, arrived, and receded.

ELENA - CAPITOL FOREST EAST

Elena hit her stride, pace steady and respiration even. Hypnotized by her breathing and the rhythm of her pounding feet, she relaxed.

This is ridiculous. That was nothing.

Elena increased her speed. Ducking now and then, she avoided striking her head on overhanging limbs.

Behind her, something thundered through the brush. Elena whirled to meet the attack.

A guy in uniform exploded onto the trail, a rifle at ready and a black and white dog at his feet, tail wagging.

"Stay back." Elena took a wide stance and waved her arms. "Get away from me."

"I'm sorry to frighten you." He shouldered the rifle "This area was closed to the public, so I wasn't expecting to find anyone."

Her fear transformed into irritation. "What are you trying to do? Give me a coronary?"

"Again, I'm very sorry to startle you," he said. "I'm Sergeant Anderson with Washington State Department of Fish and Wildlife." He pointed to the badge hanging from his belt. "I'm tracking a dangerous animal that was seen in this area," he said.

The dog trotted toward Elena, offering his best grin.

"Ohto, get back over here," said the man.

The dog sat in front of Elena and raised his paw to shake.

"Ohto, come here, now."

"You shouldn't jump out and scare people, no matter who you are." Elena knelt in front of the dog. "At least *you* have good manners."

The dog's eyes sparkled, dissolving her anger.

"Today, a predator attacked and badly injured a man, less than a mile away. I'm sorry, a woman shouldn't be out here alone."

Hands curled into fists, Elena rose. "A woman? And what is that supposed to mean?"

"I meant to say a member of the public. If you were injured or lost, no one would be here to help," he said. "I'm sure you see how unwise that is?"

"You know nothing about me." She forced her hands to unclench. "This forest is a safe place." Her voice was quiet. "Nothing will hurt me here."

"As I said, there is a vicious predator hunting here. Until we remove it, it's not safe for you or anyone else." Boone took a deep breath. "Please, return to your vehicle as soon as possible."

"You got it, officer." Elena whirled, taking off along the pathway.

"Who does she think she is, Mother Nature?" he muttered to his dog.

"Something like that," she shouted.

CHAPTER SIX

MINA - HOSPITAL

When the elevator chimed and the doors hissed open, the children's ward nursing station was quiet. Mina, wearing her official Saint Luke's Hospital Volunteer's badge, exited the lift pushing a cart. It overflowed with picture books, middle-grade paperbacks, and a sizable collection of animated films on Blu-ray. She approached the nurse's station.

LPN Marie Johnson, covered the telephone handset. "Hello, Mrs Lukas. Always a pleasure to see you." The receiver in the nurse's hand erupted in the buzz of a voice. "Yes, I'm still here," said Nurse Johnson then she rolled her eyes. "Okay, I can hold."

RN Joy Isham, wearing her favorite SpongeBob scrubs, looked up from the workstation where she was updating charts. "Marie, why don't you hang up and go downstairs? I can cover."

"I'm committed. I figure the minute I hang up they'll answer."

"Plus, if you wait long enough, I'll finish the updates." Joy winked.

Nurse Marie laughed and turned back to the phone.

"Good afternoon, dears," she said.

"Checking in on the babies?" asked Joy, with a grateful smile. "Our young Ms Zahra was asking for you this morning."

"You look tired." Mina patted the senior nurse's shoulder.

The woman's tense body relaxed in response. "Two more hours and I'm off shift." Joy rolled her shoulders. "I'll make it."

"How is your mother settling into Northwoods, Marie?" Mina asked the other nurse.

"Although I feel guilty about removing my mother from her home, it's a relief to know she is getting quality care." The sound of repetitive hold music drifted up from the phone. "She mentioned you dropped in for a visit. Thank you for taking the time to see her."

"I'm always happy to help." Mina straightened a tall, lopsided pile of books threatening to topple. "Did Noah come out of his coma?" she asked.

Joy shook her head. "It's two months without a sign of brain activity." She stared at the screen as she typed. "The boy's family accepted the inevitable."

"Oh, no," Mina said.

"They plan to take him off life support tomorrow morning." Marie sighed and forced her face into a professional mask.

"Such a tragedy," said Joy. "They intend to donate his organs, so good may grow out of misfortune."

Twelve-year-old Noah McGinty's go-cart descended an eighteen percent grade at full speed and flipped. Thrown from the vehicle, the boy landed on his noggin. It was serious. From the day he arrived, his doctors held little hope for a full recovery.

"I'll drop in to say goodbye and offer a prayer," Mina said.

"Can't hurt," replied Marie. She pointed to the receiver. "Pharmacy," she mouthed, then said, "I'm

Marie Johnson on the pediatric ward. This morning, I submitted a prescription for cefpodoxime. Yes, for the patient in room 55B. Any idea when it will be ready?" Her fingers drummed the counter. "Please, check on it. Yes, I'll hold."

"Ta-ta, ladies," Mina mouthed and twiddled a wave.

The cart's wheels squeaked as she moved through the hallway. Mina stopped at an open door. The board outside read, "Jonathan Peale, Tonsillectomy." A boy slept in the hospital bed.

She selected a volume from the stack, tiptoed in, and placed a copy of *Max and the Midknights* on the over-bed table. Jonathan stirred but rolled on his side and returned to sleep.

She returned to her book cart.

"Miss Mina. Miss Mina." A dark haired child with a sling on her right arm scampered along the corridor. "I getta go home tomorrow. Dr Muller says I'm all better from getting squished in the car." The child wrapped her good arm around Mina and hugged her.

"That's wonderful, Zahra." Mina touched her shoulder.

No need to heal this one, my priestess, whispered Žemyna, the goddess mother. *Zahra's body will complete the work on her own. Her limbs will be straight, eyes bright, and her life will be long and happy. She will serve me someday.*

In Mina's internal vision, an amber glow surrounded the child's body. A warm pink light pulsed over her injured arm. "You're looking well today."

"The lady is helping my bone knit faster, isn't she?" She giggled. "That's a funny word, isn't it? It's knitting, but not with needles like socks and sweaters."

"Healing yourself. You have a gift, my young friend." Mina arched her brows. "What lady? A nurse?"

"Your friend. She comes to my dreams. The lady says I will become an important nurse or doctor someday."

"You can become anything you choose. Right?"

"I guess so," Zahra said and shook her black curls.

"I'm checking on Noah. Do you want to come?"

"Will you make pretty lights?" Her voice hushed. "The secret ones?" Emma held out her cast.

"We'll see." Mina parked her cart against the wall. Hand-in-hand, they walked down the long hall to the injured boy's room.

A blue curtain surrounded the bed on three sides. At fifty pounds, Noah was thin and very pale, with a blue-gray tinge to his skin.

Click, click, clink, hiss, a blood pressure cuff inflated and deflated.

Shhh-plunk. Shhh-plunk, the ventilator breathed.

Transparent plastic tubing tethered an IV bag of fluids to the needle in his frail arm. Everywhere, machines monitored his beating heart, temperature, and oxygen level.

Mina knelt, meeting the girl at her eye-level. "What can you see, Zahra?" She gestured toward the boy.

The girl squinted and contorted into a scowl of concentration. "Not much. Maybe some blue light around his head." She smiled into the older woman's eyes. "Is that right?"

"There is no correct way to see. Everyone is different. Some folks witness nothing. That is okay, too." She met the girl's smile with her own.

She is spot-on. This child is so powerful. If her gift doesn't fade as she grows, she may become one of the strongest healers I've ever known.

Mina approached the bedside and held her palms an inch over Noah's chest and prayed. *Žemyna, mother goddess who nourishes life, this is your son, Noah. He needs your help.*

I healed his brain, the goddess replied. *I can do no more for him. Noah's lost his way back to this world. You must lead him, my daughter.*

I will bring him home, Mina replied.

Take care, the boy stands at the watery boundary. You must hurry, said Žemyna. *My brother Velnias comes for him this day. Don't let the trickster catch you, my daughter. He doesn't appreciate his prizes stolen.*

"Zahra, I'm going to try to help Noah. You can stay, but you must be quiet. Can you do that?"

"Uh-huh," the girl said.

Mina touched the child's dark cheek and smiled.

Mina approached the boy, knitting her brows and squeezed her eyes shut. Mina reached for her divine and willed her life force to surround Noah's form, grasping for the eternal in him. *Noah? Noah? Can you hear me?*

The *in-between,* a permeable barrier between them shimmered and dissipated as Mina moved forward. Light dimmed, and her stomach rolled as she sank into the stratum. Gloom enveloped her. She shivered with cold and fear. *Am I already too late?*

Her body curled into a ball before extending into a downward plunge. The pressure increased as she descended, and she scoured the gloom for any sign of the boy.

There he is. A pale blue spark sputtering, a candle in a draft. The boy's visage preserved a recollection of his earthly form. He hung suspended, his arms and legs, limp and lifeless, swaying in the currents.

Mina breast-stroked, speeding her descent. Soon, she reached the boy. *Noah? Answer if you can hear me.*

His quiet voice reverberated in the void. *I'm sleepy. Go away and leave me alone.*

She willed a warm authority into her words. *Little lad, you must wake. Come back into the world.*

Noah yawned and asked, *Is it time for school?*

Yes, and much more. Now wake. Reach for me, and I will carry you.

My mama will be angry, he said. *I promised I wouldn't take the flyer out. I did anyway and...* His deep sobs overwhelmed his words.

She pulled the boy to her, and he nestled in her arms. *No, son, she'll be thrilled to see you, and she will forget all past mistakes.*

Noah relaxed, his tears subsiding.

Mina kicked like a deep-sea diver. Together, they drifted upward, but the light of Real-Time remained elusive.

From deep in the bowels of this boundary land, a low rattling bleat, like the discordant song of tone-deaf whales, reached her ears. The relative gravity of the place tugged against them, and she kicked frantically for the surface.

Damn. The phantom King of Death and his retinue seek the boy. They are close. She tightened her grip on the child, and the bonds of his body gave way, now crumbling in her hands. *He responds to Velnias' call.* Mina forced her will into Noah and envisioned every particle in his form fusing back together.

By concentrating her energy, Noah's form coalesced, but Mina sensed her reserve of Žemyna's boon reaching its end. *If I hold his soul in his body much longer, I may surrender my life and join death's realm.*

The emanations of Real-Time broke through above them. With everything Mina possessed, she struggled upward. They shattered the membrane, and Mina heard the angry scream of the god of the underworld.

Mina collapsed into the guest chair, exhausted.

"Don't worry, Miss Mina. I can help." The girl reached for her, and a pink glow jumped the air gap between them.

"Thank you, Zahra. I'm not hurt." She kissed the tiny hand and nudged it away. "You are generous, but you will need your strength to heal your arm. Never forget every act has a cost, and you must always guard your own life." Mina gestured to Noah. "Tell me what you see now?"

"Gold." Zahra's eyes widened. "He's gold all over." She danced in place, the soles of her slippers shuffling on the linoleum.

The boy's eyelids fluttered open. *Where's my mom?* Mina heard Noah think. The pinky-peach of wellness replaced his blue pallor.

"Don't worry, my darling. We'll find her," Mina said as she pressed the call button.

GABBY - SCHOOL

Which is more irritating? Mr Wade's voice or the sound he makes when he scribbles on the whiteboard?

"What is the coefficient of the variable $3x$?" The algebra teacher surveyed the room, a raptor searching for prey. "Anyone?" The students shuffled their feet and concentrated on their nails, neighbors, or the world outside.

The teacher's stubby fingers ran through his ex-military flat top. "This is a simple concept, people." His bowtie bobbled up and down with every movement of his Adam's apple.

Why does he wear that thing?

"Humm-hum." The teacher cleared his throat.

The room was preternaturally quiet.

With effort, Gabby transferred her attention from the tie to the teacher's face.

"What is it, Miss Lukas?"

"What is what?" Gabby's cheeks burned as she glanced around.

"The answer to my question?"

One of the mean girls shared a smirk with her friend.

Gabby, frantic, searched her memory for the solution. "Umm. I'm sorry. I…"

A boy on her left snorted while her friend, Janie, inclined her head toward the equation on the board.

I'm in big trouble. Gabby leaned forward, then bounced against her seat, crossing her arms. "Ah, can you please repeat the question?"

Mr Wade frowned. "What. Is. The. Coefficient. Of. the. Variable. 3x. Miss Lukas?"

Gabby inventoried her brain. *Coefficient? Co means another, like co-owner. Another Efficiency? That doesn't help.*

"Any answer, Miss Lukas?"

Maybe the 3x part? Choose one and you have a fifty / fifty chance of getting the answer.

"X, Mr Wade," her reply was inaudible.

"I can't hear you," he said in a singsong. "Please, repeat your answer."

In Gabby's peripheral vision, Janie shook her head and flashed three fingers.

"Th-th-thr-ree?" Gabby said.

"Are you certain?"

He can't treat me like this. Her palms warmed. *My family has powers. You'd never talk to Gabija that way. She would burn you up.*

"Miss Lukas?

"Like I said, three. And that is, like, my final answer." Both her forearms from fingertips to elbows burned.

"That is correct." Mr Wade's eyes narrowed.

Gabby grinned and stared back.

"Perhaps you should thank Miss Bates for her assistance," he said.

The bell rang.

Gabby stuffed the algebra book into her backpack, sprinted for the hallway, and merged into the deluge of students drifting toward the last class of the day.

"Gabs, wait up." Janie's shoulder bumped her. "Mr Wade was ab-so-not-ly okay just now. It was positively gym-teachery."

At her locker, Gabby spun the combination lock's dial. "His stupid bowtie had me twisted." The metal door opened with a *clank*.

"Ancient history, GF. Mass impor-tan-tay, did you check out Jacob Brooks? He was absolutely correlating your binomials." Janie Groucho'ed her eyebrows.

"Jacob Brooks? When did I say I liked him? I never liked him. I can't believe you think I care. He's so last Wednesday." She glared down her nose at Janie, then twirled around, red hair flying.

"Last year, you wet your pretty pink panties every time he passed in the hall. Now you're all, 'he's a swipe left?'" Her nose wrinkled.

"I am not interested in freshman boys like Jay-cob. They're all children." The locker muffled Gabby's voice.

Janie nodded. "Love the sweater. I never thought of you as a green girl. V-lush. New?"

Gabby nodded. "Thanks, the sister gifted me." She removed her algebra book. "Mr Brooks was a last-year. I'm looking for Mr This-Year."

Thump. Her math book landed on the locker floor.

"I'm almost fifteen, Janie. I'm tired of roller rink lemming fests." Her pack settled over her shoulder, and she slammed the drab gray door.

"I am not a child. I want romance. I want excitement. I want-" Her cheeks flushed. "You know what?"

"A senior with a car?" Janie dragged out the 'r' in car.

"Exactly."

The second bell droned as the hallway emptied.

"Text me later, J-net."

"Later," Janie said, watching her best friend stroll away.

CHAPTER SEVEN

GABBY - SCHOOL

The yellow paint washed off her palms into the locker room sink. "Why did I sign up for the stupid decoration committee?" Tempera caked her nails. Holding them under water couldn't dislodge the color, and she picked at it with the other hand.

"Thanks for coming to help," Stacey the Freshman Class Vice President called through the door. "I don't know why no one else showed. I sent a text and posted on the school's social media."

"No problem. Happy to help." Her back to the exit, Gabby rolled her eyes and stuck out her tongue.

"I'm leaving. See you in English," the girl said, ending her sentence on an up note.

Gabby examined her pale face in the mirror. She ran a comb through the hair hanging in clumps around her square-jawed face. Cat-shaped pale blue green eyes peeked out under her thick fringe, storming with anger. "Janie didn't even bother to show," Gabby muttered.

The hydraulic piston hissed as the heavy fire door shut with a final *thud*. Although she knew she was alone, Gabby flinched.

She told her reflection, "You are such a pushover, Gabby Lukas." She headed out of the restroom.

Olive drab lockers lined the long, empty hallway. The long hand of the hall clock thumped into place as it reached twelve.

"Four o'clock. Damn, it'll be easier to walk home than wait for the stupid bus."

The overhead lights along the passage went black.

Gabby jumped. "Yikes. They're on a timer, stupid." Her pace quickened the closer she came to the fire door. She burst outside and stood on the narrow cement steps breathing heavily.

Clouds in gray, white, and black clotted the sky, obscuring the sun, and a chill damp wind blew off the sound.

Gabby wrapped her arms around her torso to stop shivering. She turned toward the school where her warm coat waited.

She glanced back. "No way I'm going back there."

On cue, the sky darkened. At her feet, a fat raindrop splatted on the pavement, and then another.

Bolting up the concrete steps, she wrenched on the handle, but nothing budged. *Locked.*

Gabby held her bookbag over her head like an umbrella. The deluge pooled in puddles on the ground and overflowed the gutters and drains in seconds. She detoured around or leapt over as much rainwater as she could, but soon, the rain drenched her, big toes to dripping hair.

"Dammit." Hot tears formed in Gabby's eyes.

A flicker in her belly ignited the kindling of her anger. This tiny flame erupted into a bonfire, heating her skin, covering her body. She stopped shivering.

"Everyone gets hot when they run," Gabby muttered. "No big deal." Suddenly, it struck her, *Gabija is a fire goddess.* "I wonder?"

She envisioned the goddess' power filling her and fanning her internal flame. Soon, clouds of steam billowed off her body as every rain drop landing on her flesh sizzled and evaporated.

When she shouldered open the front door of Swan House, Gabby was bone-dry and grinning.

ELENA - CARRIAGE HOUSE

As the clock on the mantle chimed six, Elena scoured the flat for the proper place to erect her altar.

In the sitting room dormer window. She gave the sill a quick dust, then she located the box marked 'Altar'.

Your goddess is first to enter your home and the last to leave it. See, Nana Regana, I honored one of our traditions. That should please you.

A wisp of copper hair escaped Elena's high pony-tail. She released the tortoiseshell barrette, and her mane tumbled to her shoulders.

Elena squeezed her eyelids shut, keeping any tears at bay, and slid her fingers through her hair. Elena divided it into three sections and plaited a braid.

When I consecrated my shrine in our Boston condo, Colin laughed and said, "I can't understand an intelligent woman like you falling for superstitious nonsense."

It all came back. *An empty flat. Footsteps on hardwood floors. The aroma of musty plaster. Shafts of cold sunlight striking his empty corner.*

Colin saying, America doesn't work for me anymore, and leaving, taking his books and favorite chair back to England without her.

"I should be happy and planning my wedding, dammit," she said, sighing.

Elena surveyed the suitcases and cartons cluttering the bedroom floor. *The rest can wait until tomorrow.* She carried the single carton into the compact living room.

Zipppp. The masking tape detached from the cardboard, and she tossed it aside. With two fingers, Elena opened the flaps and unpacked the contents.

The linen altar cloth fit the space well. Elena smoothed its rough weave and prayed. *Laima, goddess of fate and providence, help me find my way.* "I could use the luck."

Removing the bubble wrap, Elena placed her World Tree in the altar's central position and sat the three firestones, engraved pillar candle, and a wooden ladle nearby. One piece after the other, Elena emptied the carton until only a lidded pottery bowl remained.

Apple-sized with three stubby legs, the container was rustic but elegant.

Mama carved the rune the day I was born. "Bless us, Mediena, goddess of all that dwells in the forests."

The clay lid rasped as she removed it and set it aside. The contents glowed pale-yellow, illuminating her face. Inside, an ancient pendant nestled in cotton wool.

Years ago, I stood in the endless line of your priestesses, she prayed. *Never questioned my destiny until I met Colin. I gave everything up to be with him. So foolish.*

Her slender index finger stroked the gleaming talisman.

Seven years and still not tarnished. The goddess' power keeps it bright. Elena smiled.

A harmonic resonance rang through her body, and every cell took up the song. *Mediena is near.*

"Goddess, I open myself to you," she said. Her human spirit stepped aside, and Real-Time shifted. A breeze ruffled the wisps of her hair, and the fragrance of evergreens and fresh earth enveloped her.

"Mano Taurė, my vessel," Mediena whispered in the Lithuanian of their ancestors. "I stand at the barrier between us."

Delight filled Elena's heart as the Deivė Mediena enveloped her like a child's favorite blanket. "I have need of you, my chalice," she whispered, her tone the rustling of autumn leaves. "We have much to do. Will you serve me?"

I will, if there is still time, Deivė. I thought I lost you.

"Mano mylimas vaike, beloved child. I am eternal. To me, all time is one."

The amulet longed to return to her. An urge to take it up niggled. But Elena resisted, removing her hand. "I need time to consider my recommitment, Mediena." She bit her lip. "I will help you, if only for this task."

"Our bond is eternal, flesh to my spirit. I will call on you again soon."

Mediena withdrew until her presence was distant music, a tune barely distinguishable.

"Praise you, Deivė." Elena smiled, spreading her hands. The symbol of her future with Colin encircled her ring finger. *Other decisions may have to wait, but I can make one today. Goodbye, Colin.*

The diamond solitaire in its yellow gold setting resisted for a moment, then released with a jerk. Elena placed it in the bowl.

My future is a blank canvas now, but I don't know what the hell to paint. Elena tapped her finger against the bowl. "I don't need to decide anything now. I've come home to rest, work, and think."

She slid her phone out of her back pocket and selected Dr Richard Norton's phone number. After ten rings, it went to voicemail.

"You have reached the dean's office of the Rainforest State University." The recording rattled off the standard list of requests and instructions. The woman's accent had a Northwest patois, part-California Valley Girl and part-Canadian lumberjack. "Leave your message after the beep."

"Hi, this is Elena Lukas." She forced a warm professionalism into her words. "I've arrived in Washington State, and I'm settling in. As I mentioned in our recent conversation, I'm honored by the invitation to lead an ecology seminar this summer. I've begun course planning, and I'd appreciate meeting with the department head at your offices as arranged. I look forward to coming in tomorrow morning. Thanks for the opportunity." Elena disconnected.

Everything will be okay. I'm visiting home for a rest, not a family drama.

DAY TWO

THURSDAY

CHAPTER EIGHT

BOONE - WDFW OLYMPIA OFFICE

Brring, *brring*. The electronic buzz of a phone carried through the hallway, drowning out the steady plodding of his footfalls.

"Five forty-five a.m.," Boone groaned, unlocking the door of his Olympia office. "What idiot calls this damn early?" He glared at the industrial wall clock.

All the desks sat empty. The other conservation officers would arrive closer to eight when the department officially opened.

He grabbed the receiver and barked, "Anderson."

"And a good morning to you, too, my friend. Sitton, here." The vet's tone reflected his customary mischievous smile.

"G'mornin'," Boone replied. "Ohto, bed now."

Like it was his own idea, the dog ambled to his burgundy cushion on the floor under Boone's desk.

"Since my carrier pigeons are vacationing in Cabo, I went old school." The sounds of papers rustled across the line. "Up for a mystery? Dust off the fax machine."

"Why?" asked Boone.

"It was the fastest way to deliver this report to

you, naturally. For God's sake, man, join the modern world. Get a smartphone or tablet."

Boone wedged the receiver between his ear and shoulder. He reached for his service weapon. Snapping the retention strap, he removed it from the holster and secured it in his file drawer. "Sure. Um, okay. Shoot." He winced at his unintended pun.

"I'm sending over the preliminary DNA results from the bird watcher's attack. You won't believe what we found."

Boone picked up the mug from his desk and checked the contents. "That's awful fast, isn't it? I thought it took weeks for DNA to come back." Boone depressed the speakerphone button and replaced the receiver in the cradle.

"Usually." The speaker's tinny hiss filled the room. "The test isn't the full workup. It corresponds to a human paternity test, so I can get something back in three days. Shorter if I put a priority rush on it. I did."

Boone rotated his chair and blew any possible dust from the cup.

"This test gives enough information to identify the species. In this case, a bear."

"I could have told you it was a bear attack based on the description of the old guy's injuries."

A pile of briefings waited in his wooden inbox. Boone scanned each memo, then wadded most into a ball and shot them, NBA style, into a wastebasket on the other side of the room. He set aside a few to read later. "So, what's the enormous deal?"

"It is a bear, but not just any bear. Here's a riddle: when is a bear a bear but not bear?" the vet chuckled.

"What are you saying, Dan?" Boone frowned and gritted his teeth. "I'm in no mood for puzzles."

"Pull up a chair. You'll need some backstory first. Scientists at the US Department of Energy's Genome

Institute sequenced DNA from the molars of extinct bears."

"What's this got to do with-"

Sitton pushed on. "They compared the DNA sample to a catalog of living species to uncover the evolutionary path and to compare with other animal attacks on file."

The dog crept away from his pillow, approaching the trashcan.

"Ohto, leave it," Boone said. The dog slunk back to his bed. "This is fascinating, Mr Spock, but what does any of it have to do with our case?" Boone stood and sauntered to the coffee urn, mug in hand.

Used paper cups, napkins, and plastic spoons littered the kitchenette counter. Boone policed the area around the coffee station. "Pigs," he mumbled.

"Urus americanus antifrontalis didn't attack our victim. Our predator was, wait for it, an *Arctodus simus*, commonly known as the Bulldog Bear."

Boone placed a paper liner in the metal basket, filled it with coffee, and slid it into place. "I suppose that is interesting, but why should I care?" Boone placed the glass carafe on the burner and pushed the button. "Another invasive species inclusion. So what? That's happening more and more. Take the Asian Murder Hornet."

"Because," Dan Sitton interrupted, "the Bulldog Bear has been extinct for over twelve thousand years."

The coffee gurgled as it filled the pot. "An extinct species of bear attacked our victim?" Boone turned back to the speaker. "You're kidding, right?"

"There are precedents. Someone discovered an Alaskan bear with unique DNA. The working theory is the animal is a polar bear, black bear hybrid. It's called the Kerdome, Spirit Bear, a white subspecies of American black bear. The experts believed it a myth, until they found one." The veterinarian paused. "I'm offering you a mystery."

Boone poured coffee in his mug, then sauntered to his workspace, snatching the fax along the way. He read in silence, then slapped the sheet on the desktop. "I'm not even sure what to do with this, doc." He massaged the bridge of his nose.

"You're a detective, Boone. Go into the world and detect."

"Go where? A natural history museum?"

"Not the worst idea," said Dan.

"Then what would you do?"

"A hotshot biologist named Lukas joined the RFU faculty. I'd start with one of the experts on rare species and genetic mutations."

Boone took a swig of coffee. "That's as good an idea as any, I guess. I've got time this morning. I'll head over there and see if I can find this professor. Call me if you discover something - useful."

The vet's laughter silenced when Boone's handset fell into the cradle.

He chugged the last of his coffee, then grabbed the report and said, "Ohto, let's go see a scientist about a bear."

GABBY — SWAN HOUSE

Sunlight poured through the bedroom, directly into Gabby's eyes. Dried saliva coated her tongue, and a small wet spot collected on her pillowcase.

"Yuck," she said, smacking and licking her lips.

Gabby pulled the Pink Flamingo duvet over her head. *What day is this? It's Saturday, right?* Oh, poo. *Today is Thursday.* Gabby grimaced. *Poop, I have school.*

Her math homework remained unfinished. *No time to do it now. Great, more humiliation.*

Am I sick? A headache? Fever? Gabby peeked out.

Stuffy nose? Nope. Stomach Flu? Bitchie Witch Week? Nothing.

"Dammit. I'm healthy."

What do I wear? The laundry basket overflowed in the corner.

Choices are limited. Jeans? Jeans are so... whatever. The bedding, clutched under her nose, offered protection.

Wait. She scanned the bedroom. "Where is the cat?"

Her mother threw her tomcat outside after the fight last night.

"I'm sorry, sweetheart," she'd said. "You can't keep him. He has a home, and if we ignore him, he'll go back there."

"Mama is so mean," she twisted her comforter. "I showed her."

After Mina marched to bed, Gabby found the animal waiting in the side yard and smuggled him upstairs.

The bedcovers flew back, and Gabby scanned her bedroom. "Kitty, kitty, kitty." Her voice was hushed.

"Prrtt." The cat perched on the bookcase watched the front walkway outside.

"There you are, big boy." A grin sprouted on her face. "Come here, big man. Come to mama." She held out her arms.

The animal stretched and turned toward her.

"Come on, flirt. Come here. You know you want me."

The cat leaped from the bookcase to the desk, tightrope walked the windowsill, and jumped to safety on her dresser. Eyes narrowed, he wrapped his tail around his feet and stared at Gabby.

"Why are you mad at me?" she asked.

The cat licked its paw, long claws bared.

Flopped back on the bed Gabby said, "It's so not

fair." She stared at the ceiling. "Did you hear what Mama said, kitty?"

The cat began his spit bath.

Brandishing her arms, continuing her award-worthy impression of Boris and Natasha, "Zis is our home but alzo a businezz. Zere are many things we vant, but zis animal you can't have. Such bull-sh-rubbish."

Her lower lip thrust out. "Who cares about one stupid guest with lame allergies? I don't care what she says, what she thinks. I do what I want." Gabby pounded her fist against her leg. "You are mine, and I'm keeping you."

Her phone chimed. Gabby grabbed it from the bedside table.

"Are you up?" her mother's text read.

Her eyes widened. "Crap. School." Gabby launched off the bed, almost stepping on the cat at her feet. "How did you get there? Teleport?" she asked.

He blinked his eyes twice, yawned, and resumed grooming.

Gabby dropped the phone on the table. A heart-shaped locket hung by a silver chain from the reading lamp.

"Thanks, Mama, I just might forgive you." Gabby snatched the necklace and dropped it over her head. It slithered down and encircled her throat.

ELENA - UNIVERSITY

"Where the hell is the main campus?" Elena's MINI paused on the empty forest road. She gripped the steering wheel and squinted right then left. "Which way?" She scratched the hairline at her forehead.

Her finger pointed from one direction to the other as she chanted, "Eeny. Meeny Miny. And *Moe*." Downshifting, Elena took a hard right.

"This is a damn maze, not a college campus." The

stick shift ground into second gear, and the vehicle lurched. "Would it break the budget to post signs?"

As much state park as university, the grounds covered over a thousand acres of wilderness.

Toto, you're not in Boston anymore. No red brick and ivy here.

Ferns and wild native plants replaced her former employer's flowering trees and manicured flowerbeds.

Where are the armies of gardeners? A lump formed in her throat. *The cherry trees are blossoming on Washington Avenue.* Native rhododendrons the size of houses lined the roadway. *Beautiful here, too. Just different.*

The MINI pulled in next to the small guardhouse. A carved wooden sign spelled, "The Rainforest State University."

"Praise the goddess. I'm here." Elena cranked open the driver's side window.

"Hello, anyone home? Hello? Anybody?" She leaned out and said, "Nobody?" The car seat squeaked as she slumped back. "Why am I not surprised?"

The transmission ground into first gear as she shifted. "I'll pick up a parking permit later," she said to the invisible attendant. "You better not tow me."

Peeled logs divided the nature-park-themed parking lot into neat rows. Only imagination defined the spaces. Every stall was empty.

Elena parked, extracted a brown messenger bag from the front seat, and placed her keys inside.

Main Campus, she read. "Here we go." A yellow arrow carved into a wooden sign pointed into the woods.

The forested path ended in front of another location sign. "Grassy Knoll".

Rainforest University was the height of Northwest futurism in 1970. Campus buildings constructed of angular concrete slabs, expanses of glass and thick hardwood beams, surrounded the red brick plaza.

Even on spring break, a few students should be lurking around campus. Her eyes narrowed, and a shiver ran along her spine. Anxiety raised its hand, but Elena dismissed it. "Get a grip, woman. It is seven a.m. on a Thursday."

From the depths of her messenger bag, Elena unearthed a campus map. "That clock tower must be Evans Library," she said, pointing to the diagram. "And the seminar buildings are there, so the lab buildings must be-" Elena poked the paper with her index finger then pointed into the shrubs. "Over there. Now I'm making progress," she said and returned the map to her bag.

Caw, caw. From high overhead, Elena sensed the warm tug of her pranašas, Varnas.

A raven circled above her head. He orbited twice, then dive-bombed. Arching his body and spreading his tail, Elena's familiar landed on her arm.

Indignant, his sharp eyes glared; shorter feathers at his neck bobbled with his tail-feathers keeping time.

With a low series of rattles and clicks, he scolded. His blue-black feathers shone iridescent in the spring sunlight.

"Where have you been?" asked Elena. "I've missed you."

The bird turned his head away while he edged his way up her arm. When he reached his mistress' shoulder, Varnas nipped and tugged at her hair.

Elena snorted. "Okay, you're forgiven." She stroked the bird's head with one finger.

"Why weren't you at Mama's, old man?" she said.

The bird stomped his feet and chattered into her ear.

"I wish I could understand you, Varnas," she said,

running her hand along his back. "Go home, buddy, and I'll be back for dinner."

The raven hopped the length of her arm and pushed off into the sky. She watched Varnas until he turned into a spot and disappeared.

The fern-lined path led to a cement bunker. A sign implanted in a bed of beauty bark read, "Lab Two."

"Where is the entrance?" Elena followed the perimeter until she located a fire door.

I made it. She smiled.

The fire door groaned when she pushed it open, revealing a long dark hallway. Throughout the empty building, Elena's Cuban-heeled boots clacked on the tile floor.

Something's not right. Her senses whispered, "Listen." Nothing. *What the hell is wrong with you?* Elena shuddered and increased her pace.

A half-open door marked, "Office," lay at the end of the long hall. "Hello?" she called.

Overhead fluorescents lit an unmanned reception counter. Somewhere out of sight, a filling coffeemaker gurgled.

Someone must be here.

Her phone declared it a quarter to eight in the morning.

I'm forty-five minutes early.

She rubbed her eyes and patted her mouth, stifling a yawn.

"Someone will claim that coffee. I'll wait." Elena slumped on to a lumpy plastic couch. Notices for studying abroad and corporate internships covered the end table. *What, no magazines? This might be a long wait. I might as well make myself at home.* Elena's eyelids drooped.

ELENA — UNIVERSITY - LATER

Slam. Elena's eyes flew open.

In front of the fire door, a gamine woman juggled a super-vente latte, a muffin, and a bulky satchel while dabbing her coffee stained shirt with a napkin. "My Aunt Fanny. Why does this always happen to me?"

She moved to the reception area, and her briefcase zipper burst, spilling papers on the beige carpet. "Why me? Why me?" Bending to retrieve her documents, she spilled her drink on the counter.

"Let me help you?" Elena said, stifling her laughter.

"I'm a mess," the pint-sized woman said with a sheepish smile.

"It happens to the best of us." Elena picked up the fallen test forms. "I'm Doctor Lukas, visiting summer faculty."

"You're you, aren't you? I'm here to greet you." Her words stumbled. "I'm Alice Jackson from the dean's office. Not from so much as for them." Alice closed her eyes. "He, the dean, missed his flight, so he couldn't be here to greet you, and somebody had to, so he called me."

"Nice to meet you, Alice," Elena replied, handing back the papers.

"What would you like to do first? The full tour of the campus or to settle into your office?" She stuffed the notes in her neoprene satchel.

Elena attempted to answer, but Alice continued, "You could have a partial tour and move into your office later."

"I-"

"Or perhaps we could—"

"Just my office today," Elena cut off the lengthy list of options.

"Great, great, great." Alice deposited her jumble

on the counter and brushed her hands together. "Okay, follow me." She sped out the door.

Elena did her best to keep up with Alice until their near collision at a second-floor office door.

"Here we are." Alice patted her jacket pockets. "I had it here somewhere." She checked her pants pockets next. "Ahh, ahh. Okay, here they are."

A wad of keys filled her hand, and she squinted at one after another. "Nope, that isn't the one. Nope, nope, here."

She held the key up for inspection, then shoved it into the lock. *Thunk.* Alice removed it from the lock and thrust it into Elena's hand.

"There, you have it. Home sweet home. Or maybe, office sweet office." Her laugh evaporated. "Well, you know what I mean."

The door opened with a long slow creak worthy of a horror movie. *What an anticlimax,* thought Elena.

A vanilla room with beige walls and empty bookcases waited for a new occupant. A standard rolling chair sat behind an ordinary wooden desk.

"This office was Doctor Smyth's. He taught physical chem. That isn't right. He taught botany." She smacked her palm against her forehead. "No, his office was in that hall. Jinjing Hong used this office and taught organic chem." She shook her head. "Wait, Jinjing's space wasn't here either, it was- where was it?"

"Thanks, Alice," Elena answered. "This is perfect."

Alice shrugged. "I'm sorry. I talk too much when I'm nervous."

Elena cocked her head. "Alice, why should you be nervous?"

"I'm a fan," Alice said, thrusting her hands into her pockets. "I've read all of your papers."

"I'm glad somebody did," Elena said, smiling. She patted the other woman's shoulder. "No reason to be nervous, Alice, we're both scientists and educators. Right?"

"You're the top of your field. You earned a PhD before twenty-two, for heaven's sake." Alice ran her fingers through her short, mousy blonde hair. "Look at me, I'm thirty-five and a lowly assistant genetics professor." She drooped. "If I don't get publishing soon, that ol' tenure door will slam in my face."

Before Elena could offer encouragement, a masculine voice asked, "Is this our visiting superstar?"

A man, on the short side of tall with a runner's build, leaned against the doorframe with his arms crossed. His pale blond hair fell, consciously casual, around his face, and wire-rimmed glasses framed his eyes.

"Hello, Doctor Capello," said Alice.

His eyes fixed on Elena, ignoring the other woman. "I'm Seth Capello, anthropology." He slid his wire-rimmed glasses into the neck of his white linen shirt.

He's a stud, and he knows it.

"Elena Lukas, visiting professor of ethnobiology." She pointed to herself and to the guest chair. "Take a seat, doctor?" Elena maintained a calm and professional tone. "I understand we're working together."

"I certainly hope so." The man remained in the doorway. "Perhaps we can get together and explore the possibilities."

"Please, call me. I'd love to… um, chat." *Look out for this one, he's trouble. A classic Don Juan.*

"I have another appointment in…" Seth glanced at a thin gold watch, "an hour." He shook his head, then brightened. "Maybe I'll call you." His green eyes sparkled. "We could get to know each other over dinner? Do you think that might be possible?"

"That will be nice, Professor Capello."

"Seth, please."

"Of course. Um, Seth." Regret flooded Elena. *This guy is a player. The last thing I need right now.*

"You'll be hearing from me, Elena," Seth winked.

CHAPTER NINE

BOONE - UNIVERSITY

Boone pulled the truck into the half-full lot and parked in a shady spot. *Why do people get lost? This campus is simple to navigate.*

He rolled down the window a crack and left Ohto sleeping on the seat.

This is nice. No red brick, white columns, or blasted ivy.

Red cedar shavings lined the short trail, which opened onto the central plaza. A spattering of students rested on benches or sprawled on the freshly clipped grass, enjoying the weak spring sunshine. Robins hopped in the flower beds shopping for breakfast, and an oversized crow or raven watched from the branch of a fir.

On his way to the labs, Boone ran into a few students milling around. *I guess the university is not in session.*

Boone opened the lab door as another man his age rushed toward him. "Excuse me," Boone said, moving aside.

The man in wire-rimmed glasses leaned away. His lip curled. "If I must," he said.

Stick it up your ivory tower, a-hole. Boone watched him round the corner.

Inside, Boone paused and considered where to start his search.

"Hello, are you lost?" said a plain woman with short, pale hair.

"Have you seen Dr Lukas today?"

"Up the stairs, follow the hall, third office on the left," she smiled.

"Thanks," he said and bounded away. *She is cute in her own way.*

The door was closed. He knocked, and a muffled voice replied, "Come in."

He opened the door and found bookshelves and an empty desk. "Professor Lukas?"

"Yes?" a disembodied voice replied. "There you are. Got you." The youthful woman stood, mechanical pencil in hand.

Boone's jaw dropped. *Oh, my God, it's her.*

ELENA - UNIVERSITY

"You are Dr Lukas? Um. I mean, are you *the* Dr Lukas, the expert-"

Elena didn't speak.

"Of course, you are." He clasped a manila envelope under his arm, and floundering, sank into an uncomfortable silence.

"What's the matter, officer?" Elena winked. "Did you forget your gun?"

"I guess you remember me." His face warmed.

"You're hard to forget." She grinned. "I'm not on the business end of a rifle every day, officer."

"Sergeant. Or detective," Boone said.

"Excuse me?"

"My title. I'm Detective Sergeant Anderson from Washington Department of-"

"Hello then de-tective Anderson. Why have you tracked me to my lair?"

"I didn't follow you." Still holding the envelope, he stuffed his free hand into his pocket, his other arm dropped to his side.

Blue-black hair with matching lashes, and so tall. He fills that doorway nicely.

"How can I help you?"

"I represent the Washington State Department of Fish and Wildlife." He straightened his posture.

"You said that already," she said, smirking.

Boone cleared his throat and forged on. "We gathered anomalous DNA at the scene of an animal attack, professor. The department seeks the opinion of an expert in endangered species, hybridization, and mutation."

"Okay," Elena said, dropping into her chair.

Boone cleared his throat. "We believe your expertise offers insight into these important test results. We don't wish to cloud your judgment, so I'll say nothing more."

He placed the file on her desk.

She didn't touch it.

"You will serve your community and be well compensated. Are you willing to consult on this case?"

"Sure, why not?" She allowed her smile to fully form.

"I've attached my business card." He pointed to the file on her desk. "Please, email or fax your report along with an invoice. Afternoon, professor." With military precision, he marched out of the door.

"You're welcome," she called after him.

The door closed, and the sound of his footfall receded.

VARNAS — MUD BAY

The moon and sun neared alignment, and with it, the last super moon of the year. The spring low tide turned the Eld Inlet into vast mudflats. Named for a Wilkes expedition officer, the locals preferred to call the area Mud Bay. When the water retreated, they gathered the abundant native clams, mussels, and oysters which lived here.

The Puget Sound in the distance glittered, and the withdrawing bay sculpted phantom waves in the intertidal sand. Bulb kelp whips and neon green seaweed baked in the sunshine. And flotsam dotted the tidelands, joining nature's smooth stones, crab carapaces, and deserted oyster shells.

Varnas spotted a pinprick hole in the mud and waited for the next manilla to squirt. It required patience but was also inevitable. Sometime soon, the bivalve would have to breathe, passing water past its gills. If Varnas was quick enough, he might snatch it before the shell snapped shut.

Although he loved the salty, sweet flavor of the rubbery meat, Varnas couldn't stop worrying about the vessel.

He'd found her in a place covered with a dusky film of magic. Not all was dark, but he spotted one location pulsing with evil working, this forging recent. Worst of all, she was blind to it.

"Not safe, not safe," he cawed. *Unclean.* Varnas cocked his head and twitched his neck feathers.

Sea water geysered through the mollusk's funnel and sprayed an inch into the air. Varnas' movement was a blur. Like a magician's parlor trick, the clam materialized in his sharp beak. Unfortunately, he was a millisecond too slow, and the locked valves protected the raven's potential lunch. He would have to find another way to open it.

Check for threats, stash food. Varnas spread his

wings. *Return to goddess sanctuary.*

Close to the shoreline, a driftwood log lay buried in the mud. He hopped onto the grayed wood, lowered his head, and launched skyward, rising until the whole estuary spread out below him.

Large swatches of dark green forest scarred by squares of gray stone the people used to build their homes. Here and there, Varnas spotted glowing pockets of common magic but little else.

He followed the inlet until it crossed the human's stone river, where moving metal boxes sailed. Flapping his wings, he ascended to the altitude of eagles and glided over the city. On a hill above the village, the shrine of the goddess glittered like a star.

He found the vessel's rookery and dropped his bundle as he flew over the roof. The clam struck the stone patio, cracking on impact. Varnas circled in for a landing. When his feet touched the slate plaza, he hopped over to the broken shells.

Save? Store? The raven poked at his prize. *Choose? I choose.* Varnas chortled and snatched up the clam. He hopped to a brick bulkhead nearby and stuffed both meat and shell into a crack.

The raven admired his new pantry and thought, *More? Save?* Fresh-tilled vegetable beds offered an excellent worm hunting ground. A quick hop across the courtyard, and he touched down on the rich dark soil. A few minutes of rooting produced a tidy stash of segmented earthworms.

After hiding them, Varnas strutted and vocalized in celebration until it was time to begin his genuine work.

The turret made an acceptable observation tower. But the crown's pitch was too steep. Varnas opted for the roof ridge and landed on the iron cresting. This decoration discouraged roosting birds but wasn't a deterrent for the raven. From this perch, he surveyed the sanctuary grounds.

Chartreuse eddies of natural magic created trails of intention across the lawns and landscaping. Varnas gurgled and croaked as he jumped from picket to picket along the ridge, the gentle wind ruffling his feathers. *Common. No threat to the vessel.*

The fledging fire goddess slogged down the box trail, leaving a contrail of red and orange in her wake. Her power sparked and crackled while her spirit's inner light, her *siela*, strobed in erratic patterns.

Wildfire, wild magic, no harm to the vessel? Masks other darkness? He cawed five times, and his harsh call carried for a considerable distance.

Below, the girl stopped and glanced up but didn't recognize the pranašas and continued into the shrine.

The corvid took off and circled the building, then landed on a finial.

Through the giant rhododendrons, he spotted the distinctive purple of dark working. He fanned his tail feathers, screamed, and rocketed into flight.

Varnas glided over the lawns, gardens, and a tiny shrine to the earth goddess.

The evil magic emanated from a garden of stone and effigies.

The unwelcome maker of discord had disappeared, but its intention hadn't dissipated. Only hours ago, it stood here.

The raven landed on a statue of an unknown goddess' shoulder. "*Prruk-prruk-prruk,*" he cried. Furious, every ebony feather puffed and quivered. No sign of true ritual marred the garden, but the trespasser's obsession left an afterimage in shades of violet marbled in black.

A threat to what? Who? The raven shifted.

Carrion decay, the smell of death, swirled in the air currents, but didn't tempt Varnas to feed. The danger to the vessel was his only focus.

The interloper left no ritual artifacts, bits of clothing, hair, or personal possessions behind. Their target wasn't evident. This one craved something out of reach, tasted violence, and sought domination.

Unmask? Hide. Watch. Protect.

Chuckling, Varnas took off from his perch and went in search of the vessel.

ALICE — UNIVERSITY

In her tiny office, Alice studied an Excel spreadsheet tracking her research paper submissions.

Six tabs spread across the bottom of the application window. She clicked on the one marked "Arsenic." It tracked her paper "Arsenic Exposure Monitoring Using Biomarkers," an analysis of old and new research. The title was too long for the tab.

She scanned the extensive list of peer-reviewed academic journals in the first column.

The letter from *The Journal of Genomics and Mutational Research* sat on her desk. Their message was simple.

"We are sorry to inform you that your paper isn't suitable for our publication," it read.

Staring at her hands, Alice's chin trembled, and she chose "Reject" from the status drop-down. The last remaining journal turned her down. There were no more chances.

"Six papers submitted to two hundred and thirty-nine publications and nothing accepted." She pulled a handful of tissues from the flowered box on her desk and blew her nose.

She was glad to be alone. Being caught weeping wouldn't help her reputation. Her colleagues liked her, but most considered her an academic lightweight.

Her tenure committee reviewed her progress next month, and this would not please them. *If I can't get it together soon, I'll end up teaching high school biology in some rural backwater. Oh my, not Yakima.*

After filing the letter in the bottom desk drawer,

the correspondences graveyard, Alice slumped into her broken chair.

I need a new topic for my next paper.

She'd read two papers this week, and they mirrored her research. All too similar. *That's two years of investigation wasted.*

Alice cracked her knuckles and thrust out her chin. *I will find a new topic, something new and so unique there won't be five hundred other researchers already working on it.*

I betta getta thinkin'. Like her late father often did, she dimmed the light, hoisted her feet onto the desk, and leaned back.

Crash.

Alice sat up so quickly she almost fell out of her seat. "What was that?" she said.

The start of summer quarter was still a few weeks away and campus was sparsely populated.

Alice crept to the door and peered down the abandoned hall. Music wasn't playing and any glow of fluorescents and desk lamps absent.

Thud.

Maybe it's a security guard. Alice left the safety of her office. The industrial gray carpet muffled her footsteps. She tiptoed down the hallway toward the dean's office. A knock on each door and jiggle of the knobs convinced her she was alone.

Alice reached the executive offices. Light escaped through the side light mini-blinds on either side of the dean's door. Although he often worked late, this week he was attending a conference in Atlanta.

Who's in there? I have the only key. She squinted through the shades. *Maybe the admin forgot to turn off the lights.*

She rattled the latch. *It's locked.* The key hung on

her massive ring, so Alice located it and opened the door.

Seth Capello stood over the dean's desk, reading the open file folder before him.

"What are you doing here?" he said, eyes flashing.

Alice's cheeks flushed. "I, um, I…"

"What do you want?" He slapped the folder shut.

"Oh, I'm so sorry, doctor." Her shoulders slumped. "The lights were on, and I was worried someone had broken in."

"That explanation's ridiculous. What if it was a burglar?" Capello wrinkled his nose in disgust. "What could you do? Nothing," he spat.

"I'm sorry. So very sorry." She swallowed, her face beet-red. "You're right."

He moved toward her, and Alice lowered her eyes and shrank back.

His sudden smile returned warmth to his eyes. "That's all right." He squeezed her shoulder. "No harm done."

"Thank you?" she replied, stepping back.

Capello knit his brow and said, "You changed your hair?"

"I don't know, I guess so." Alice ran her fingers through her short bob. "Why?"

"It's lovely. Keep wearing it that way." Grinning, he continued, "I'd love a longer visit, but I must be on my way." He patted her cheek, his hand lingering.

"Thank you," she squeaked.

Seth Capello walked out, leaving Alice with her mouth agape.

The file folder remained on the desk. She picked it up and checked the label. "Professor Elena Lukas."

"Hum?" Alice hesitated as she fought the urge to read the private file. With a deep sigh, she returned it to the file cabinet, turned off the lights, and locked the door.

CHAPTER TEN

NEWLYWEDS - FALL CREEK CAMPGROUND

The newlyweds of three months pitched their tent moments before the drizzle began.

Gloria raised the hood of her pristine North Face parka. *I'm surprised we set up that monstrosity without another fight. Camping gear is the stupidest wedding present ever.*

Her husband, Rolly, pounded in the last stake and set to cinching guidelines.

Why did I bother registering? His family is hopeless.

Her fashion-forward rain boots weren't keeping her feet dry. *I'm freezing. I want to go home.*

Rolly dusted off his palms and stood back. "This Quarter Dome's a work of art." He circled the tent, smiling. "Check it out. The sides are near vertical."

"Uh-huh," she said.

"We sure could have used this last year when Dad and I scaled El Capitan-"

Gloria stopped listening. *It is my fault we left Seattle a few minutes late.* She considered her spouse's steel-blue eyes and nodded with mock enthusiasm. *It was so hard to decide what to bring. Then again, it took longer driving here than mountain man expected. That is his fault. Even if we left on time, it would've been dark when we ar-*

rived. So, arriving after dark isn't my fault. Gloria took a deep breath and dove in for a sound bite.

"-climbing Rainer at twelve. Now that was an eye o-"

Not interesting. Her nose ran, and she sniffed. *Our first real fight ever.* A lump formed in Gloria's throat.

That bumpy dirt road to the campground trail covered our brand-new Subaru with dust and mud. Daddy gave us that car for a wedding gift. Rolly won't even take care of it.

We arrived at that empty guardhouse after four, and it was full dark at the trailhead.

Gloria pulled on her matching mittens. *When I suggested we stay with the car and hike in the morning, he laughed, and that bastard called me a little chickie chicken.* She smiled at her husband, but she doubted it reached her eyes. *Wait, what did he just say?*

"-I understand this trip is your first time roughing it," said Rolly.

Did he know I wasn't listening? Her heart skipped a beat. "I'm not a complete city girl, Pooh," Gloria said. "My mom and dad loved the outdoors. We went to the cabin every summer weekend, and I'm an exceptional skier."

"You're an amazing skier, bunny." He removed another wedding gift, a camp stove, from his pack. "We have this whole campground to ourselves." With a grin and a wink, he added, "Isn't that romantic?"

"I guess." Gloria's teeth chattered, and she moved closer to Rolly and his body heat. "Why isn't there anyone else here?"

"We're early, and Fall Creek's not even crowded during the summer."

"Okay," Gloria squeaked.

"Don't you enjoy being alone here with me? I enjoy being here with you." With a *click* and a *whoosh*, the mantle caught fire.

Rolly stood. "Our campsite is the only one with a view of the night sky."

Rainwater dripped from the trees, and flame sizzled. Gloria rolled her eyes.

"If the sky was clear, we'd see the galaxies in Leo and Virgo there." Rolly gazed upwards.

"Joy." Gloria pulled her jacket in tight.

Rolly wrapped his arm around Gloria and drew her to him. "Imagine you see the blue giant, Spica, the brightest star in Virgo right there above those trees." He pointed into the night sky. "Just think, the starlight we see left the star two hundred and sixty years ago."

Gloria twisted into his embrace, giving him a peck on the nose. "I'm trying." She snuggled in his arms. "I'm sorry I took so long to get ready."

"You are always worth a wait." His kiss, intimate and searching, told Gloria their first fight had finished.

"I'm hungry. You?" Rolly asked, releasing her.

"Starving, but not for food." Gloria turned off the stove.

He held open the flap of the two-person tent. "Come on in, baby, I'll show you something special." Rolly leered comically.

"Wildlife?" Gloria, eyes wide, batted her lashes.

"See for yourself." Rolly disappeared into the tent. Gloria followed, and soon, their soft sighs and murmurs merged with sounds of the forest.

GLORIA - FOREST

What's that? Gloria jerked awake. She had to pee.

Rolly's heavy breathing verged on a snore.

"You awake?" she whispered. His breathing continued, unchanged.

I can't wander into this wilderness alone. For over an hour, she lay awake, ignoring her urging bladder. *I don't have to go. I can wait.* Her thoughts circled, a carousel returning to the place it started.

Unable to wait any longer, Gloria slipped out of

the sleeping bag and wiggled into Rolly's flannel shirt. The tent's zipper opened with the roar of a chainsaw. She paused part way, then inched the zip along until it opened. Her husband's shirt fell to her knees, and as she bent to retrieve her rain parka, she felt a draft.

Her damp boots sat outside. Laces undone, she donned them without socks and shuffled away. *Which way are the restrooms? Do they have any?* She peered about for a latrine. *I can't go here. I'd die if Rolly heard me tinkle.*

At the edge of the campsite, Gloria peered into the woods.

The sky cleared. Moonlight bathed the clearing, but beyond was pitch dark. Gloria located the small flashlight in her pocket and pointed the faint shaft of light into the timbers. The dim beam brightened with a shake.

"This is not scary," Gloria said. "Wild animals are more frightened of me than I am of them."

Salal and blackberry vines pushed in from either side of the trail, little more than a deer path. The way narrowed, and Gloria struggled through the wild foliage, fighting for every yard.

A stray bramble snagged her sleeve, the nylon ripped. "Damn." In the pale beam of her flashlight, tufts of goose down escaped from an L-shaped tear.

Tears filled Gloria's eyes, and she charged forward, catching her foot on an exposed root. She fell, landing on her hands and knees, still clutching the light. Brush scratched her face, and wet leaves showered over her body.

Her cry caught in her throat. She clambered to her feet. Muck and wet fir needles clung to her bare legs; her frantic attempts to wipe them off only smeared and ground dirt into her wounds.

Gloria planted her feet and set her jaw. "I'd better pee and get back." She panned her flashlight, and it illuminated a clearing surrounded by lanky firs.

Far enough.

At the center of the clearing, Gloria dropped the flashlight into her pocket. Its faint beam illuminated the treetops.

She lifted her coat and shirt to her waist and squatted, balancing on the balls of her feet. "I'm not scared." Gloria relieved herself, liquid sprinkling the ground.

Leaves rustled, and branches creaked. Her head snapped up. "Wind, only wind blowing," she mumbled, but with less confidence. She strained to hurry, but the stream kept coming.

The brush behind her rustled. "Hurry, hurry, hurry." She whistled a tuneless little song. The sound of rustling rotated to her opposite side.

The light in Gloria's pocket flared and went dark. She sprung up, yanking her shirt and coat over her hips. Behind her, a twig broke with a *snap*. Gloria's heart pounded, and the hair on her arms rose to attention.

"Rolly, are you trying to scare me?" Her cry came out in a squeak. Gloria waited for her husband's warm chuckle, but it didn't come.

Gloria jiggled the flashlight, but it remained dark. "Calm, be calm," she said, taking a step back.

A low feral growl rumbled.

She froze and sucked in a breath. Heart racing, a sour taste filled her mouth.

Two red eyes glared at her.

A putrid, sickly sweet stench overwhelmed her. Her stomach lurched.

She stepped away. "Stay calm," Gloria muttered under her breath.

The growl escalated, louder and more primal with each step she took.

What am I supposed to do? Talk in a calm monotone and move slow. That's it.

"Whatever you are..." she said, her voice shaking, "you're more afraid of me than I am of you. You are more-"

A deafening bellow.

Knocked off her feet, Gloria Poole tumbled to the ground.

She screamed.

DAY THREE

FRIDAY

CHAPTER ELEVEN

BOONE - OFFICE

"Parts are difficult to hear," Dan said. "It helps to read along." The doctor handed Boone a transcript.

The government office was stuffy. Gray metal desks hosted elderly monitors, wired keyboards, and mice.

Under the buzzing fluorescents, the twenty-pound bond paper took on an unnatural brightness.

"Start the recording please, Martha," the doctor told a middle-aged classified employee sitting at the computer. With a soft *clack* of the enter key, a recorded hiss invaded the workplace.

Boone read the document as the distress call played back:

911: "Nine-one-one, what is your emergency?"

Caller: [heavy breathing] "My wife is out there. She's screaming. Gloria. Gloria. I'm coming, baby." [Movement]

911: "Calm down, sir. Where are you?"

Caller: [cries in the background grow louder.] "Fall Creek Campground. We're at Fall Creek Campground. Oh, my God, she's screaming. Someone is killing her. I'm coming. I'm coming, baby."

911: "Sir, are you hurt?"

Caller: [Wailing and unknown animal sounds.] "Oh, oh, God. It is eating her. It's eating her. Stop it, get away from her."

911: "Sir, sir, listen to me. We have dispatched emergency responders to your location. Sir? Are you still there? Are you hurt? Can you describe your wife's injuries?"

Caller: [Sound of struggle.] "Let go of her, you son of a bitch." [Unintelligible.]

911: "Are you there, sir?"

Caller: [Phone dropped, and the voice muffled.] "Gloria, I'm here, baby. Oh, God, part of her chest is missing, and her legs. It tore off her leg. She might be dead. God, I hope she is- Don't look at me. Get back. Ahhhhh. Get away. Stop. No. No." [Sound of roaring and a man's screams.]

911: "Sir. Sir. Talk to me."

Caller: [Struggle and shrieking.] "Help me. No. No. [Screaming fades to silence.]

911: "Sir, are you there?"

911: "Officers are on the way." [Silence]

911: "Sir? Sir?"

Caller: [Gurgling, uneven breathing, whispering] "It doesn't hurt anymore. It's eating me, but it doesn't hurt-"

911: "Sir?"

Caller: [Silence]

The technician stopped the recording, her hands trembling.

Hush. No one spoke.

The rustle of Dan Sitton's notes broke the silence. "The victims are Gloria Giselle Poole, twenty-two, and her husband of two months Roland Alexander

Poole, twenty-eight, both of Seattle," Dan said. "EMTs med-evaced within twenty minutes of receiving the call. Mrs Poole, the wife, dead at the scene, her limbs detached, torso eviscerated, and parts of her body masticated. Rescue workers couldn't find her head."

Pale green, Martha rushed out.

"Mr Poole was barely alive, bitten through the chest. His lung collapsed." Dan turned to the next page. "The attacker dislocated his left arm, covered it in puncture wounds, and mangled both thighs and calves. It wounded him and planned on coming back to finish. We have photos."

The vet sat in the metal office chair relinquished by the clerk; laying his notes on the desk. He closed the folder with reverence. "It is a miracle he didn't bleed to death before help arrived." He placed his palm on the file. "Roland Poole is in intensive care at West Sound General. Surgeons amputated both legs and one arm. He hasn't regained consciousness and remains in critical condition."

Boone fixated on the space before him, the pages still in hand. *Humans kill over religion, ideology, greed, and envy. Those things make a perverse sense.*

Savage, primal, and indiscriminate, Roland and Gloria Poole were murdered for food.

ALICE — UNIVERSITY

The envelope wasn't red hot and burning her hands. Alice knew it. A wave of hopelessness rolled over her as she tore the letter open and removed the contents.

The engraved masthead read *Office of the Dean, Rainforest State College.*

Dear Ms Drinkwater,

The American Association of University Professors, 1940 Statement of Principles on Academic Freedom and

Tenure guidelines for academic tenure prescribes a limited period for candidates to demonstrate a record of published research, ability to attract grant funding, academic visibility, teaching excellence, and administrative or community service.

As a tenure track instructor, you must prove and document your qualification by the start of the next academic year. This correspondence is your official notice, and failure to meet these criterions may cause immediate termination.

The institution reserves the right to cancel your contract or offer you a non-tenure position such as adjunct professor, research professor, or lecturer at a lower rate of compensation and benefits.

In the interim, you remain an associate professor of genetics.

The Rainforest State University and your tenure committee wish you well and the best of luck in meeting the objectives set out before you.

Sincerely, Blah, blah, blah.

The pages dropped from Alice's hand as tears rolled down her cheek.

ELENA — CARRIAGE HOUSE

This morning, the Fish and Game Department report remained untouched on the dining room table where she'd dropped it.

Elena checked in at the main house last night and discovered an energetic argument over Gabby's feral cat. Crying, her sister ran upstairs to her room, and Elena retreated to the peace of the guesthouse, the detective's mystery forgotten.

Her crumpet popped out of the toaster. "Ouch." Elena snagged it, burning her fingers. She took her first bite, butter escaping over her chin.

She dabbed her face with a paper napkin and scanned the *Boston Globe* on her iPad, but each sideglance at the discarded envelope prompted waves of guilt. Elena deposited her tablet next to the unread report.

"The look on officer Anderson's face," she chuckled.

It surprised me to see him, too, but I didn't choke. That ranger stammered like a teenage boy, very cute in a Tarzan the Caveman way. She reached for the sealed report.

The new Bluetooth intercom beeped.

"Elena, you have an admirer," Mina's voice teased across the hollow tinny speaker.

She depressed the lighted "Talk" button. "What makes you think so, Mama?"

"Because a florist delivered a dozen yellow roses and a card."

"What does the card say?"

Cellophane and paper rustled. "Flowers of friendship. Welcome to a most charming colleague," Mina read. "Dinner? Tonight at 7:00? Seth." Her mother laughed. "And who is this person?"

"It is nothing. Another professor I might collaborate with on my summer seminar."

"In my day we called it something else."

Elena laughed. "I'm not in the market." *And not interested in a player. Professor Capello or that dumb ranger.*

Mina chuckled.

"Mama, that is enough out of you."

"Nothing more will be spoken," Mina said.

"Good. Last night, you and the kid were still arguing over that cat. Have you two made up?"

"Your sister ran to her room crying. I think she slipped out without breakfast because I've haven't seen her this morning."

"She'll get over it. She always does. Hey, may I use your office?"

"Žinoma, my daughter."

"*Ačiū,*" replied Elena. "I'm coming now."

Elena left the remains of breakfast on the table,

grabbed her sweater, and descended the stairs two at a time.

On the landing, a metallic flash caught her eye, an antique silver and malachite pin in the shape of a lizard.

"Strange," she said, turning the pin over in search of a maker's mark. *I'll ask Mama later.* Elena dropped the brooch in her pants pocket.

CHAPTER TWELVE

ELENA - UNIVERSITY

T*hump.*
The apple crate of books dropped on the floor. "That's the last load," Elena said.

Her third trip from the parking lot, Elena's blouse, damp with sweat, stuck to her skin, her breathing labored. Her laptop balanced on top of the box, Elena took it to the desk.

Bright sunlight dimmed the screen. Elena squinted as she entered her password. The operating system desktop sprang into view, but the network icon displayed zero bars.

"Damn, no Wi-Fi," she said. "Now what?" Elena scanned her desk.

A post-it written in block letters hung on a gooseneck desk lamp. It was the password.

"Thank you, Alice, you angel."

Elena set up her workstation.

The doorway where Seth Capello slouched, stood half-open. *I should have brought those roses in with me, just in case.* "I really should thank him."

The email login prompt blinked seductively.

"It *is* only polite, right? I'll write him a brief note."

Elena rubbed her earlobe, lips pressed together. "I could say something innocuous: 'Thanks for the flowers.' No, email is impersonal-" Elena glanced at the landline. "Look up his number in the college directory, make a quick call, and leave a message. Not a big deal."

Bringing the receiver to her ear, Elena dialed his office phone number. As it rang, her stomach flipped. "Dumb, dumb, dumb," she muttered. The call went to voicemail.

"You have reached Seth Capello, Professor of Anthropology, please leave your number, and I'll return your call." His voice, smooth and seductive.

"Thank you for the beautiful roses," Elena said, "What an unexpected surprise. The roses, I mean."

She slapped her hand to her forehead. *Just say goodbye and go.* "Um, I'll be here this afternoon if you are at the college, too." *I'm an idiot.* Her cheeks, and ears burned.

"Dinner tonight is, ah, a delightful idea." She turned away from the receiver, shielding an embarrassed cough. "So, I'm going to be home soon, so you can contact me there... later. If you want? Oh, it is Elena Lukas, but I guess you know that already. So, okay. Um, bye." She hung up the phone.

"Unexpected surprise. What an idiot." Elena groaned and unpacked the nearest box. "Suave, Lukas. It's never too early to announce you're a dork."

Like bullets from an assault weapon, she slammed books into the metal bookcase. After twenty minutes of shelving, she'd dissected the call as if it were a frog in high school biology class.

Elena collapsed in her guest chair. *There's nothing left but Ranger Rick's report.*

"You can't put it off any longer." She extracted the papers from the envelope. "I'll just scan the dumb thing and shoot off a brief reply."

Elena read the pages, then she read them a second time. She dropped into her chair.

The report comprised five typewritten pages. Elena spent the next hour making notes on a yellow pad. For another hour, she performed more and more frenetic internet searches.

Elena set the documents on the table and stared ahead.

"It can't be," she said. *It is bear DNA. No doubt. It has some of the right markers. But not* Ursus americanus, *an Olympic black bear, or* Ursus arctos horribilis, *a grizzly.* Elena nibbled on her upper lip. *Maybe a hybrid? A polar bear,* Ursula maritimes, *and one of the other native species?* Her pulse played a tattoo at her temple. *Maybe it's an undiscovered species or a genetic mutation?*

A broad grin grew, and she wiggled in her chair. "This is exciting." In her imagination, thoughts chased each other's tails.

"Wait." Elena froze, and her eyes widened. She snatched the map from the pile and, checking the collection's location, confirmed her fear. The most recent animal attack was less than half a mile from where she heard, *I see you.* A wave of nausea overwhelmed her.

Could this creature be from the mystical world?

Elena almost missed the soft rap at the door. "Come," she said as she straightened the pages and slipped them back inside the envelope.

Alice poked her elfin face around the frame. "Hello? Hello?"

"Hi, Alice. What's up?"

"I stopped to see if you're settling in all right. Are you? All right, that is?"

"Yep. Thanks."

"Great, great." Alice turned to leave.

"I got this report from the Fish and Wildlife department." Elena passed Boone's folder to Alice. "Review the genetics and give me your thoughts?"

"My thoughts? You need *my* thoughts? Gee, it means a lot you think I might have thoughts. Thoughts of value." Alice smiled, then blurted out, "I forgot why I'm here. Your voicemail isn't configured, so he didn't know how to find you. He called the front office." She peered at Elena, expectant.

"Who called? Seth Capello?"

"Nope," Alice said, "This call was from the Fish and Game guy."

Elena beckoned her to continue.

Alice excavated a wadded blue memo from her overall pocket, straightened, and held it out to Elena. "He wants you to go there." She tapped the note. "He said it's urgent."

MINA - SWAN HOUSE

Mina's hands yearned to be busy. "Today will go well," she muttered.

Forty-five minutes ago, her special guest called from Seattle.

An excellent review could keep us from losing the inn. "A car traveling on Interstate Five this time of day." The hands of the fireplace clock read six fifty. "They should be here any moment."

She plucked an errant thread from the brocade sofa upholstery.

Maybe the flower boxes need watering? Copper watering can in hand, Mina hustled out to the porch and tripped. *What in the world?* A garden gnome lay on the mat. Her thirsty plants abandoned, Mina picked up the statuette.

Dressed in red lederhosen and a green cap, the figure held a trowel in one gloved hand. "Hello, who are you?" Mina. She shivered, regardless of the warm spring day. "Your smile hints at madness, little friend."

A pale blue Infiniti QX56 glided to a stop in front of the walk. Mina placed the gnome on the chair next to the watering can.

A tall, gaunt man with a goatee opened the passenger side door and stepped out. He scratched notes in a leather-bound notepad in his hand with a black Cross pen, then placed both inside his navy blazer.

"Welcome to Swan House," Mina said.

The man squinted along his aquiline nose. "Tobias Stephens, travel columnist and blogger," he said. "We're expected."

His limp hand reached out, and she took it.

A round woman with a curly blue-gray perm exited from the driver's side. With a bustle in her every step, she removed several monogrammed valises from the trunk.

"This is our first visit to the south sound." His broad smile gleamed, revealing square, straight teeth. "Only the best places in Seattle, Port Townsend, and the San Juan's." His relentless gaze scoured the mansion. "What will this humble community offer my discerning fans?"

The older woman carried a valise up the stairs, then turned back for another.

Stephens noticed his wife on the porch.

"This is Cecily, my wife," he said with a dismissive wave.

"Let me help," Mina stepped forward.

"Not to worry, Cecily takes care of such things," he said. "Won't you, my dear?"

The woman nodded.

"Now, show us to our room." Stephens steamed inside, pulling Mina and the overloaded Cecily along in his wake.

From the swing, Gabby's cat surveyed the trio's exit. He leapt to the porch decking and, stealthy as a panther, stalked the unwanted statuette. The cat pounced, hissing with claws brandished.

The little man burst on impact, scattering shards of pottery everywhere.

CHAPTER THIRTEEN

GABBY - SCHOOL

The small, narrow window in the classroom door framed Mr Wade. He'd propped both feet on his desk, his legs crossed at the ankles. He clutched a white bread and mystery lunchmeat sandwich in one hand, and a brown paper lunch bag squatted on the desk blotter.

Last night, Gabby marked a few answers on her worksheet, but the majority remained undone. She folded the paper in half and placed it in her math book.

If I asked for help, throw myself on my knees and beg for mercy, maybe he won't flunk me.

The door hinges screeched as she pushed it open.

The teacher considered Gabby but didn't change his position. He continued to chew.

"Mr Wade, do you have a minute?" Gabby lowered her eyes and began her approach.

"Can't this wait for class, Miss Lukas?" He took an oversized bite of his sandwich, leaving a dollop of mayo clinging to the corner of his mouth.

"No, sir. I have questions 'bout yesterday's assignment, and I need help." She cracked open the book and removed her homework.

His lips smacked as his jaws ground his lunch to paste. He swallowed. "I see." He inhaled another mouthful.

"I didn't understand most of these questions."

He swallowed again. The tip of his tongue flicked out fast as a lizard, removing the condiment from his lip. "Class is in less than thirty minutes, Miss Lukas, and you interrupt my lunch with last minute appeals." He licked his fingers one at a time. "That's called locking the barn door after the cow was stolen."

"But, Mr Wade…"

"You may leave, Miss Lukas. Oh, and I suggest you inform your parents you plan to repeat algebra in summer school."

Perspiration collected along her hairline, and she shifted, uneasy. "Okay." Still clutching her assignment, Gabby plodded mechanically out the door and into the hallway, the door hissing as it closed. Her breath came in quick gasps as she crushed the worksheet in her fist.

Gabby opened her hand, and the wad burst into flame and incinerated on her palm. She watched the ash float aloft.

BOONE - WDFW OLYMPIA OFFICE

Ohto rose from his bed, a burgundy cushion under Boone's desk. The dog stretched his front legs in the downward-facing-dog yoga position. He sat back on his haunches, tail wagging, and focused on the office door.

Boone watched from his desk but didn't see. Even now, he couldn't block out the husband's terrified voice. He shook his head once and squeezed his eyes shut as a grimace of pain distorted his face.

Nature red in tooth and claw. His body flinched. Phantom shelling fell all around, and the screaming.

Grabbing the mug on his desk, it took all Boone's control to repress the memory of friendly fire without shattering the ceramic mug against the wall.

The dog's ears cocked toward a sound only he could hear, then let out a joyful bark and ran to the doorway.

"What's up, fella?" Boone said. He released his death grip on the cup and replaced his placid mask.

The squad room door opened, and Elena walked into the room. Ohto barked and danced in circles.

"Hello." Elena laughed and crouched to offer her hand, palms down.

Ohto sniffed and licked her fingers, then sat with his head tilted to the side.

"Good dog," she said.

Boone blinked in disbelief. "Ohto. His name is Ohto," he said. "He is usually standoffish to strangers."

"What a beautiful name."

The dog closed his eyes as she scratched under his chin.

"Finnish for *spirit of the bear*. I guess you know that." She grinned. "It's wonderful you're allowed to bring him to work."

"He's not a pet. He's my partner." Boone joined Elena and his canine partner. "We've been together since he was a pup, and we'll be together for the rest of his life."

"So, you're a police dog."

Ohto wiggled with pleasure.

"His primary role isn't law enforcement." Boone joined her, kneeling on the floor with Ohto between them. "He's a Karelian Bear Dog, bred to hunt and capture big game, bears and cougars. You're a tracking superstar, aren't you, boy?"

"Perhaps I'll see him in action someday."

"Be careful what you ask for, professor." Boone smiled.

"I will, sergeant." Elena's eyes twinkled.

"Thank you for agreeing to meet me with little notice."

"I studied your report this morning and found it fascinating," she said. "Sorry, I'm still working on my response."

"That's all right, I have a more serious matter, and I could use your expert opinion." His earlier somber manner returned. "There's been an attack with a confirmed fatality."

Elena accepted the office chair he offered.

Boone depressed a key on the keyboard, and with a *click*, the elderly desktop's hard drive ground like a cement mixer. The thick monitor's screen blazed into life, displaying a screensaver popular in the mid-aughts.

"Emergency Medical Dispatch recorded the attack, and I left the scene photos on the table. I'm sorry, Ms Lukas, I'm going to play the recording but, be warned, this will not be pleasant."

ELENA — WDFW OLYMPIA OFFICE

The 911 recording ended in a silence that hung thick between them.

Elena held the photos. *You can do this.*

Flip. Flip. Flip. The grisly images were the worst she'd ever seen. Her stomach rolled, but she allowed no outward sign of distress.

She turned the final photographs facedown. "The Poole's are the second and third people attacked in the past two weeks," Elena said. "Is that correct?" She placed her palm on the pile of photos. "Violent attacks don't come out of nowhere. Were there any others?"

"A recent livestock mauling. The clerk pulled everything within a hundred miles of Capitol Forest borders." He pointed to the towering stack of folders at his elbow. "Want to help?" He grinned.

"Don't your people use computers?" Elena asked.

"Sure, we've got loads of them. Loads of old slow ones," Boone replied. "The records group brag they're only six months behind now." He held a handful of files out to Elena. "I could use your help, Doctor Lukas."

"I suppose I can help just this once." Elena shook her head and admired her nails to hide her smile.

Boone gestured to the opposite desk.

Together, they read in companionable silence for the next few hours.

As she worked, Elena sorted her assigned reports into two piles. "I found three likely accounts. The oldest was in early March," she said, placing the last file on the shorter pile.

"Here are a couple more," Boone added his cases to her stack. "These animal attacks fall into the same timeframe and locale."

"Let me get this straight," Elena said. "Two months ago, an unidentified predator shows up and begins ripping apart larger and larger animals until it worked up to people. Is that it?"

"That's about it."

Their eyes locked, and neither spoke for several seconds.

"You're the specialist, what do you think?"

Elena pinched the bridge of her nose and sighed. "These are our options," she said. "One: a sick or hurt native bear on a rampage. Rabies?"

Boone shook his head. "Not inconceivable but unlikely. Black bears appear to be resistant to the infection.

"A rabid arctic fox attacked an Alaskan brown bear and seriously injured it. A buddy of mine, a local conservation officer, searched but couldn't find it before hibernation. The following spring, he recaptured that bear and, sure enough, the bugger tested negative for rabies." He grimaced with eyes squinted. "He thinks the bear was of such mass it would require a much larger dose of virus to become ill. A little fox bite just wasn't enough." Boone cocked his head with raised eyebrows.

"Don't like that option?" The corners of Elena's mouth twitched, and she pursed her lips. "Number two," she held up her index and middle finger, "an invasive species, maybe a polar bear or grizzly, migrating into the habitat."

"Less likely but still possible. What else you got?"

"Number three, an escaped zoo or circus animal. A lion or tiger comes to mind."

"We would have a record. I checked, and there isn't one. I suppose if somebody smuggled an exotic animal into the country and it escaped, but it would come to our attention pretty fast. Next?"

"Four," Elena cringed, watching from the corner of her eyes, "a previously unknown genus driven out of the wilderness by human encroachment."

Boone's guffaw erupted. "You mean Bigfoot or the Chupacabra? Are you kidding, Professor Lukas?"

Elena snorted, returning his laughter. "Hey, guy, it's not impossible. Biologists have discovered several..." she made air quotes with her fingers, "extinct species alive and well."

Boone cradled his chin in his hand and waited.

"In 1996, several zoologists traveling in remote Laos discovered a *Laonastes aenigmamus*, commonly called a rat-squirrel. Most biologists assumed this rodent disappeared eleven million years ago. Their find forced researchers to reclassify the entire family."

Elena stood and crossed to the coffee station. "Closer to home, we've rediscovered the Giant Palouse Earthworm in Eastern Washington. It's an albino worm, over three and a half feet long, that burrows as deep as fifteen feet underground." She poured coffee into a paper cup and carried it back to the desk.

"Fascinating as this line of inquiry is becoming, professor, has Rocky the rat-squirrel or Casper the friendly earthworm eaten anyone?"

"I appreciate your skepticism." Elena's eyes twinkled. "I'm sharing every possibility with you, detective." She paused and nibbled her lower lip.

Boone cocked his head and stared into her blue-green eyes. "Elena, what aren't you telling me?"

She took a drink of the coffee and winced at its bitterness.

The desk phone rang.

Boone pointed at her. "You stay right there. I'm not done with you." He answered the call on speaker, "Anderson."

"Hi, Boone, Sitton here." The connection crackled.

"I'm glad you called, doc. I'm here with the expert you recommended. Professor *Elena* Lukas. She's sharing several interesting predator theories."

"Great," said the vet in a rush. "I look forward to meeting her and hearing her ideas."

"What can I do for you, Dan?" Boone shifted in his chair.

"I'm over at the hospital. Our first victim is awake, and he's telling a strange story."

Boone leaned forward, arms crossed on the desk. "What's he saying?"

"You need to hear for yourself. Can you get over here soon?" Urgency was clear in Dr Sitton's tone.

"Okay. I'll be there as fast as I can." Boone hung up, then said, "I need to go meet our wildlife vet at the hospital in the next hour. Are you game for a field trip, professor?"

GABBY — SCHOOL

Despite the oscillating rumble of the pep rally in the gym, Gabby's kitten heels clacked loudly on the empty hallway's beige linoleum.

"Today is the worst day of my life." Gabby shuddered at the memory of her algebra class.

———

"Ms Lukas didn't hand in her paper today," the demon Wade said. "Can you share your reasoning with the class?"

"No, thank you," she said, but the teacher would not let it go.

"Perhaps you should teach the class today since you obviously understand the material better than the rest of us." He continued until all the students were laughing at her.

Then she lost her temper and screamed, "Shut up, shut up, shut up."

The teacher smiled when he ordered her to the vice principal, Mr Lyons. After a short talk and a long wait, the VP referred her to Mrs Summers, the school's licensed psychologist.

An attractive older woman with a mane of auburn curls, Nora Summers-Irving used every tool in her ample toolbox to encourage Gabby to talk.

"Your teachers and the other children like you, and your grades over your academic career are good, Gabby. This year, Mr Wade says you are uncooperative and rebellious. Do you know what is prompting this change in your behavior?"

Gabby stared at the rustic folk-art and photos of exotic locations, wanting to speak but not knowing where to start. *She must travel a lot. I want to go somewhere. Anywhere?* She stared at her shoes.

"Is there something going on at home we should discuss?" Nora, a half-smile on her lips, waited for her to continue.

Gabby crossed her arms over her chest. She considered telling the counselor Mr Wade hated her and picked on her. But common sense told her he'd been a teacher for a hundred years and no one would believe her.

She shifted in her seat.

Telling anyone she was pissed because her mother wouldn't let her keep a stray cat sounded childish.

Telling outsiders about the goddess, her new powers, and her crazy family was not permitted. And if she broke the rules and talked, no outsider would believe her. They'd send her to the crazy kids' home. It was hopeless.

"Everything's okay," Gabby said, angling her body away from the counselor.

"Good to hear. Are you having a challenge with a classmate? A boy?" Nora said.

"I said, 'No.'" Gabby swept her arms out, her nostrils flaring. "Are you listening to me? Nothing is wrong."

"I hope you know you can talk-"

"Can I go?" Gabby said, cutting the older woman short. Gabija's fire kindled, all the way to her toes. "I have to go," she said. "I have a class." Bolting to her feet, Gabby didn't wait for permission to leave and fled out the door.

A few minutes later, Gabby reached her locker and spun the dial: left, right, left, right. *Clunk.* The hasp released. She opened the door and threw in her backpack.

Catching a glance of herself in the mirror inside the door, Gabby stuck out her tongue at her image. "Ugly. Hideous," she said.

Her scarlet cheeks and the perspiration on her forehead showed that Gabija, goddess of home and hearth, the fire-bearer, was close to the surface. The girl's limp hair hung around her face. She bent at the waist, shook it out, then straightened, flipping her locks back.

"Hello, hot stuff," a male's voice whispered in her ear.

Gabby spun to face him.

Dressed in black jeans and a skin-tight white shirt, his thin hips, broad shoulders and sculptured pecs artfully displayed.

Jacob Brooks stood too close. The warmth of the boy's body and aroma of Versace's Eau Fraiche caressed Gabby, and an unfamiliar sensation of need rose in her. Like an hourglass, her angry heat drained from her chest to settle in her pelvis. Gabby stepped back, but the locker door blocked any hope of escape.

"I waited for you in the gym," he said and selected a hank of her long red hair. "Where were you?" He twiddled the lock between his thumb and forefinger.

"I was studying in the library." Gabby placed her palm on his chest and pushed the boy back. "Not that it's any of your business."

"I was gonna walk you home after the rally." Jacob stepped aside, allowing access to her locker. "I'm not so sure now."

"My loss," she said and flipped back her hair. Gabby grabbed her pack from the floor of her locker and pushed the door shut.

"Bye." She turned to leave, but the tall boy grabbed her arm and jerked her to him.

"Where do you think you're going?" He released her. "If you're my girlfriend, you do what I say," Jacob whispered as he ran his finger along her cheek.

Gabby squared her shoulders and said, "Then it's good I'm not your girlfriend."

The boy's eyes, now flinty with anger, narrowed. But the happy pep rally crowd burst through the gymnasium fire doors, drowning out his hissed reply.

Gabby grabbed the opportunity. "Janie, wait up," she called and disappeared into the mass of her fellow students.

CHAPTER FOURTEEN

ART - LACY, WA

"We'll play," bellowed the redneck yokel as he scampered back to his family.

Shifting in his Barcalounger, Art Morton reached for the remote and decreased the volume.

Most days, Art spent the day in his snagged blue terrycloth robe but, this morning, he donned his only pair of gray sweatpants and a gray XXXXL shirt with "Wildman" printed in block letters on the front.

A small cake with white cream frosting, yellow roses, and "Happy Birthday" swirled in yellow icing rested on the card table in front of his favorite armchair. A Kraft green field notebook lay nearby.

"Today, I'll eat the entire cake while watching my shows. Damn the diabetes," he said.

Judge Joanne Justice, Art's favorite program, played on his sixty-inch television. A fifty-something woman with a nasty dye job filled the screen. She was suing her unnaturally buxom daughter and her skinny boyfriend for two hundred and fifty dollars in back rent.

I love this shit. Art watched the angry faces. *It's a*

fuckin' looney bin out there. I'm never leaving the house again. Animals are better than people any day.

Picking up the remote, he muted the volume and configured close captioning, then placed it on the card table next to his Mac. Art opened the laptop's lid, launched a browser, and selected the State Department of Fish and Wildlife's Wild-WatchCams live feeds from the field from his favorites.

"Think I'll watch the Seal-cam today," he said.

Last spring, Art spotted an abandoned seal pup on a sandbar. He reported the sighting to the Northwest Marine Mammal Stranding Network.

The man smiled at the memory. *Those rangers must have picked up the baby and taken it to a rehabber because it was gone when I checked back. Maybe I saved a life.* A grin spread across the man's broad face. "Did you know I'm a hero, Judge?"

The web cameras refreshed every ten seconds. Art switched focus between Judge Joanne and the Seal-cam, never missing a thing.

Sporting a baseball cap and missing a front tooth, the loser boyfriend testified. Dialogue displayed at the bottom of the screen read, "I never promised to pay the old bat nothing."

Art slid an oversized forkful of cake into his mouth and grimaced at the sickly-sweet frosting.

Seal-cam displayed an abandoned gravel spit extending into the bay. Art frowned.

"That's a lie. He is a liar, and he cheated on my daughter." The mother mugged for the camera.

Here comes my favorite part. Carefully, Art scraped off a rose and popped it into his mouth and unmuted the sound.

"Madame, it's not your turn," blared the Judge. "When I want your opinion, I will ask for it."

"You tell her, Joanne." He laughed through a mouthful of cake, then muted the volume.

Gabby bounded up the stairs like a doe and sprinted through the sitting room toward the door.

Who is this? Our horrible guests are out, Elena's at school, Grandmother's napping, and Mama won't get back from her stupid errands for another hour.

Gaby slid into the entry. The bell rang again.

"I'm coming, I'm coming."

Gabby yanked the double doors open. "Yeah, what do you want?"

A blond man with beautiful eyes waited on the porch.

"Um, I mean, can I help you?" she said.

Gabby ran her fingers through her tousled hair.

"Hello, I'm Seth," he said. "I'm here to take your sister to dinner."

"I'm Gabby, her younger and cuter sister." She giggled then straightened. "Sorry, Elena isn't here."

Seth's face fell. "How unfortunate, there must be a misunderstanding? I guess I'd better go." He turned to retreat down the steps, then paused and said, "I could wait."

"I don't know," Gabby said, her words quiet. "Elena should be back soon." She tucked a strand of hair behind her ear. "She didn't say when she'll be back." Gabby's cheeks flushed red, matching her "Kiss me, I'm the cook" apron.

"I don't mind how long it takes." His warm smile pushed her doubts away.

"I guess it would be alright," she said.

"Thank you, how kind." Seth Capello held out his hand.

His grip was firm, dry, and warm. When he gave her hand a gentle squeeze, Gabby's tummy tingled.

Seth glared toward the porch swing. "I can wait out here, but..." His smile drooped.

His eyes were dark brown like chocolate. *Yum. I love chocolate.* Self-conscious, Gabby looked away, then made her decision.

"Come in, sir. Can I get you a cup of tea or coffee?" Gabby gestured for him to enter.

"Why, thank you, Miss Lukas," Seth smiled with a twinkle in his eyes.

With an elaborate flourish and curtsy, Gabby gestured toward the dining room. Seth walked past her into the entry. "The sitting room is on the left."

Gabby pulled out her phone and texted, "U nt bleev w@ I'm doin."

With a tug, she released the ties, tossing the apron on the entry bench. Gabby flipped her hair, stuck out her chest, and sauntered through the door, swaying her hips as she went.

JANIE — RALPH'S FINE GROCERY

Short with thick glasses, Janie Bates might bloom after high school. But today, she was the little brown wren singing an ordinary song.

She and Gabby became friends in sixth grade, and from the moment they met, Janie understood she was the sidekick to a tall, slender girl with beautiful red hair. Resigned to this most of the time, today, it bothered her.

The grocery checker, a college student, stared at the cash register when she handed him five dollars. He ripped off the receipt and threw it on her purchase. "Thanks," he muttered. "Next." Janie grabbed her item and headed for the door.

Gabby found a boyfriend. And I can't get this ugly old guy to look at me? She's flirting with her guy right now, the little skank. Giggling, she blushed at her language.

Whoosh. The automatic door opened, and Janie walked through, unwrapping a large organic Brazilian chocolate bar. "The cure for everything?" She took a bite of candy, letting it melt in her mouth.

In the parking lot, Jacob Brooks sat on the hood of a Toyota Celica. Another boy she didn't know sat behind the wheel. Jacob slid off and beckoned her to come.

Oh, my God. He means me. Janie crammed the chocolate bar in her purse and trotted over to meet the boy.

Wordless, Jacob looked her up and down.

Fighting an urge to cross her arms, Janie waited for him to speak first. He didn't. When she could wait no longer, she said, "Hi?"

Smiling, he opened the backseat door. "Get in."

Her words stumbled. "I don't think I... um. My mom, she wants…"

"Sit for a minute, I only want to talk to you." The boy Cheshire Cat grinned.

"All right," she squeaked and got inside.

Worn seat covers, discarded fast food wrappers, and the odor of marijuana yelled this wasn't a parent's car. The driver watched her in the rearview mirror and smirked.

"You're Gabby Lukas' friend, right?" Jacob glowered at her.

"Yes, I'm her best friend." She raised her chin to see him better.

Jacob lazed with his arm flung over the door.

"Why?" she said, adjusting her glasses.

He placed his other hand on the opposite door frame, blocking her escape. "You know my man, Keshawn?"

"Yes. Last year, he was in my English class." A lump formed in Janie's throat. "I really gotta go."

"He thinks, maybe without glasses, you'd be cute. But I'm not sure." He leaned closer. "Take 'em off."

Reluctant, Janie removed her spectacles and, heart pounding, squinted at Jacob through the fog.

Appraising her, the boy stepped away. "I guess you'll do," he shrugged his shoulders. "Be at Skateland on Saturday and Keshawn will meet you there."

"Like a date?" she asked. Her stomach fluttered.

"Sure, why not?" Jacob stepped aside. "And bring Gabby Lukas with you or don't show."

Janie jumped out, but Jacob caught her by the wrist.

"Don't tell her we talked." His voice was stern.

"Okay," she said.

He tightened his grip. "Promise?"

"Yes, yes. I won't tell her. I promise," Janie yelped. "Can I go?"

"No one's stopping you," he said, releasing her. "Be there Saturday. My boy likes you so don't disappoint him."

I've got a date. Her self-esteem rising, Janie rushed away.

CHAPTER FIFTEEN

ELENA - HOSPITAL

Despite their voices in the hallway, the old man's eyes remained closed. The hospital bed threatened to swallow the frail elderly man.

Boone, Elena, and Dan Sitton clustered in the hallway, listening to a doctor.

"Patrick Moore presented with long gashes across the right side of his back and buttocks," said his doctor, a man in his sixties, with a badge reading Eric Jensen, MD.

"He's concussed, with broken ribs and a clavicle. Cuts and abrasions from a fall." Consulting a computer tablet, he went on with the faint remnant of a Boston accent. "The patient's been in and out of consciousness for the last twenty-four hours."

Dan Sitton took up the story. "Mr Moore had a minor stroke brought on by his injuries and hasn't regained full use of his right side. Mountain bikers found him. It is fortunate he didn't spend the night alone and risk exposure."

"My patient's taking pain medication," the doctor said. "Don't take what he says as gospel." Dr Jensen peered at the dog through the half-glasses perched on his nose. "Please, make it short, and try not to upset him Mr Moore needs his rest."

"We'll keep that in mind," Boone said.

"Excuse me." The doctor nodded, then strode off down the hall.

"I'll wait here with Ohto," said the vet.

They entered the room. Boone led the way.

Elena crossed to the guest chair by Mr Moore's bed with Boone circling to the opposite side.

Late afternoon sun filled the room with amber light. An IV pole with two bags hung by the bed, and a bedside table held tumblers of water and juice, waiting with straws bent and ready.

"Mr Moore," Boone said.

The man opened his eyes.

"Sir, I'm Detective Anderson from the Washington Department of Fish and Wildlife." He gestured to Elena.

"My colleague, Doctor Elena Lukas from the Rainforest State College is with me. Dr Lukas is a wildlife specialist."

Elena smiled and opened to the Penumbra. Reading auras wasn't her native ability, and the throb at her temples was immediate. Her breathing slowed as the Penumbra brightened.

Burgundy tendrils of pain swirled around the room, mixing with indigo swatches of grief; lightning bolts of amber anger alternated with the sickly chartreuse flashes of fear.

I must hurry before this working takes too much of me.

Elena sorted out the shades of the patients who suffered or died in the space distorting her view. She concentrated on the color and flavor of the old man, separating his palette from the spectrum of others.

Mr Moore returned her smile with a weary one of his own.

"May we ask you a few questions?" she asked.

"Please, hand me that glass of water, miss?" he asked, his voice cracking.

Elena lifted the water glass and held the straw to his mouth. Mr Moore took a long draw.

"Thank you."

His eyes shut.

"Sir," Boone said.

"I don't remember much," he said.

"Tell us what you can, Mr More. Everything is helpful." Boone cleared his throat. "What happened to you in the Capitol Forest?"

Elena offered the glass to Moore again, but he waved it away with his good left hand.

Viewed from the *in-between*, the old man's internal flame sputtered, a wick drowning in a well of wax.

His words struggled out as if he couldn't easily locate them. "For years, I've been trying to collect a Pacific-Slope Flycatcher." Moore shook his head. "They migrate up from Mexico in the spring, you know. They prefer, what do you call it…" Moore stared at his twisted right hand, raised blue veins standing out against his translucent skin. "Those green needle trees, Douglas fir?" The old man smiled. "Conifers, that's it." His words flowed now, and his inner light shone brighter. "Flycatchers are a fascinating species."

"The birds wait on the branch, you know, until they spy a tasty insect." He licked his lips with a smack. "At an impressive speed, they swoop down and catch it." He reached out and snapped his fist closed.

"And your attack?" Boone's smile was fixed, his hand tensed but didn't clench.

Elena glanced at Boone, then shifted her gaze away. She didn't wish to see what aura surrounded the officer.

"Inexperienced birders often mistake a Cordilleran Flycatcher for the noble Pacific-Slope. The difference is subtle."

Elena nodded as Boone moved into a rigid parade rest.

"The Cordy has a two-note call, and the PacSlope calls with a single up-slurred note."

"That's fascinating, isn't it, officer?" Elena said.

"Uh-huh," Boone said.

"Go on, Mr. Moore." Elena touched his hand and smiled into his watery grey eyes. In her sight, the old man's blue life-force danced around his body.

"The Packy I located was a perfect specimen. White oval eye ring, orange lower mandible, wing bars, everything. Spectacular." A distant look formed in the man's eyes, and he stopped speaking.

"So, you were watching the... Pacific-Slope Fly-catcher," Boone prompted.

"Her nest sat in the hollow of a tree downslope. I set up my tripod on the edge of the embankment and had her in my long lens. She was feeding flies to her chicks. Remarkable, don't you know." The old man took a sharp wheezy intake of breath.

"Did you recognize the animal that attacked you? What species?" Boone asked.

Moore stared into space, a vacant look in his eyes. "There was a ripping sound like fabric tearing," he said. "The blow spun me around, and I fell backward."

"What was it?" Elena whispered and took his pale hand. The contact with his icy flesh increased her sense of him.

Psychic blowback hammered in her skull, and the coppery scent of blood filled her nose. With two fingers, Elena pressed her temple.

"It was massive and looming above me. His, her, or its? I don't know, just glowing red eyes." His speech was halting.

Moore's terror crashed over Elena once more, and she flinched.

Am I hurting myself? Her jaw tightened as she

struggled to hold on to the Penumbra for a moment longer. *I'll let go soon.*

"There was something wrong with its face," the man said.

Boone slid his chair forward.

"I only got a glimpse," Moore said. "Hunks of flesh were missing. But the stench. Meat rotting in the sun."

A black and purple mottling erupted beneath the old man's fragile skin, malevolent squid's ink swirling under the ocean's surface.

What the hell is that? Elena was grateful Boone couldn't see the evil permeating the man.

"The beast bellowed, and I thought my eardrums would rupture. Teeth, there were long yellow teeth." The old man groaned, and his eyelids drooped.

For a moment, Elena thought he might pass away, but the even rise and fall of his chest showed he was asleep.

The skin mottling faded.

Elena released Mr Moore's hand, breaking her connection to the Penumbra.

Mediena's blessing. Give him our strength.

Boone gestured to the door.

Elena nodded and rose from her chair. Her head spun, stomach rolled, and she grasped the chair.

"You okay?" he asked.

"Low blood sugar, I skipped lunch." She shook her head. "I'm all right now."

Placing one unsteady foot in front of the other, Elena lurched toward the door after Boone.

"You get anything?" asked Dan.

"Maybe." Boone watched Elena lean against the doorframe. "Ready to go?"

Elena nodded.

Three abreast, they returned to the elevator at the end of the hall.

No one spoke. Boone pushed the down arrow.

There's a whiff of darkness clinging to him. She wrinkled her nose. *Just like the smell of smoke from an occult bonfire. No sick animal or invasive species attacked Mr Moore. This was magic. Blood magic.*

"What do you think?" asked the vet.

"I think I need a drink," Boone and Elena said in unison.

BOONE - HOSPITAL CAFÉ

Boone placed the orange tray on the hospital cafeteria table. Coffee sloshed over the lips of the paper cups.

"What happened to your doctor friend?" asked Elena.

Ohto leaned against Elena's leg, watching Boone.

He handed one to Elena and placed the other in front of his chair.

"He had to get back," Boone said. "Have something?" He gestured toward the breakfast pastries on the tray.

Elena's hands shook as she removed a blueberry muffin.

"Thanks," she said, taking a bite. "Stale hydrogenated oil and high fructose corn syrup, my favorite."

Boone slid into the chair. "Sorry. There wasn't much of a choice."

"I'm not complaining. Wait, I guess I am complaining. Sorry." She took another bite and chewed slowly.

She is beautiful. Silky hair and extra-long legs. Boone felt his physical response to her and shifted in his seat. *Damn it.*

"What? Do I have food on my face?" Elena brushed her hand across her lips.

"I, ah, I was wondering why you became a biologist." Boone gulped his coffee. It tasted of bitter hours in the pot.

"My field is *ethno*biology." Elena returned the half-eaten pastry to the tray. "I study the relationships between people, biota, and environments and changes throughout human history."

"An unusual field," Boone said. "What drew you?"

"You could say I joined the family business," Elena said. "My mother specializes in… home remedies and such. Regana, my grandmother, was a healer, too. My entire family is, ah, close to the land." She rotated her mug of coffee around and back to its original position. "I'm from a lengthy line of herbalists, healers, and religious leaders. They assumed I'd follow in their footsteps. I did, but with a twist. Not very interesting." Elena batted the question away with her hand.

"What about you? Why not become a big-city police detective? Why choose Bambi and Nemo over perps and skells?" She winked.

"I was a patrolman back in Helena for two years," he said. "I enlisted when we invaded Kuwait." He scrutinized the tray, his mouth a line.

"How long were you in the military?" she asked.

"I did two tours with the Rangers. The other kind." Chuckling, he touched the uniform insignia on his chest.

"What was that like?" Elena picked at her pastry, her eyes averted.

"Intense. Sometimes there was," he paused, "heavy action." Boone swallowed. "When I got back, I needed more space. Each WDFW officer covers five hundred miles, give or take, so I got what I wanted."

"Helena, as in Montana, right? Did you grow up there?" Her bright eyes watched him.

"Twin Bridges, a hundred miles southwest of Helena. A crossroad with a gas station, feed store, and a tavern. Guess which one does the most business."

Laughing, Elena tilted her head. "Are you from a big family?"

A hint of a smile formed on his face. "I grew up in an orphanage. My mother abandoned me at birth, so I never knew my family."

A bank of plate-glass wall-to-floor panes covered the far wall, and the pale sunlight of dusk cast long shadows on the floor.

"You? Husband? Kids?" he asked.

Elena stared at her coffee. "I was engaged, but it didn't work out." Elena paused, then shook her head and smiled at Boone. "No kids, just the four of us: my sister, mother, grandmother, and me." Elena cleared her throat. "My mother was born in Lithuania but lived all over Europe. My sister and I were born here in the States."

Elena lay her hand on his, then pulled it back. "Foster care, that must have been hard."

"The orphanage closed when I was six." He stared at his hand for a long moment. "After that, I never stayed with one family for long. When I was twelve, an elderly rancher and his wife adopted me. I'm not complaining. They weren't unkind. They just needed a farmhand, not a son. The Andersons fed and educated me. They gave me a warm bed."

"Are you still in contact with them?" Elena asked quietly.

"They're both gone." He sipped his coffee. "What about you?"

"I never met my father," Elena said, her voice a whisper.

She reached to him once more and touched his forearm. Boone felt a spark jump from her hand to his skin. He shuddered.

With a quick intake of breath, Elena pulled her hand away.

ELENA — HOSPITAL CAFÉ

Elena's cell phone trilled. "Excuse me," she said to Boone, then picked it up from the table and answered. "Elena Lukas."

"Doctor Lukas, its Alice Drinkwater from the university."

"Oh, hello, Alice."

"Sorry to call, but I've done something that might make you angry."

"Okay, tell me." Elena looked at Boone, then pointed to the phone and mouthed, "I'm sorry."

Boone dug into his breast pocket and removed a dog biscuit. He held it out to Ohto. The dog stretched forward as far as he could without leaving Elena's side and took the treat.

"It is the DNA report. That DNA sample you gave me," said Alice. "My specialty is genetics." She giggled, "You know that."

"Uh-huh." Elena tapped the back of the phone with her index finger.

"After I reviewed my results, I instructed the lab to run more specialized tests."

"Lab?" asked Elena. "What lab?"

"The Forensic Animal Genetics Laboratory at UC Davis." Alice's voice lowered to a whisper. "I used your name, Dr Lukas." Silence hung on the line. "The results are fascinating, and I'll find the budget somewhere."

"Not a problem. I'd have done the same. Alice, Sergeant Anderson is here with me and I'd like him to listen in. Do you mind?"

"Not at all. I don't mind, I mean," said Alice.

Elena turned on the mobile's speaker. "What are you telling me?"

Boone leaned forward.

"My initial test showed DNA from more than one

animal. I think it's a chimera, but I won't know until we get the next round of test results back."

"A what?" Boone said. "Like the Greek myth thing?"

"No," Alice said. "It's a genetic chimera, a single organism composed of cells from multiple genotypes." The pure joy in Alice's voice was infectious.

"This *is* very exciting," Elena replied.

"It would be great if we could get more samples," Alice said. "Is that possible?"

"I'm planning to go out to the Capitol Forest tomorrow," Elena said. "I'll look around the site of the attack," Elena said. "Maybe I can find more for you. This is great work, Alice, keep it up."

"Bye, Dr Lukas," Alice said and terminated the call.

As she dropped the phone in her purse, Elena looked up to Boone. His narrowed eyes, pinched mouth, and flushed face told her something was very wrong.

"What?" she asked.

GABBY — SWAN HOUSE

Gabby threw her head back and laughed a bit too loud. "You are so funny, Seth." She settled her elbow on the table and balanced her head on her hand.

"As charming as the company is," Seth said. He smiled, displaying straight white teeth. "I must be going." The smile faded. "I'm sorry I missed your sister, but I enjoyed our chat and the refreshments." He gestured to the plate of cookies on the table.

"Oh, no, you don't have to leave, do you? I can make more tea? Coffee? Orange juice?"

"Tempting, Gabby. Very tempting." His voice dropped to a deep rumble. "Sadly, I've other people to see this evening." He rose. "None of them half as pleasant as you, Ms Lukas."

Gabby followed Seth to the door. Grabbing for the door handle, her hand brushed his. She gasped. Seth lifted her hand from the knob, saying, "Allow me."

"Thank you, kind sir." Gabby model-walked through the front door.

On the porch, Seth took her hand, bringing it to his lips. "Farewell, my young friend. Until next time."

"Goodbye," Gabby whispered. She held her breath and wished the moment might never end.

The older man released her hand, and it floated to her side.

Just like in a movie.

On the front walk, the black cat skidded to a stop in front of the man, hissing. His back arched, his fur standing on end.

"Trouble, stop that. Leave Seth alone."

The tom jumped sideways in challenge, hissing and spitting.

The man pointed. Trouble froze. "Go." His voice was quiet yet commanding.

Trouble growled low and slunk away into the Hydrangeas.

"I'm so sorry." Gabby ran down the stairs. "He's a nice kitty most of the time."

"Pay no mind." Seth touched the tip of her chin. "Please, tell your sister I came by."

"I will," she said.

Without opening the door, he hopped behind the wheel of a red vintage MG and departed with a roar of the engine.

Gabby unlocked her phone to text Janie, her best friend, never wondering how the cat got out of her room this time.

BOONE — HOSPITAL CAFÉ

Elena stared into his eyes. "Is something wrong?"

"It's nothing," Boone said. "Now, explain this all to me again. What is this chimera thing?"

"In the strictest sense, a mythological monster often depicted as having a goat's body, a lion's head, and a serpent's tail," Elena replied. "In this case, Alice uses the genetics definition, a single organism with the genetic material of two or more distinct individuals: could be both male and female, or a lab created specimen with several contributions."

"Can that even happen?" Boone asked. "I've never heard of such a thing."

"Occasionally, human embryos merge in utero," Elena rubbed her eyes. "Lab researchers produce chimera by transplanting the DNA from one creature into the ova of another."

"That's sci-fi isn't it," Boone said with emphasis.

Elena ran her hands through her hair as she sat back in her chair. "In 1984, a team in Cambridge, England, commingled the genes of a goat and a sheep, transplanted the fetus into a donor animal. A few months later, an animal with both wool and hair was born."

"This is so wrong," Boone said, scratching and rubbing his left eye.

"It gets worse. In 2007, at the University of Nevada, they injected human DNA into a ewe's egg. The adult was fifteen percent human and eighty-five percent sheep."

"Damn it," Boone said. "Why the hell would they do that?"

"Organ transplantation." Her face was passive, unreadable.

Boone closed his eyes and shook his head. "I don't get it."

"Think," she said. "Imagine someone you loved,

let's say your child, waited years for a new liver, heart, or kidney." Elena spread her hands. "Then someone told you they can grow a replacement organ that is a *perfect* match. No one has to die, and they save your child."

During their visit, the cafeteria filled. A lone doctor in scrubs sat in a corner eating a sandwich and reading a newspaper. It was quiet, but for one toddler objecting to his mother's menu choice and a group of nurses laughing.

"Your colleague believes a lab-created monster attacked Mr Moore?"

"I suspect Alice believes it's a naturally occurring phenomenon, but it's still too early to tell."

Boone sighed. "This case gets more and more disturbing."

"We'll know more when I gather more samples."

CHAPTER SIXTEEN

BOONE - HOSPITAL CAFE

"I'm afraid we'll have to find another solution. The area is closed to the public." Boone folded his arms across his chest. "No one can go out there."

"There is no other way. I'm a scientist, and I have to see things for myself," Elena said, matching his movement.

"The hell you do," he burst out. "I'll bring you more crime scene photos, casts of prints, everything you need. Examine those."

"It isn't the same, I need to see and touch everything for myself and experience the place first-hand." Her jaw set, her gaze held.

"Things? What the hell does that mean?" He squeezed his biceps and shifted his weight back and forth. "The whole idea is foolish, and I won't permit it."

"I do not need your approval, Detective Anderson." Elena's palms struck the table. "You came to me. You asked for my help. And you need my expertise." The diners sitting behind them scowled. Elena lowered her voice. "Well, this expert is going to the Capitol Forest tomorrow morning, and she is not asking for anyone's permission."

"Wake up, Dr Lukas. I told you the area is closed, and for a very good reason. A vicious predator mauled a woman to death, put two men in the hospital, and it is still hunting in those woods." Boone slammed his fist on the table. "I need to protect the public and you are the public. That's my job, damn it."

Facing off across the green Formica cafeteria table, they glared at each other with clenched fists.

Elena broke their gaze, snatched her purse from the table, and sprang to her feet, almost upending the chair.

Boone rose. "Where are you going?"

"I'm leaving, and you won't stop me." Elena twirled away.

"Doctor Lukas?" he called.

"What?" she spat, her back to him.

"You rode to the hospital with me." His deadpan was perfect.

Elena's shoulders shook with repressed laughter, the surrounding diners watching.

"Would you consider a compromise, Elena?" he said, sotto voce.

"I'm listening." She turned to face him.

"We *could* go together. I pick you up, drive to the scene, and show you everything." The ghost of his smile threatened. "What do you say?"

"I'll consider it." She smirked, pulled a rough brown napkin from the holder, and scrawled her address and phone number. "Here. Pick me up at this address tomorrow at seven a.m."

Boone folded the paper and stuffed it in his pocket.

She smiled, and his heart skipped a beat.

"We'd better head back," she said, gathering up the cups and napkins and depositing them on the orange tray.

"I'll police this for us." He took their trash and

dishes and walked over to the trash cans and the conveyer belt along the back wall. He sat the tray down and watched until it disappeared into a hole in the wall.

On the way to Boone's truck, and later on their drive back to the WDFW parking lot, Elena and Boone kept to safe topics like the weather, new construction, and traffic.

Boone pulled in next to her yellow MINI, and Elena slid out of the cab to the ground.

"See you tomorrow," she said.

"Okay, Bye." He placed his hand on Ohto and stroked the dog's back.

Boone remained behind the wheel until Elena's car receded into the distance. As it disappeared around the bend, the invisible bond between them tugged, snapped, and broke. The thread severed, pain stabbing his gut.

Ohto's whimper prompted a rush of cold in his empty core.

The dog felt it break, too? Boone turned away. "Don't worry, fella." Boone rubbed Ohto's head and scratched the bridge of his snout. "We'll see her tomorrow."

ELENA - SWAN HOUSE DRIVEWAY

Purple, red, and yellow tulips lined Swan House's curved driveway. Elena sat behind the wheel, staring. The plants nodded in the light breeze. She didn't recognize their beauty.

Images of the attack haunted her like a slasher movie villain refusing to die. Images of delicate limbs mangled and bleeding. The vision assaulted her spirit. Elena closed her eyes, and her stomach turned.

Both her hands gripped the wheel. With effort, Elena slowed her breathing and pushed back her grief.

Alice's DNA results, the old man, and those incident reports of escalating animal attacks add up to something. But what? Elena pressed her back against the seat.

Her slouchy russet handbag rested on the passenger seat. Elena picked it up and rummaged around until she found lip balm. She adjusted the mirror and spread the gloss across her full mouth. She snapped the cap on the tube, then tossed it into her bag.

Rap, rap.

Mina's face appeared in the window. Elena jumped. She lowered the glass. The handle squeaked. "You scared the bejesus out of me, Mama."

The older woman stooped, eye-to-eye. "I spotted you from the dining room window. You sat here for so long I worried something was wrong."

"I'm fine." Her sigh was deep and long.

Mina cocked an eyebrow.

"I'm consulting on a wildlife problem. There have been some very violent animal attacks, but I can handle that. I'm worried it might be something more *complicated*."

"They are difficult to work with?"

"A little. The guy I'm working with, Detective Sergeant Anderson, is charming, but also a bit macho." An image of Colin popped in her mind. She was immediately flooded with guilt and loss. "I can handle him, too. We'll finish investigating tomorrow, solve his mystery, then I can run as fast and far away as possible."

"Then what was so complicated?"

Elena's fingertips touched the base of her throat. "This afternoon, this detective and I visited an attack victim in the hospital. He'd been badly mauled." Elena took a deep breath. "I sensed something off. So, I decided to try and read him."

A slight breeze ruffled Mina's hair. "What did you see?"

Elena shivered. "Blood magic sign. The old man was saturated in it."

Mina's eye widened. "Oh, no. This is serious. Did you drain it from him?"

Elena's shoulders sank. "No, Mr Moore's reading weakened me so much. I couldn't even try," she said.

"It makes perfect sense," Mina said. "You're out of practice, and true seeing isn't Mediena's gift. Using an unnatural gift levies a much higher personal price."

"It was stupid. I jumped in with no thought of the cost." Elena massaged her temples.

"Indeed. If your gentleman were a bird or tree," said Mina, "it would have been easy to read and cost near nothing."

"I've taken the gifts for granted. Foolish. These days, I don't know what I'm doing much of the time. I could have easily paid for that party trick with my life." Elena looked into the rear-view mirror then sagged in her seat. "Look at these bags, they weren't there this morning." Her eyes drifted closed, and her voice drifted away.

"You're exhausted." Mina placed her cool palm on Elena's cheek.

Her mother's hand warmed. Elena's own exhaustion dissolved. She opened her eyes, sat up, and watched as bags formed and darkened under her mother's eyes.

Elena removed her mother's hand and kissed the back. "No need for you to take any more. I'm better now." Elena's head bowed. "Thank you for Dievė Žemyna's blessing."

Mina swayed and stepped back.

"Are *you* all right?" Elena asked. She got out of the car. The closing car door thumped.

"There is something on my mind, but I suppose it's nothing." Mina hesitated.

"You can't fool me. Come up to the carriage

house," Elena said, taking her mother's arm. "We can talk there."

STEPHENS - SWAN HOUSE

Tobias Stephens wrote in his travel journal.

The large guest suites are elegant, welcoming, and comfortable. Queen-sized, four-poster beds leave ample room for period nightstands. Dressers, armoires, and writing tables wait for visitor's convenience.

He went on.

The excellent condition of the antiques would fool a novice believing them replicas. Should Mrs Lukas maintain this quality and service level during my visit, I will give Swan House a passing review.

He finished with a flourish, then scowled at the plastic novelty ballpoint in his hand.

He missed his favorite. He bought the black stylograph, once owned by novelist Graham Greene, in London at a Christy's auction. For the last ten years, it brought him luck, fame, and financial success. Or so he'd come to believe.

Frowning, he snapped the leather-bound notepad closed.

"Cecily. Cecily, come here this instant," Stephens called. *I hate raising my voice, it's so common.*

The plump woman bustled into the room, out of breath and gasping.

"Where had you gotten off to, my good wife?

Cecily opened her mouth, but he continued speaking. "Did you find it, my pen?" asked Tobias Stephens. "Did you check the sitting room? The vehicle?"

Out of breath, Cecily shook her head after each question.

Stephens wrinkled his nose. "The downstairs *facilities?* Where do you think it went?"

She shrugged.

Our hostess better locate my property soon. Or Mrs Lukas might not appreciate my review.

MINA — CARRIAGE HOUSE

Mina considered her daughter bustling around the kitchenette. *I love this little flat, so cozy and warm. Elena looks at home here.* Gratitude for her daughter's home-coming filled Mina.

Carrying a wooden tray overflowing with coffee and crockery, Elena said, "I made decaf. I hope you don't mind."

"Thank you, that will be delightful," Mina said. "Shall we take it in the lounge?"

"Certainly," Elena said. She led the way into the living room.

They unloaded the tray onto the coffee table.

"Okay, Mama, spill," Elena thumped a cup in front of her mother.

Mina fingered the rune charm hanging around her neck. "This could be nothing," she said. "I trust her, but she has been so different." Mina lifted her hand to her cheek. "I don't know what to think."

"Who's different?" asked Elena. "Do you mean Gabby?"

"Yes, Gabija." Mina sipped her coffee and placed the mug back on the coffee table as if she feared the porcelain might shatter on contact.

Her daughter licked her lips.

"I think she took something from our guest." Mina's voice was thick, and her eyes welled with tears. "Perhaps she found the pen somewhere."

Elena held the coffee cup to her mouth but returned it to the end table without taking a drink. "Oh, she would never do that. Not our Gabs. A brat maybe, but not a thief. What would make you think such a thing?"

"For several days, things have gone missing, then

I find even sillier things." Her hand rubbed the twill of her beige capris. "Yesterday, I found the neighbor's garden statue on the front stoop. When I spoke to Mrs Murphy, she said it was hers and other things had disappeared."

Elena averted her gaze, resting her forehead on her fist. "What things?"

"Nothing of great value, a garden trowel from her shed, a wire whisk from her kitchen drawer, that sort of thing. There is one item of sentimental value missing, her mother's antique brooch, a piece of costume jewelry. Poor woman lost her mother in childhood."

Elena picked up the purse sitting on the coffee table. "Describe the piece for me?"

Mina's voice trembled. "A leaf carved from green stone-"

"Set in silver?" Elena said, finishing the sentence.

Mina breath caught. "Yes, how did you...?"

Opening her handbag, Elena removed the brooch. "I found it in the carriage house stairwell this morning." Elena placed the pin on the coffee table in front of her mother.

"This is the one." Mina sighed, picked up the piece of jewelry, and turned it over. "I'll find a way to return it in the morning." Mina slipped the brooch into her pants pocket.

Neither spoke, sipping coffee. The loud *tick-tock* of the captain's clock on the mantelpiece measured time creeping forward.

"I agree, it's weird," Elena finally said. "But what makes you think Gabs is our thief?" She batted the idea away with her hand. "No, not possible."

"There's more. Gabby is wearing a heart-shaped pendant." Mina poured cream into her coffee. "Like another of our neighbor's missing things."

"Oh." Elena's voice dropped several decibels. "No." A violent shudder shook the idea from her head. "I'm sure she found it somewhere in the house and forgot to give it to you. What did she say when you asked her?"

"Nothing. I haven't spoken to her since we argued. Gabija's been either at school or hiding in her room." Mina shrugged. "Now she's got that animal hidden in her room, and I'd rather not catch her disobeying me."

"Confront her," Elena said. "You don't have a choice."

"Could we keep that cat downstairs away from the guests?" Mina said, then shook her head. "That will never work."

"Do you want me to talk to her?" Elena asked.

"No, I'll talk to her." Sadness showed in Mina's eyes. "I hope- I'm *sure* there's an explanation."

"Me too," Elena said.

Mina rose from the couch. "First, I must check on your grandmother." She opened the door. "She worries me, too, but let us leave that until later." Her mother left the guest house, pulling the door shut behind her.

"Tell me what you discover?" Elena yelled after her.

GABBY — SWAN HOUSE

Mina tapped on the door to Gabby's room, then pushed it open. "Are you busy?" she asked.

Gabby sat on the bed reading a textbook with her legs crossed. She narrowed her eyes. "Yes, I'm studying," Gabby replied. "And I don't need anyone to check up on my homework, thank you." She licked her finger and turned the page.

Mina remained in the doorway. "Is there something you wish to tell me, Gabija?"

She never calls me by my proper name unless I'm in serious trouble.

"Nope," Gabby said. Frowning, she closed her algebra textbook.

Mina wrung her hands. "Is there anything you need to say to me?"

Oh, poo, I hope she doesn't know I've still got Trouble. "No, not a thing, Mama." Gabby stuck out her lip. "Algebra's gotten me worried. I need a B+ to keep up my GPA. If you're flunking, they send home a note, and I haven't gotten one. So, I suppose I'm okay." She returned to her book.

Mina gripped the door frame and drew a deep breath before she spoke again. "Gabija, I'm just going to ask straight out."

Here we go, she knows. Gabby's stomach wrenched. She opened the book, but the numbers on the paper dissolved into random squiggles.

"Did you take Mr. Tobias' black pen?"

"Huh?" she muttered, her head in her textbook.

"Our guest's pen is missing, have you seen it? It's precious to Mr Stephens. Our neighbor, Mrs Murphy, is missing things, too."

"Some things are missing?" Gabby relaxed. "Gosh, I'm sorry about that. Describe them to me? I'd like to help keep an eye out," she offered with a smile.

"His pen is expensive, made of gold, and fits into his leather notebook. You haven't seen or touched it?" Mina's gaze bored directly into her eyes.

"No." She scrunched her face. "I said, 'No.'"

"And you're sure?"

"I don't know why you're asking me, Mama. I didn't even know he lost or even owned a special pen."

Her mother smiled. The mood lightened, Mina swept into the room and kissed Gabby on the forehead. "Goodnight. Don't stay up late," her mother said, and she left.

"Adults are so weird," Gabby muttered.

DAY FOUR

SATURDAY — 12 A.M. - 12 P.M.

CHAPTER SEVENTEEN

GABBY - SWAN HOUSE

Gabby awoke with her heart racing. Sweat drenched her novelty pajamas. Around the darkened room, shadows of wolves, deer, cougars, and otters danced on their hind legs.

Where the heck am I? Her hands wiped the sleep from her eyes, and the hallucinations faded away.

"You're home in your own bed, stupid," she muttered, her breath, mixing with the frigid air, turned to fog. The room was freezing. She'd left the window open, and Trouble's favorite spot was empty.

"Kitty, kitty, kitty," she called but kept her voice quiet.

I'm not getting in Dutch with Mama again. She is already wigging, and she'd kill me if she knew I'm sneaking Trouble in at night.

Gabby abandoned her cozy blankets and slid to the edge of her bed to check the time. The minuscule desktop icon on her phone read 3:00 a.m. *No one will be awake.* She dropped the phone on the bedside table.

Pulling her hand from the overhead light switch – *better not, might wake someone* – Gabby removed a teeny red flashlight out of the drawer and turned it on.

Its slender shaft of light cut into the bedroom's dark empty corners.

Where is he? Her tummy rolled. *What if something happened to him?*

At the open window, Gabby crossed her arms, as much from worry as for warmth.

The dew sparked on the lawn in the empty front yard. No cars on the street. No people on the sidewalk.

Where is he? She leaned her elbows on the windowsill.

A black streak catapulted over the porch swing and into the hydrangeas.

"You little devil," she whispered. "Are you going to make me chase you?" Gabby straightened, rolled her shoulders back, and took three steps toward the bedroom door. She paused.

"This won't do for going outside." Her flannel pajama bottoms decorated with cows dressed as waitresses and white *Got Milk* tank were not climate appropriate. She added a loopy oversized brown cardigan from the closet and slipped into a pair of turquoise flip flops. "Good enough."

Gabby opened the bedroom door, and peeked into the hall. No one was there.

On tiptoes, she navigated the hardwood floor. She surveyed the two squeaky flights of stairs standing between her and the front door.

Her right toe touched the first step. She eased her weight to the ball of her foot and lowered her heel. Step by step, she inched downstairs to the second floor. Halfway. Gabby fist-pumped, celebrating her accomplishment.

Click. A narrow slash of blazing light escaped from beneath the door of the Odette suite. Heavy footsteps tromped across toward the en suite bathroom. Gripping the banister, Gabby waited for the toilet to flush and the guest to stumble back to bed. A lifetime passed before the light evaporated under the door.

Gabby descended the next flight and slipped across the entry hall to the door. The last obstacle.

The three locks barred the way. *You taunt and mock me, but you will not defeat me. I accept your challenge.*

Gabby dispatched the simple brass bolt with the élan of a safecracker. The security chain's bolt inched until she extracted it from the slider without a clink.

The temperamental deadbolt remained. Gabby blew on her fingertips and rubbed them against her thumbs. Her master criminal imitation ended with a giggle.

The lever fit in her palm. She lifted it while depressing the night latch. The lock didn't release.

"Fudge," she said through gritted teeth. *You can do this. Okay, inhale and hold it.* Applying torque to the knob, she wiggled the handle until-*clank* – *CLANK* — the lock released.

There was no movement from the downstairs family area where her mother and grandmother slept. Nothing. The door groaned as it opened. Gabby didn't wait this time. She dashed to the porch and drew the door closed behind her.

In the distance, quiet freeway traffic whooshed, but the street out front was deadly silent.

At the bottom of the steps, Gabby switched on her flashlight. She illuminated the manicured lawn, lit the tops of every tree and under each bush. *It looks like the fairy from Peter Pan is dancing out here.*

"Trouble, come here, Trouble," Gabby hissed. "Kitty, kitty, kitty." Her tone ascended and volume rose as she called out to him. "Trouble," she shouted in a stage whisper.

Culinary and medicinal herbs hid amongst ornamentals and fruit trees in the yard. A meandering walkway curved around the side of the house.

The fragrance of the rich black earth and green

growing things filled her with the thrill of being alone in the night. Scared yet excited, Gabby trembled at her wickedness.

I'm sure he went that way. A rhododendron thicket and ornamental grasses concealed the backyard gate. "Trouble," she called on her way to the gateway leading to her mother's kitchen garden and the two-acre back yard.

"There." A cat-shaped shadow sprinted toward the greenhouse between the raised beds. The wrought-iron gate stuck. Gabby shouldered her way through it and stumbled toward the vegetable beds, three rows of raised wooden boxes her mother filled with soil, mulch, and compost. Recently seeded, tender shoots of radishes, carrots, and onion erupted through the earth. Pots of beans and peas would soon crawl up trellises along the back fence. The thick spring bounty made it difficult for Gabby to decide which way Trouble may have gone.

Gabby walked around to the flagstone patio abutting the house. Hand on her hip, she waited for a rustle in the underbrush. The sculpture fountain gurgled.

He ran past the apple trees and flower beds toward the summer house.

"Stupid cat." Gabby took off at a trot. Reaching the pergola, she climbed to the platform, calling in a loud singsong, "Kitty, kitty, kitty."

Following the marquee's scalloped brick wall, she squinted into the darkness. The abundant foliage blocked any view of the house. "Darn it." She stomped her feet on the redwood planking, and she pulled her sweater around her midsection. *It's freezing, and no fun anymore.*

"Poo on you, Trouble," she said and took a few steps away. "Stay out here, I don't care." Gabby paused. A suspicious cat shape perched on the apex of the roof.

Is that the weathervane?

Thump. Something jumped from the gazebo's conical roof and scampered away along the path toward the sculpture garden at the back of the property.

Gabby struck off, the bright focus of her flashlight bouncing along the trail.

The gravel crunched under her feet as she reached the arbor entrance to the statuary court. She swung the flashlight back and forth in a search pattern, illuminating the closest figure, one old god or another.

The moon rose, and the garden brightened. No longer needed, Gabby flicked off the flashlight and yawned. She sat on a stone bench waiting for her eyes to become accustomed to the night.

Crunch, rustle, crunch. Gabby turned toward the noise. "Come on, boy. Here, kitty."

A statue stood silhouetted against a backdrop of trees. Clouds gathered in the night sky, the moonlight faded, and stars disappeared. Goosebumps rose on her arms. "Trouble?" Gabby got to her feet and stepped forward for a better look.

It took her a moment to recognize the sound; air rasping in and out. Something very close breathed.

Then the statue moved. Gabby froze.

That's not made of stone. It's someone. Adrenaline hit her bloodstream with an electric jolt. Her heart sped. Gabby squeaked, short and high as a rodent in a trap. She turned and sprinted toward the house.

Her lungs burned. She gasped for breath as she ran as fast as she could.

Thump, thump, thump. Footsteps pounded behind her. *They're catching up to me.* Moving around one more curve, she'd arrive at the patio, back door, and safety.

Gabby scrambled across the dew-covered flagstones. The security motion sensor triggered, flooding the patio with bright light.

Gabby twisted and pulled the knob. It didn't

move. It didn't turn. She knew it was hopeless, but she tugged on the locked door again.

It's coming. It was right behind you. Spinning around, Gabby searched for her pursuer.

In the halogen light's halo, the patio remained empty, but beyond, darkness threatened. Tears poured. *I'm trapped.* The rainfall began in earnest. The security light flickered out, and the night swallowed her.

ELENA - DREAM

It was an old dream. Always the same. A slim crescent moon perches in a field of stars. Tree limbs droop with heavy snow. White crystals cling to the bark. The thin crust of ice frosts the snow-covered forest floor. It cracks with each footfall. Her fur-covered boots sink into the drift below.

She sprints through the forest with a huge white wolf at her side. She ignores the two-snowshoe hares loping with them. They run. Time stops. Minutes or hours, she neither knows nor cares.

Lub dub-dub. Lub dup-dup. Her heartbeat plays counterpoint to her pace and breathing. The cold is their welcome companion. Crisp air fills her lungs, and plumes of steam marked her exhalations. The skin of her face tingles with life and vitality.

She reaches an ancient oak. Ice and snow encrusts its skeletal branches. The gnarled branches twist out from a massive trunk. It would take ten men to encircle its girth.

The hares disappear into a burrow at the foot of the tree.

She pushes back the fur-covered hood on the full-length shearling coat. The wolf stands at her side. She removes her mittens and runs her fingers through the animal's thick, coarse coat. He lifts his head and howls.

Owooooo. Owooooo. Ow ow owooo. From every direction, the pack returns his call.

She smiles, knowing her family is with her.

The wounded bark of the oak draws her closer. She reaches for it. Her hands caress the trunk. The branches glow a bright lime green. It warms and transmutes into the scarred flesh of a man, The burns like melted wax flowed from right shoulder to waist.

She wraps her arms around him, her cheek presses against his back. He leans into her embrace and places his feverish hand over hers. His scent, spice and musk, intoxicates her.

He turns, stepped away from the oak tree, and kisses her.

Their tongues touch, tentative at first, then playful. He presses against her, and her body responds.

He releases the bone toggles on her coat.

The cold wind warms, gentle breezes caress them. The snow melts. Green buds burst from the oak's branches. Tender shoots of grass erupt from the black earth.

She laughs and shakes her hair free.

Her wolf nips at her finger. She strokes his head. "Go find your mate, my friend."

He howls, and pants, he disappears into the forest.

The man pushes her coat back from her shoulders. Falling, it forms a woolen nest on the earth.

Their gazes caress every inch of each other's flesh. His hand touches her face, and their lips meet once more. Their kisses long, probing, and intimate. She wraps her arms around him and holds so close she fears their bodies might fuse for eternity.

Her heart races. He lowers her to the bed of spring grass and clouds of wool. He kneels over her, his face in shadow.

Wildflowers, yellow star-shaped Ruta, blooms around their bower. She smells the strong, bitter scent.

Lightning flashes.

The tan skin of his muscled chest is smooth brown leather. She touches him. The familiarity of his flesh brings tears to her eyes.

She extends her arms out to him. Falling to his hands and knees, he kisses her neck. She quivers with desire for him.

"I want you," she says. "I need you."

Thunder rumbles.

Elena's heart shudders. The horned moon disappears, and blinding sunlight fills the glade. Something is wrong. She pulls away. He reaches for her, grief in his eyes.

Her eyelids squeeze shut to block the glare, but Elena forces them open.

In the intense brightness, her lover evaporates.

I'm in the carriage cottage. A bright light blazed through the naked window. Something's wrong.

Elena bolted to the window. Below, Gabby pounded and pulled on the back door. Then it went dark.

Without stopping for robe or slippers, Elena heaved her door open and bolted down the unlit stairs to the garage. Running full out along the back fence, Elena passed through the covered walkway to the main house.

The deadbolt and chain fought her until she got the door opened.

Gabby huddled against the frame, weeping.

"Gabby, what are you doing out here?" Elena lifted the girl to her feet.

"It is coming." Gabby screamed, grabbing her sister and pushing her into the house. "We have to get inside. Close it. Close it."

"What is coming?" asked Elena. She slammed the deadbolt back into place.

"I didn't see it," she sobbed. "It was coming to get me, and I ran. It was big and chased me." Gabby's nose ran.

"Honey, you're all right." Elena searched the patio through the window in the door. "Nothing is out there. You're safe. I'm here."

Gabby buried her face into her big sister's shoulder and collapsed into gasps and tears.

Elena rocked the girl. "Slow deep breaths, sweetie, or you'll pass out." She cradled her until an exhausted Gabby could cry no longer.

Arms around one another, the sisters returned to the guest house. The moment they crawled into Elena's bed, the girl dropped into a deep sleep.

But Elena remained awake, staring at the ceiling until the amber of dawn crept through the bedroom window.

LOGGER — CAPITOL FOREST

Heavy rain fell all through the night. In the predawn, the tall man watched rivulets of runoff eroding the bank.

"Shit, just what I needed," said Josiah McGowen, muttering under his breath. The logging trucks would arrive in two hours. The profit margin for this job was slim, so he had to stay on schedule. They must have the timber loaded and on the road by six.

McGowen, a quiet man with a crew cut, walked every inch of this tract, selecting each evergreen they cut.

If the guys cut timber until six-thirty, we might make it in time.

Soon, the sky would lighten, becoming pale gray on the horizon. A translucent mist rolled over the ground, pooling in low places, and the air was thick with the pungency of peat. This was his favorite time of day.

"Get to work, McGowen." The rods in his back broadcast a painful background static. Today, his pain was on the wrong side of tolerable. *Keep moving even if it kills you.* "We *will* be ready for loading."

McGowen Logging won the bid on a large government parcel. Back then, the company went through some lean times. To cut expenses, Josiah and his father, Jacob, didn't hire rigging rats for the job. They worked alone that morning.

It was a day just like today, cold, wet, and one hundred percent humidity when he tangled with the widow maker.

Loggers called them widow makers, dead trees that fall silently. Sometimes it's rain destabilizing the ground, or the root systems dies, but other times it's fate.

That morning, Jacob yelled a warning but was too distant to pull his son out of danger. The tree crushed Josiah's back and blocked the only road back to civilization. With no cellphones back then, his father jogged all twenty miles for help.

An old Northwest logging family, Josiah's great-great-grandfather felled trees as big as houses. Josiah wasn't even the first McGowen logging victim. In 1944, some fool dropped a tree and crippled his grandfather.

I'm the last logger in this damn family.

Josiah finished plotting his load and checked his watch. "I better get that crane moved," he said, patting his slicker in search of keys.

Water splashing in puddles, rushing to join the creeks and river below, and the rain pounding on the hood of his rain parka, Josiah never heard the animal attack.

BOONE - HOME

"Yip," Ohto cried.

Boone looked over his shoulder. "Don't follow so damn close, and I won't step on your paw."

The dog looked from his master to the refrigerator, to his food dish and back. Ohto's stomach growled.

He opened the dishwasher and removed a cup from the upper rack. Boone looked inside and made a grimace of disgust. A small stack of dishes waited in the sink. He added the cup to the pile.

Ohto tapped Boone's calf with his foot.

"What do you want?" He looked down at the dog. "Don't pull that 'sad eye' crap on me." He pointed at Ohto's cushion. "Get in your bed."

Head lowered, the dog slunk away to his cushion.

"Stupid dream meant nothing," Boone muttered.

He opened and slammed cupboard doors, looking for the coffee. "Damn coffee." Boone banged the last cabinet.

While deep in the refrigerator, rummaging for an egg or some juice, Boone knocked over a milk carton spilling it on the galley kitchen floor.

Ohto sprang to help, his tail wagging.

"Don't even think about it," Boone spat. "Get back on your bed now." The dog slunk back and threw himself on his pillow with an expressive flop.

"Don't give me that look, dog." Boone wadded up an entire roll of paper towels and soaked up the mess. "It's the last time I get a whole gallon. Either it spills, or the damn stuff spoils." He threw the dripping paper into the sink with a *plop*.

"Screw breakfast, I'll pick something up on my way."

The dog sighed, rolled on his back, legs splayed in the air. He fell asleep, snoring.

Boone stomped into the bathroom and slammed the door. Stripped out of his gray USMC sweats, he bunged on the water and jumped in without checking the temperature.

Hot water poured over his shoulders and back. He tried not to think of Elena. Boone kept his eyes open. When he closed them, that damn dream rushed back in lightning flashes. Her mouth enveloping him, the taste of her skin and smell of her hair. Like the water from the shower, memories bombarded him.

Boone stiffened. "Don't you start," he growled at himself. He twisted off the H tap and bowed his head into the icy water.

GABBY — THE GUEST HOUSE

The thick quilt engulfed Gabby. In the bathroom, Elena's shower pattered. Golden morning light chased away her midnight fright and left the memory of a foolish dream.

"You're such a scaredy-cat. There was no one after you."

Her stomach churned, and she closed her eyes. "I can't face Elena."

Earlier, when the alarm rang and her sister got up, Gabby pretended to be asleep.

"I don't want to explain anything to Mama, either." She craned her neck to better see the clock on the nightstand. "Right now, she'll be up and cooking for the guests. I better get to my room."

Throwing back the blanket, Gabby leapt out of bed and tiptoed out of the guest house. She didn't stop until she was behind her bedroom door.

"*Prrt*," the cat said from his customary perch on top of the bookcase.

"Trouble," Gabby cried out and ran to him.

She cuddled the cat in her arms and cooed. Then Gabby crawled into her bed and soon returned to sleep.

CHAPTER EIGHTEEN

MINA - SWAN HOUSE

She juggled her stack of linens and began the long trudge up to the third floor. *A demanding guest I can handle. But accusations of theft?*

Elena strolled through her teen years. A precocious student, the only challenge was feeding her older daughter's intense curiosity. It was different with Gabby. An average student, Gabby's strong emotions led to a worldview filled with dramatic highs and lows.

Mina's shoulders sagged, and a deep sigh escaped.

The current situation with the feral cat was the perfect example. Although she wished to let her daughter keep the thing, the success of the business and health of their customers must remain paramount.

On the first landing, another wave of fatigue hit her. Restless, her mother cried out in her sleep all night, frequently waking Mina.

Open the visor of his helmet. Even in Lithuanian, it makes no sense.

Upon reaching the second floor, she scrubbed the hall bathroom and deposited used linen in her laundry basket. Usually, such simple household tasks were calming and grounding, but not today.

This morning, her mother chattered as she ate her breakfast, her night terrors forgotten.

The second floor finished, Mina continued her conquest of the staircase.

Last year, Regana was sharp and interested in world events. Most days now, her mother didn't know where she was or what the year was. This morning, she chastised Elena for missing training as if she was a child. Mina's greatest fear remained. Her fierce, strong mother was entering temporal dementia, the immersion and loss of self.

Her every heavy tread thudded.

"She'll not be with us much longer." Mina reached the third floor. Mina shifted her load to her left hip and opened the door to Gabby's room.

Posters of teen idols and boy bands decorated the walls. Stuffed animals, teen-vampire-angst novels, and valued mementos littered every surface.

In the en suite bathroom, Mina stowed fresh towels under the sink, and on her way out, dropped clean bed sheets on the white lace coverlet.

Gold flashed on the bedside table. Mina took up the object, turning it in her hands.

"Oh, dear." A heaviness formed in Mina's chest. "This is Tobias Stephens' missing pen."

STEPHENS — SWAN HOUSE

The man himself swept into the dining room, his narrow nostrils flaring, and a tight smile on his thin lips. A sweet and nutty aroma filled the room. Coffee in a silver carafe waited on his favorite table.

To the right of an embossed silver charger sat a cup and saucer bearing delicate vines and pale pink roses.

He set aside the cup and lifted the saucer to the

sunlight pouring through the six-foot casements. His long, slender fingers shadowed through the porcelain. He inspected the maker's mark on the bottom, then set it back in place. A flick to the bone china cup rim produced a chime of authenticity. He noted the quality of the china, silver, and linen in his oxblood leather journal.

Today was his last day in Olympia, and he considered the possible next destination. Mount Rainier National Park could make a nice sidebar, but Paradise Lodge might not be open while snow remained on the ground.

He added: "Hotel closed, call to arrange a tour" to the bottom of the list. "Book a suite at the Murano Hotel" had a check next to it. "Tour the Tacoma Museum of Glass", "Call Dale C", and "Review the art glass collection" remained unchecked. Stephens nodded and placed the book on the table.

The reviewer sat in his chair, flourishing the linen napkin before placing it on his lap. He reached to pour his coffee. His pen stood out against the white linen tablecloth. Snatching it, he let out a sigh of relief.

"I see you have found your pen, Mr Stephens."

He smiled broadly. "Ah, good morning, Mrs Lukas. Yes, right here." His index finger pointed to the table setting.

"I found it this morning, but you were in your room, and I didn't want to disturb you." Mina turned toward the door. "Will Mrs Stephens join you for breakfast?"

"Yes, she'll arrive soon. I'll order for us both." In a bored tone, he said, "My wife will have an egg white omelet, unbuttered whole wheat toast, and black coffee."

He brightened when he told Mina his own order. "I'll have the banana pancakes with syrup. I presume you use real Vermont maple syrup, not some fake imitation?"

Closing her eyes, Mina bowed her head.

"What else?" Tobias Stephens punctuated each word with a flourish of his bony hands.

"Two soft-boiled eggs, two slices of nitrate-free organic bacon thoroughly browned, but not excessively crispy. An eight-ounce glass of freshly squeezed orange juice, cold without ice. This coffee is adequate for now but refresh the pot after my meal." His small sharp eyes locked on her. "Do you need to write my order on a pad?"

"I've got it," Mina's eyes performed a microscopic roll only a member of her family would recognize. "Your breakfast will be ready in ten to fifteen minutes."

"Very good." He flicked his wrist to Mina. "You may go."

Mrs Stephens bustled into the dining room and just missed clipping Mina.

"Cecily, sit." The man pointed to the chair across from his. "Is everything ready?"

His wife nodded enthusiastically.

MINA - KITCHEN

Mina descended to the family quarters, her head shaking.

"What is it?" Elena asked from the oak farm table.

"That man's wife, she is a saint." Her hands made a neck-wringing motion. "I'd have killed him years ago."

Elena laughed, choking on her orange juice.

Trending kitchen gadgets sat on the granite countertop, while herb bunches, garlic braids, and pear-shaped artisan cheeses hung in the corners. Nods to old Europe balanced the stainless-steel modernism.

The refrigerator light illuminated Mina's face when she retrieved the eggs.

"Did he ask how you found his things?" Elena asked.

"No, thank the goddess. I didn't know what to say and still don't understand how the pen got into Gabby's room."

Mina cracked the first eggshell on the edge of a beige pottery bowl. "Last night, Gabby claimed to know nothing." Mina tossed the shell into the farm sink.

"Gabs is odd, but you can explain it with hormones and teenage angst." Elena took two thick slices of homemade bread from a wooden breadbox and placed them in the toaster on the counter.

"Isn't she just-" But before Mina could finish her thought, Regana tottered out her door and into the middle of the room. The old lady's feet were bare, and she wore a floor-length linen night dress. "Mother, you shouldn't be out here without your sweater."

"I'll get it, Mama." Elena scurried to the bedroom and returned, garment in hand.

"Karys ateina, ir aš turiu paruošti jį jo žygiui," the old lady croaked.

"The fire *is* going," replied Mina.

Regana shook her head. "*Ne, Ne.*"

"Let me help you to your chair, Nana." Elena draped the soft gray sweater over the old woman's shoulders.

"*Kaip žodis angly kalban? Ah-*" Regana tsked and closed her eyes. "Warrior comes." Her thick accent was difficult to understand, even for her family to understand.

"I don't know what you mean, Mother. No soldiers are coming here today, or any other day. I'm sorry, but you're mistaken." Worry dripped from Mina's voice.

Elena caught her mother's eye, and they shared a concerned exchange.

The upstairs doorbell chimed.

"*Žiūrėti*." Regana pointed to the ceiling. "Bring him," she demanded, then shambled back to her room. She settled any questions with a firm bang of her bedroom door.

"What?" Mina asked.

"I know who she means, Mama," Elena said. "This will be very interesting," she muttered under her breath.

BOONE - SWAN HOUSE

Boone's work truck pulled up in front of Swan House. The man sat with his hands on the wheel, repressing last night's dreams.

Riding shotgun, Ohto was on full alert. "Grrrrr."

"What is it?" Boone asked.

The dog responded with a guttural growl.

"What do you see?" Boone searched the foliage for the cause of Ohto's concern.

Dead still, a black cat crouched on the porch rail, its round yellow eyes staring.

"It is just a cat, you dope."

The windows rattled as the dog threw himself against the door.

"Knock it off, Ohto."

Eyes fixed on the cat, Ohto growled louder and deeper.

"Behave, my friend, or you stay in here."

Barking, the dog dug at the seat.

"I'll take that as your answer." The door slammed as Boone exited and walked up the flagstones to the house.

From his place in the truck, Ohto continued barking.

The cat strutted along the porch rail with tail raised high.

GABBY - SWAN HOUSE

Glued to the screen of her phone, Gabby galloped down the stairs.

Bing-bong. The bell rang. She opened the front door.

Two large feet encased in a pair of dark brown hiking boots with thick rubber soles stood on the welcome mat. They disappeared into the legs of olive drab trousers.

"Hello, is this the Lukas residence?" a man asked.

Gabby looked up and found she was face to face with a camouflage flak vest. Her gaze followed the chest up past the broad shoulders until she reached the man's face. Head tilted back and mouth open, she said, "Hi?"

"This is the Lukas residence, isn't it?" he said. "I'm here to pick up Professor Lukas."

"You got the right place," she said. "You're here for my sister." *This guy is hot, old but hot. Not as hot as Seth, but he'll do for Elena.*

"Is she here?" he asked, still polite.

Gabby gaped again. "What?"

"Professor Lukas? Is she here?"

"She's downstairs." Gabby didn't move.

Boone waited.

"Should I get her?"

He nodded. "Thanks. That's great," he said, his voice sharper.

"You wanna come in and wait?" Gabby gestured toward the sitting room.

"I'll stay on the porch."

"Sorry, detective, it won't be that simple," Elena said.

His every muscle stiffened at the sound of her voice.

BOONE - REGANA'S ROOM

Boone's hand lingered on the glass doorknob. *Why the hell does she want me to meet her senile grandmother, and why couldn't I tell her no? It's barely seven a.m. and this day is already out of control.*

A deep and rasping voice cut through the heavy wooden door. "*Ateikite pas mane.* Come, come."

Who is that, Dracula meets Greta Garbo?

He glanced back at Elena. Her half-smile was serious, but her eyes were twinkling. She flicked her hand, motioning him forward.

Darkness and candlelight cloaked the old lady's sitting room. An incense haze obscured the corners and worn leather-covered volumes piled on every flat surface. An archaic cassette player, the only nod at modern life, played women singing close modulating harmonies.

On a table to his right, a haphazard jumble of seashells, faded photos, and fetishes carved in stone clustered in purposeful disarray. At the center, a single candle burned from the top of a three-foot metal tree.

"Gyvybės medis," the woman croaked. "Tree of Life. You know this?"

"No, ma'am." Boone risked a backward glance toward the door. "Your granddaughter told me you wished to meet me?"

"You sit." She gestured at the footstool by her chair. The ornate rings clinging to her gnarly fingers glinted in the candlelight.

Silver cotton candy hair floated around her face. Despite the lines and wrinkles, Boone could still make out the beauty of her youth.

A lifetime of joy and sorrow created that face.

The woman's lacy shawl and long black velvet dress overpowered her slight frame. Her eyes, shiny black like buttons, didn't hide her irritation, and she motioned at the stool again.

Contorting his long frame, Boone crouched on the ottoman. *What am I doing here?* Knees under his chin, he waited for the woman to speak.

Her breath deep and even, she closed her eyes. The music increased in volume and dissonance. The surrounding air vibrated.

A trick of the light. A dull pain throbbed at his temples.

Reopened, her eyes were the darkest emerald green.

Weren't they black when I first got here? No, it's just dark in here.

"*Jūsų rankos.*" Regana stretched out her tattooed hands and displayed her palms.

"I'm sorry?" Boone didn't budge. "You want my hand?"

"*Jūsų rankos.*" Her countenance declared this was not a request.

He held out his hand and the old woman grabbed it. Electricity jolted though him like he'd walked into an electric fence. The room tilted and spun. A cacophony of voices, thoughts from every mind in a hundred-mile radius assaulted him.

Regana swayed from side to side, muttering under her breath. Then the music stopped, and his world righted itself.

"*Aš* paliečiau *tavo sielą,*" she said, releasing his hands. "You I see." Regana patted his leg. Her smile displayed a set of perfect white teeth. With effort, she rose from her chair.

"Let me help you?" Boone leapt up, overturning the footstool.

"*Tu liksi čia.*" She waved him off and shuffled to the highboy. Pulling out one drawer after another, she rummaged through the contents until she found what she was seeking and returned to him.

Dwarfed by Boone, she held a small copper knife in her two hands. "Take," she said. Foreign symbols and characters decorated the blade and handle.

"Thank you, but public employees cannot accept gifts, ma'am." He stepped back. "It's against the law."

Regana pushed the blade toward him.

"I can't take it from you. It looks valuable."

Her eyes blazing, she thrust it to him a third time. "Take," she demanded.

"Um, thank you?" he said. The weapon was heavy in his hands. *It's... what? Familiar? Nevermind. When I get out of here, I'll return it to her family.*

Her head snapped in his direction. "*Ne-* You." A firm poke to his chest drove her message home.

"Well, thank you, Mrs Lukas." He dropped the ritual knife into his flak jacket pocket.

"Go." Scowling, the old woman slumped back into her chair.

"A pleasure meeting you, ma'am." Boone backed away as the door swung shut on her throaty chuckle.

ELENA - FAMILY QUARTERS

Elena waited at the massive wooden table. Nana Regana brought the piece to the US on a tall ship, long ago.

The descending service elevator rattled, and Mina entered the room carrying dishes on a round lacquer tray. She deposited it on the counter by the sink and turned on the tap. Steam rose from the hot water. She rinsed each dish before loading them in the dishwasher.

"Is your friend still in there?" Mina asked.

"Uh-huh." Without looking up, Elena played with a wooden napkin ring. "I am not looking forward to his reaction."

"Your grandmother has her reasons. It must be important or she wouldn't summon him. You know this?"

"I know, Mama. I just wish we were not so..."

"Colorful," her mother finished with a grin.

"I suppose that's one way to put it." Elena returned a lukewarm smile.

Boone burst into the kitchen. His mouth opened, but nothing came out.

"Thanks so much for taking time to visit my grandmother." Elena jumped up from her chair. "She's an old lady and appreciates company."

"Yes, thank you, detective," Mina said, her hands encased in pink rubber gloves.

"Yeah, uh, not a problem." He shook off his discomfort. "You're welcome." The ritual of polite conversation appeared to reassure him.

"I guess we'd better take off." Elena walked toward the stairs. "Goodbye, Mama." With a wave, she ascended the staircase, with Boone following mechanically.

"Come and visit us again, son," Mina called after them.

"Thanks for your hospitality, Mrs Lukas."

By the time they reached the front door, he'd regained his composure. "What was that about?" he said.

"It's nothing. She's old, so don't take what she said or did seriously." Elena swung her daypack over her shoulder. "Shall we go?"

"It wasn't nothing. It was-"

An elegant man floated by with a small round woman following behind.

"Thank you, my good man." He slipped a dollar in Boone's hand as he passed. Mrs Stephens smiled her apology as she rushed after her husband.

"Cecily, the car, bring around the car," he called from the street.

Elena and Boone burst into laughter.

"You're right, we better get going," Boone said, turning and striding out the door.

Unaware she was holding her breath, Elena exhaled and followed.

Gabby - Swan House

"Good Morning, Swan House," Gabby answered the phone with her best sexy voice. "And how may I help *you* today?"

He chuckled, rich and masculine. "Hello, little one, what a pleasant surprise."

"Seth." Lightheaded, she sank onto the telephone gossip bench's brocade. *Jeez, I'm a swooning princess in an old book.*

"Is your elder sister available?"

A shaft of true jealousy shattered her heart, painful, agonizing, and wrong.

Seth is mine. Elena gets everything she wants. But she can't have him. Her fist clenched, nails cutting deep into her palm.

"She left with a hunky forestry guy. They left in his truck," Gabby said through clenched teeth. "Alone. They're going out in the woods. We don't know when they're coming back. I think he's her boyfriend."

The line was silent. Icy fear filled her mouth as she waited for his reaction.

"No matter," he said. "I thought about you last night."

"You did?" Her surprise was a needed balm. "What did you think?"

"I read a poem last night, Carol's, 'A Strange Wild Song.' It made me think of you."

"You read something that made you think of me," she whispered, "Wow. I love poetry."

"You appreciate fine things. I suspected you might. That trait is rare, and I'm impressed. You're a very extraordinary young woman, Miss Lukas."

"I am?" she said, glancing over her shoulder, then said, "I think you are special, too."

"Why, thank you, Miss Lukas."

"Call me Gabija." She traced the carved lion's mask relief crowning the bench. "I'd like that."

"What a lovely name, Gabija."

Her phone chimed an incoming text. She removed it from her pocket, and without reading the message, she typed, "L8R."

"Can you recommend good stuff to read, Seth?"

CHAPTER NINETEEN

ELENA - FALL CREEK TRAILHEAD

Since leaving Olympia, Boone and Elena hadn't spoken. Ohto lay on the seat between them, his head on Elena's leg.

I can wait until he is ready to talk.

Boone parked the green truck in the parking lot of the Fall Creek Trailhead and killed the engine.

"Why isn't anyone here?" Elena said.

"The department closed the area after the incident," he said.

"Oh." The dog nuzzled his chin against her thigh. She stroked his side.

Boone patted his dog. "Ohto likes you."

"He's a very good boy. Aren't you, fella?" She massaged the thick fur at his neck.

Ohto's tail thumped against the plastic upholstery.

Boone checked his watch. "Let's get going." He slid out of the vehicle, removed his rifle from the gun rack, and hung the weapon over his shoulder. "Ohto, time to work."

After a moan and another wag of his tail, the dog hopped out and joined his partner.

Thump. Elena jumped out of the cab, landing on

both feet. She leaned back in and retrieved her pack from behind the seat.

The sun shone in a clear sky. *A perfect day for hiking.* The smell of evergreens and dark, rich loam filled her with a sense of purpose. Boston was never the right place for me. *I'm more complete, more myself here in the forest.* "Detective, how far is it to the campsite?" No answer. "Where did you go?" She quickly scanned the lot.

Across the parking lot, Boone and Ohto headed down the trailhead.

She shifted the weight on her shoulders, unzipped her parka, and rushed after them.

The Fall Creek Loop Trail bore right at the first junction, past a sign for the campground. In silence, they followed up the gentle grade through a young forest of Douglas fir. For a mile, the path paralleled a creek, the icy water pooling in low places and flowing around any glacial erratic blocking its way.

Ohto scampered ahead, sampling interesting aromas and running off trail to explore.

At the ridge, the water roared. The once gentle stream now rushed through the canyon. A thousand years of erosion carved a deep chasm into the basalt.

A rustic suspension bridge spanned the gap from south to north. Decades ago, New Deal-era Civilian Conservation Corps constructed the narrow bridge deck, pony trusses, and handrails out of two-by-six planks, rusty nails, and rope. Over the years, state workers performed maintenance, but the structure showed its age.

"Do you need a break?" he asked.

"I'm good," she replied with a grin. "Let's push ahead."

Boone and the dog trotted across the swaying and bouncing structure. Smirking, he leaned against the far abutment and waited.

Elena took a few careful steps to test the superstructure. The span held. Elena grasped the railing and eased her way to the other side, never looking into the rapids far below.

Beyond, the young forest matured to old growth cedar giants and massive firs. This biosphere, rich in life and death, beckoned Elena. She surrendered herself to her goddess.

"Your vessel opens to you, Mediena," she whispered.

The joy of the forest cocooned Elena as the goddess filled her. Life glowed. The leaves and needles of all the plants rotated toward her, birdsong increased, and insects stopped their labor to honor Mediena.

"Professor? Are you all right?"

The man speaks, said the goddess.

Boone's lime green life energy blazed, forcing Elena to shade her eyes.

"I'm fine, detective," she said. The goddess' warmth radiated through her.

Boone's eyes narrowed, and his mouth formed a tight line. "You look so- I don't know what."

Ohto grinned a doggy smile, his tail wagging.

"How far is it to the campsite, sergeant?" Elena asked, lowering her gaze.

Moving away a step, Boone inspected her as if she were an exotic insect. "How? Um." He cleared his throat. "Is it what?"

"How far?" she asked again.

"Oh, not much farther."

"Shouldn't we go?" she asked.

"Yeah. Okay. Let's go." He turned away, moving down the trail. She followed.

Mediena, I wish to compress time.

The gift filled her. She watched the nearby alder and maple leaves bud, unfurl, and wither into autumn's reds, oranges, and yellows. Grass underfoot ripened to seed and blew away. A decade of seasons passed in moments.

Begin again, and show me the passage of days, not years. In her mind, she ran the illusion forward, and backwards like a film clip. White dogwood blossoms spiraled open and closed again. *That's perfect.* Elena smiled.

All around, the migratory paths of animals stood out in relief and revealed the phantoms of former travelers.

There is magic here, but only nature's magic.

In Real-Time, the foliage rustled.

Elena and the dog halted, aligning with the wind. Musk from a doe in heat told them it had passed yesterday at dusk. And oily machines and their yeasty human masters chased through the hills last weekend.

Wait. At the edge of perception, something hunkered down, waiting for prey. *Dark magic.*

I've found you again.

ELENA - FALL CREEK CAMPGROUND

"This here is where they set up their tent. Forensics took the gear away." Boone crossed the campsite. "The husband's attack happened beyond those trees. The woman lost her life nearby. Follow me, and I'll show you." Boone attached Ohto's lead to the harness around his waist.

An animal path led off into the trees. One behind the other, the trio pushed their way through the heavy foliage. Five-hundred-feet before they reached the attack site, Elena's nausea rose. Breaking through the brush, Elena and Boone stepped into a clearing of young evergreens.

Dark magic-tinged swirls of violet pain and chartreuse terror marked the massacre. Elena willed events to playback in rapid flashes. The tall afterimage of Rolly Poole was distinct, but his attacker too blurred to tell if it was man, beast, or monster.

"Mrs Poole died by that big cedar. Tracks told us the bear circled behind and attacked. First, he…" Boone paused. "Well, you've seen the photos."

"Um, I-" She stood immobilized, her eyelids fluttering and eyes darting as flash cuts replayed in her head.

"Do you need a blow by blow description?" He scrutinized her.

"No," she whispered.

"What do you see?" asked Boone, narrowing his eyes.

Damp sweat formed at her hairline. "Nothing," she murmured.

Huddled against the cedar, the shade of Gloria Poole peered into the space where she died. Her gaze pivoted to Elena, then she faded.

The story of the attack played out before her in the Penumbra. The dead woman's afterimage appeared. The monster lunged, and she flew into the dirt. It attacked again. The woman's deafening screams pierced her ears. Elena watched every detail of the massacre. Each slash and tear psychically scored her flesh.

Elena whimpered and tears poured down her cheeks. *I'm sorry, so, so sorry*, she told Gloria's spirit.

"Doctor Lukas?" Boone said, the tendons in his neck standing out. "What the hell's going on?"

"What?" she said, without looking at him.

"You've been out of it since we left the trailhead. I want to know-"

Then a fresh horror overshadowed everything. *There was something else present in the shadows.* She grasped for the source, but every time she neared, the phantom submerged. Elusive. Cunning.

I recognize you. You're the same creature of dark magic I met before. I'm sure of it. Her gruesome front-row view of the massacre ended, and with it, Gloria Poole's spirit departed.

Elena returned to Real-Time and her rigid body relaxed. She wavered.

"Doctor Lukas?" Boone pushed into her personal space. "Elena, are you listening to me?" he demanded, grabbing her shoulders.

Elena touched his hand, then pulled away. "I'm taking everything in." She swallowed. "Imagining it, like an FBI profiler." Elena shook her head. "It takes a lot out of me."

"Are you, all right?" he demanded. "You look strange."

"Don't worry about me." Elena thanked the goddess for her help and asked for release. Exhaustion hit, threatening to knock her off her feet. *It's been years since I channeled Mediena so deeply.*

Boone reached out to steady her, but she grabbed hold of a sapling instead.

Elena wavered again. "It's just low blood sugar." She feigned a chuckle. "No time for breakfast."

"We better go back to the campsite," Boone said, placing his palm on her shoulder. "Do you need a hand?"

"I just need to eat something," she said, smiling. "Lunch is in my day pack."

"Excellent idea." Boone bowed his head. "After you, professor."

Unsteadily, she moved past.

Boone shivered. "This place gives me the creeps."

VARNAS - IN THE SKY OVERHEAD

It was no challenge to soar along with the truck. *Why is the vessel with the man from the forest and his wolf? What drew them to her?*

With the wind behind him, the raven glided. *Is this the work of the goddess?* Over the trailhead, he circled and flew up the slope to investigate. He found no other humans, only reflections and trails.

In subtle variations of gray, clouds rolled and tumbled over the ridges and pooled in the basin. A wide swathe of clear cut stood out like a scar in the land, the dormant metal monsters of men lazing there.

The vessel is safe. Safe for now. Tilting into the wind, he performed a smooth about-face, returning to the truck. Varnas watched them exit the vehicle and move away into the forest. As they hiked up the trail, he continued scouting for threats, ranging up and down the mountain.

Then, bright as a beacon, the goddess manifestation burned. *The chalice is filled, and my lady walks.*

Kraa. Kraaaa. Against the cliff faces and down the hollows, his alarm call announced Mediena's presence.

Varnas landed on the highest branch of an old growth cedar, observing the vision playing out below him.

Indistinct afterimages blazed when the deity's powers animated them. He responded to the revealed action with repeated clicks and bell-like tones. *An ugly death, but not pointless. Something fed on flesh and power there.*

The vessel's life-force flickered. She had reached the end of her store of Mediena's magic. *My lady, she consumes herself. Stop her now or death.* He spread his wings. *Varnas fly.*

"Stay, old friend," said Mediena. "The new mate watches over our vessel, and the wolf perceives her true visage." His lady's voice was like a breeze ruffling his feathers. "They protect her even from herself. See?"

The man reached out to the vessel, and his touch gifted his own pale green lifeforce to her. The woman's aura brightened.

Not enough. Too little. Agitated, Varnas' head bobbled, and a rattle rose from deep in his throat.

"Fear not, she will feed and replenish," said Mediena. "I have an important task for you. Darkness is near, Varnas. Can you sense it?"

He bobbed his head. *Something hidden prowls. Old? New?*

"Uncertain," said the goddess. "Find this evil, my soldier. Uncover its nature and purpose." Mediena's voice melted away until the forest sounds supplanted her.

Varnas hopped along the branch, determining the best location for the launch. The limb bounced when he sprang into the air, and with wings flapping, he climbed skyward.

CREATURE (LƏ'NÍ) - THE BURROW

The snug burrow Lə'ní dug in the side of a hill was deep enough to back into and wide enough to hide his full form.

Becoming weak and more vulnerable now, they must not find me. In the dark of his den, a gnawing need for food possessed him.

Separated from her kind, the female was easy prey. She was an insubstantial meal, and fighting her mate weakened this body. I left the feast unfulfilled. Foolish. Insects and berries hold off death, but not for long.

He snarled.

It is difficult to find prey in this barren territory. Leave, find somewhere plentiful?

His head rested on his massive front paws. *Where to go?* Since Lə'ní woke from the cold long night, memory and instinct failed him. Everything was unfamiliar, strange. His eyelids closed, and he drifted in the dark toward sleep.

Riding the draft, a scent wafted in from the cave's mouth. Every muscle tensed. He recognized the rich musk, another female. Like the other, she was not for mating, but she drew him. "She's ripe with power." He chuffed. "The maker will enjoy her power."

His body screamed when he pulled out of the burrow. Balanced on his hind legs, Lə'ní inhaled deeply, pinpointing her position. *A little way toward the dying sun. Near the first sacrifice. Good.* Chuffing, he dropped to all fours.

Not alone, this one, but her mate was insignificant. The hunger and pain forgotten, Lə'ní, the ritual knife, loped away.

ELENA — FALL CREEK CAMPGROUND

A granite outcrop marked the center of the campground.

"Stop here?" Boone asked.

"Uh-huh." Elena scrambled up a giant granite boulder and perched on top. Crystals studding the black and white stone glittered in the sunbeams.

After circling three times, Ohto lowered to the forest floor. Boone rested on a nearby log.

"Isn't that damp?" One arm at a time, she slipped off the daypack.

"Water resistant." His palm slapped his thigh. "Trust me, I'm a professional."

A lovely smile when he uses it. She opened the pack. "What did Mama prepare for our lunch?"

Ohto's ears perked.

Elena pulled an enormous sandwich from the red knapsack on her lap. "Rare roast beef on fresh homemade bread. This would be for you." She lobbed the plastic baggie into the air. Boone seized it.

Elena unwrapped and bit into her chicken salad croissant.

Boone removed the sandwich from the bag and examined it. "Wow, an inch of mayonnaise, just the way I like it." He took an oversized bite and chewed with enthusiasm. "M'anks," he said.

"You're welcome." Elena swallowed. "But our feast wasn't my doing. My mother left the full pack by the door." She extracted a bottle of water and held it out to him. "Thirsty?"

"Thanks." Once again, he caught the projectile like the perfect outfielder.

Another bottled water and a collapsible fabric bowl out of the back appeared from the pack. Elena slid off the rock. Water gurgled into the dog's dish. Like magic, a dog biscuit appeared out of her pocket.

Ohto, tail wagging, took the treat like it was a fragile treasure.

She returned to her comfortable roost and resumed her lunch.

Boone finished, licked his fingers.

She extricated a freezer bag of chocolate chip cookies and shook it at him.

"Oh, yeah," Boone nodded. They made an airborne transfer.

He sorted through the bag until he found the biggest one. "How did your mother know about Ohto?"

"She has her ways." Elena smiled.

"He waited in the car so she couldn't have seen him. You must have told her."

"She is perceptive."

"I get it. She spotted me when she was upstairs serving breakfast."

"Perhaps?" Elena said, her eyes twinkling.

"Is everyone in your family weird?"

"My mother calls us 'colorful'. How would you describe your visit with my grandmother?"

Boone selected a second cookie and spoke between bites. "I'm not sure how to describe it. She is an interesting old gal."

"She is old country. In Lithuania, she was a seer, a mystic. Today, new-agers would call her a shaman." Pride showed in her smile. "Going back hundreds of years, women of the family followed this tradition. People came for miles to ask for her advice and to hear their future. When she summons someone, we've learned to go with it."

Elena pulled out a red delicious apple and polished it with a cloth napkin.

"Do you know what she told me?"

"No. The message was for you alone."

"Do you want to hear?" The third cookie consumed, Boone took a bite of his fourth.

He offered the bag. She waved it away. "You can tell me."

"I couldn't understand a lot of what she said. She was all... ah..."

"Lithuanian."

Boone shook his head and pulled the dagger from his vest. "She held my hand and gave me this." He held the weapon out to Elena. "Please, take it back. It looks like an heirloom."

"It's a durklas, a ritual dagger, and now it's yours. Did she tell you why you needed it?"

"Nope. She dropped it on me and sent me packing."

Elena's looked down, her brows knit. *Regana must believe he has a role in this mystery. Can I tell him the truth?*

"That lady is one scary customer," he said.

"She can be," Elena said.

The clouds burned off, and small patches of pale blue sky peeked out here and there. Like the sky, the oppressive malaise of tragedy also retreated.

Elena tossed the apple core into the daypack. She heaved a sigh and relaxed back on the boulder.

A black bird circled in the sky above her. "Varnas," she whispered.

The raven circled lower and lower, perching on a branch of an evergreen at the edge of the campsite. The bird cawed twice and went silent.

Sliding off to her feet, Elena walked forward and

held out her arm. The bird glided to a landing on her outstretched limb.

Boone watched, eyes wide and mouth hanging open. "Who the hell are you? Snow White?"

"This is Varnas," she said, as though his name answered all questions.

Ohto, watchful, remained in place.

The raven sidled up to her shoulder to chortle in her ear.

What do you want, my friend?

Varnas spoke to her for the first time, in images, not words. She understood his warning, and it wasn't good. "Sentinel," she called.

Varnas launched from his perch on her shoulder and flew out of the clearing.

Elena's pulse raced. Her cheeks reddened. "We need to leave, Boone. I hope you are ready to hear this, because something is coming."

DAY FOUR

SATURDAY - 12 P.M. — 6 P.M.

CHAPTER TWENTY

LƏ'NÍ - THE FOREST

A rabbit crossed his path. *Meat.* His mouth filled with saliva. *Not worth the effort. This insignificant thing won't feed the hunt.* Find the true martyr, and her flesh will sustain this flesh and the working.

The female's scent grew stronger. *She's close.* Drool overflowed and dripped from the corners of his mouth. Lə'ní groaned. A slight alteration in her aroma's direction and intensity told him his quarry was moving away. The hunt's thrill dulled Lə'ní's agonizing pain, but it still survived, an ache beneath the surface.

Lə'ní filled his lungs and caught the musk of a male. He cuffed and sniffed again. *Wait. A wolf. But no pack. It is alone. I will kill it and gobble it down.*

The leaves quivered as the winds changed, and he lost their scent. *Not close enough to track by sound or sight.* Uncertainty niggled at him. If the breeze changed again, his powerful scent might betray him. *Continue on. Trust the maker's power will guide them to you.*

Which way will the trespassers take? Lə'ní considered their probable route. *They'll take the migration path back to their mounts. Take a shorter way, wait, and the offering comes to us.*

His prey-drive strengthened, and his focus narrowed toward the hunt's bloody end. Ləʼní praised her and celebrated the coming gift. She took her food, and soon, she will be our sustenance.

ELENA — THE FALL CREEK CAMPGROUND

"What're you talking about?" Boone said. His hands jumped to his rifle, and he glanced into the woods.

"We've got to get out of here." Elena's face paled. She scurried around, gathering the remains of their meal.

Ohto stood at attention in the center of the campsite, every muscle quivering. He stared at his master, then Elena.

"Calm down and tell me what's going on," he demanded.

She turned to face him. "Nevermind. It's nothing," she replied, puffing. "I want to return to town now." Hands trembling, Elena stuffed the trash into her bag.

Motionless, he studied her. "I thought you wanted to hike over to the other attack site."

Elena groped for the knapsack strap until she found it. "I changed my mind." She threw her rucksack on her back. "Listen to me, Trust me."

"How can I do that?" Boone snorted. "First, you must come up here. So, we arrive, and you walk around in a daze, then converse with the damn birdies like a cartoon princess." He threw up his hands. "Now, for no reason, you insist we leave." He still didn't move. "Elena, you're not acting rational."

"I'll explain it all later." Shoulders hunching, she boosted the pack into its proper place. "Believe me, Boone. We must go now." She regarded his narrowed eyes, and in a hushed tone said, "Please."

Boone relaxed. "Okay, okay, professor," he said.

"Thank you, detective," she said, her shoulders relaxing, too.

Elena scanned the campsite for the last time, nodded to herself, then bustled toward the trail.

"Geez." Shaking his head, Boone stuffed the empty cookie bag in his pocket.

With Ohto on point, scanning for threats, she double-timed down the footpath. Clenching her fists, Elena fought the urge to run.

BOONE - THE FALL CREEK TRAIL

Boone watched her recede into the huckleberry. There's nothing around here. He checked his weapon. Then, still reluctant, he followed.

The north half of the Fall Creek Loop Trail climbed through red alder and black cottonwood trees. The incline mild, they made good time. They reached the ridge and the halfway marker at 2:20 p.m. Low gray clouds gathered in the once bright sky, threatening drizzle. A rising wind tugged at their gear. Their journey's next leg spread out below. Tight switchbacks descended to a forested plateau and the parking lot.

Ohto moved ahead of them but stopped dead. He raised his nose and rotated his head, inhaling. The dog's hackles rose. He growled long and deep.

Boone brought up his firearm.

"Does Ohto think something's down there?" she asked.

"Cougar or bear maybe." Boone gave her an encouraging smile. He joined his dog. "They're all over in the reserve, but Ohto can handle them."

"Let's go," he told the dog. "Come on, boy." The big dog didn't move. Frowning, Boone stepped forward. Ohto whirled to face him, blocking the way. Ohto barked three times, sharp and urgent. The man stepped forward again. The dog came forward to meet him. They stood at loggerheads.

"Not you, too," he said, his jaw clenched.

Ohto whipped behind Boone and nipped his heel.

"Hey, watch it," he said.

Barking, Ohto bolted up the trail past Elena and turned. He faced them both, baying in alarm.

"He's never disobeyed me or turned away from any fight." Boone shaded his eyes and scanned the valley below.

Her voice cracking, Elena said, "It isn't safe there. We must find another way."

A raven's cry sounded. Varnas sailed over the hillside, skimming the treetops. Reaching Boone and Elena's location, he dive-bombed, passing a few feet above their heads, then flew north toward the summit of Fuzzy Top.

Elena never flinched. "Varnas sees something down there. We need to follow him." She turned back, drawn away by the retreating bird.

"This is ridiculous," Boone said, his arm still protecting his head.

In the distance, Varnas' alarm called. Ohto whined.

"Hell," Boone said. "Who can argue with a dog and a bird?" He scratched his forehead. "If we head north overland, we'll hook up with the road." He sized up Ohto. "Will that work for you, pooch?"

Lə'ní - THE FALL CREEK TRAIL

This is an honorable sacrifice, Lə'ní thought. *They see me not until I fall upon them from my hide.* Spittle dripped on the fir needles at his feet. *I rise, and foolish prey freeze.* He puffed. *This amuses us.*

I slap your male away, mount him, and take out his throat. Lə'ní quivered and dug his claws into the dirt. *His hot blood covers us, and if the stupid wolf protects, I'll release it to rebirth.*

His prizes paused on the crest of the hill. He waited in his hiding place.

Descend to me, love. With your mate dead, you will run, but not far. He huffed. His heart drummed in his chest. *Covered in the blood of your male, I fall on you. Fear makes sweet meat.*

From the sky, a huge black kaw'qs swooped upon them. *What happens?* He rocked and bore his fangs. *That wolf bars the way. No.*

Their protectors caught my scent and herds them to safety. Lə'ní wriggled out of the brush. *Why do they turn away and leave me?* Terror and fury tore through his tortured body. *I will punish that beast if they elude me. I will not honor him with a clean death.*

His prey moved away. Lə'ní despised the wolf with his whole being.

Wound him, pull out his entrails, and let him bleed out, kicking. Grinding his teeth and shaking his pelt, Lə'ní suppressed a roar of rage. *I'll prevent scavengers from feasting, the body rots, and insects take it. I will deny the wolf's ascension.*

They disappeared behind the hill.

I will track them until either they or I meet death. He leapt from the hide. *Move faster with greater stealth. Circle and cut them off. Ignore pain. They will be ours, and I will make them our flesh.*

CHAPTER TWENTY-ONE

ELENA - FOREST

Boone's Pathfinder watch read four o'clock when they topped the next promontory.

The forest, a dense jade tapestry, carpeted the valley. Scores of creeks, bloated by spring runoff, waterfalled over rocky outcroppings. Cutting channels into the bedrock, they cleaved their ways to the basin below, settling in ponds and wetlands.

"Look. Beyond the valley," Elena said, pointing. "Is that the road?"

"Yep." He took in their surroundings. "But we're still miles away."

"Can we stop for a minute?" Elena removed her aluminum canteen from the pack and gulped the contents. "Juice?" She held the flask at arm's length.

"Only three hours of daylight," he said, taking it. "Thanks." Boone drank.

Scratches covered every bare inch of Elena's skin. She cleaned them with alcohol pads and applied antibacterial ointment. "Want some?" She offered the first aid kit to Boone.

"No, thanks, but I'd take some bottled water. Any left?"

"Take whatever you want." She threw the knapsack. It landed at his feet.

Elena searched the sky, scanning for Varnas. During their escape, he'd flown ahead. Ohto took the rear guard. When they fell too far behind, he'd circle back.

Boone rummaged in the backpack. "Has your buddy, the raven, seen anything?" He removed two waters and a bag of trail mix, setting them at his feet. "I'm not seeing large-animal sign, so maybe we lost whatever it was."

Perhaps I overreacted. Elena shook her head to the offered snack.

"See if you have a phone signal." He poured nuts, raisins, and chocolate candies into his hand, and dumped it into his mouth.

Elena held the cell phone over her head. She performed a slow pirouette. "What will you do when you find the animal that killed Mrs Poole?"

"It's a man-eater." He chewed. "So, we'll hunt and put it down."

"If I stand on my tiptoes, there are two bars." She craned her neck to see the screen. "Who should we call?"

"WDFW. They'll send someone out here." He held his hand out for the phone. "Do you mind?"

Elena passed the mobile, her fingers brushing Boone's hand. He smiled.

"Damn, what is the number?" Eyebrows knitted, he rolled his eyes up and to the right. "Okay, I got it now." He dialed. "It's ringing."

"Are we…?" she said.

He held out his palm. "Boone Anderson. I'm out here in the Capitol Forest with Professor Lukas."

A muffled voice replied.

"Nothing like that, we went off course." He paused, listening to the response. "Do me a favor? Send a vehicle to collect us on Waddle Creek Road

around the middle near the Fuzzy Top trailhead."
Boone chuckled. "No, we're fine. We only need a ride
to the Fall Creek Loop Trailhead to pick up my truck."

Wind out of the north sent clouds scuttling across
the angry sky. The temperature fell. Elena shuffled her
feet for warmth.

"We're two hours off the road. I would like to take
the professor back home before she freezes."

The answer sounded garbled to Elena.

"Thanks, doc." Boone ended the call.

Elena reached out, and he dropped the phone into
her hand.

"Just a nice little stroll downhill and our driver
will be waiting."

"You know, detective, when you advised against
coming alone, you had a point." She laughed and
picked up her daypack.

Boone reached out to help her, and this time, she
let him.

On the ridge, Ohto sampled the wind.

"Let's go, boy." Boone positioned his rifle and
walked down the hill. The dog checked on Elena's
position.

"I'm coming, Ohto," she said.

With no cleared trail, the steep incline threatened
to send Elena tumbling. She inched along, seizing
seedlings and tree limbs until they reached the valley
floor.

Little sunlight pierced the canopy, the gloom pal-
pable. Cold permeated her rain gear. A red huckleberry brush blocked their way. They pushed ahead.

Even with Boone at her back, every shadow and
movement increased her discomfort.

A cone dropped and landed at her feet.

Elena gasped. *It flanked us.* Freezing, she held her
breath.

The dog's head snapped toward the noise, his
teeth bared.

"We need to keep moving," Boone said, his hand grasping the stock of his rifle. "Could you go faster, professor?"

"I'd love a run." Elena ushered him off with a sweep of her arm. "Please, set the pace."

Boone nodded and sprinted off.

Ohto, returning to the point position, passed his master.

Boone check her progress. He smiled. She matched his speed. After galloping through the trees for twenty minutes, he spotted a body of water through the thinning underbrush.

Ohto slowed. Boone signaled a stop.

They arrived on the swampy shoreline of a good-sized pond. A narrow animal trail skirted the water's edge. At the far bank, tall aquatic grasses and lily-pads clustered. A matt of algae scum floated on the surface.

Boone bent over with his hands on his thighs, catching his breath. "Damn."

Panting, Elena asked, "What now?"

"That puddle is deeper than it looks. We can go around." Boone found a fallen log. "But let's rest here.

"Check it out," he told the dog.

Clockwise, with nose to the ground, Ohto paced partway around the small lake, then stopped to sniff the air. Apparently finding nothing of concern, he returned to his starting point to repeat the motion, this time moving in the other direction.

Hands on her hips, Elena stood still. Boone fingered his five o'clock shadow. They watched and waited.

Subdued, Ohto returned and sat at his master's feet. "You don't know, either, eh?" Boone patted the dog's head. "What do you think, professor?"

Elena shrugged her shoulders. "You know this area better than I do."

"I guess it's up to me." He sighed and made his

choice. "You ready?"

She nodded.

They sprinted down the right side of the pond, dodging limbs and other trip hazards.

LƏ'NÍ — WATERING HOLE

Running full out, Lə'ní reached the watering hole with an overwhelming thirst. He preferred it flowing, but he'd drunk the turbid water before, and he wasn't sickened.

The strong funk of organic decomposition wafted up from the mud. His tongue lapped up the greenish-brown fluid until he was full. His muzzle wrinkled and lips smacked at the slippery clay aftertaste.

Cattails, skunk cabbage, and dagger-leafed rushes clustered close to the shoreline. A small wooden platform floated at the center of the wetland.

Wait and watch the far shoreline.

Hidden in a cluster of salal, Lə'ní watched the opposite ingress and both approaches. *Rest, for soon I will eat.*

The shadows moved with the breaks of sunlight. His three targets left the cover of trees.

He chuffed. *The wind is with me. The guardian won't catch my scent this time.*

They stood still. Lə'ní's patience tired. *They don't understand all paths bring them to me. I let them pass by the hide, then I'll take them at their flank.* The promise of the kill thrilled him. *Come to me, little female. Fill me. Feed me, my love.* His inner voice sang in praise to her.

ELENA - WATERHOLE

The narrow trail was barely above the waterline, slippery and eroding. They rounded to the opposite shore in short order, ending at a clearing and an abandoned logging road leading away.

"A short tramp through the trees, and we reach the road," Boone said.

"Good." Elena bit her lip and scanned the clearing. *Something is off.*

"We may have to walk a mile or so to find our ride."

The breeze shifted again and brought the rank odor. It stung the back of Elena's throat. "What is that smell?" She covered her nose and mouth with her hand.

Boone sniffed and made a face. "Something died around here."

"You're right, that's it." Her body relaxed. "Many plants do have an aroma of corruption." She pointed to the western skunk cabbage growing at the water's edge. "There's some *Lysichiton americanus* right over there." She walked toward it with a broad smile brightening her face. "Although unpleasant to humans and most mammals, the odor attracts flies and beetles. They pollinate-"

Ohto focused on a clump of brush on the far side of the clearing. He rumbled.

Elena pointed to the dog. She edged toward Boone.

"Don't move. Stand still," he said. He removed a palm-sized canister from his pocket and pressed it into her hand. "Bear Spray."

"What do we do?"

"Stay alert and move back toward the road."

"Aren't you coming?" she asked.

His jaw tensed. "No, I'm the distraction. Bears are all about dominance. I'll show him who is boss."

"What if it's not a bear?"

Dismissing her question, he inclined his head toward the road. "Go."

Boone advanced to the center of the clearing. "Buddy, we know you're here. Come out, and I won't hurt you."

LƏ'NÍ - WATERHOLE

Rage filled Lə'ní. *That wolf scented me again, and the foolish male challenges, a diversion while my female escapes.* He ground his teeth. *This will not happen.* He salivated. So near he could taste her sweet meat. *Come, I will take you quick, and we will be one.* The fever to take the prey surged through Lə'ní, but he held his position. He would strike when he was ready.

BOONE — WATERING HOLE

Boone took a broad stance and watched the predator's hiding place. "I am bigger and badder than you, so beat it."

Ohto crept to his side. They would face the animal together.

Boone and Ohto stepped toward the salal. "Scat, you big dummy. I am in charge, so piss off," he said.

The underbrush rustled. Elena gasped. Boone lifted his rifle.

Up, and up, and up, a living nightmare rose from the forest floor to tower above them.

Over fourteen-feet-tall, weighing over two thousand pounds. This bear wasn't normal, the snout too broad and flat. A low forehead crowned the face, its eyes set far apart and bloodshot like a hound. The animal loomed, glared, and snarled.

Her hands clasped her ears. "Goddess, what is that?" Mouth open, Elena stared ahead.

The thing smelled of rotten meat. Bones, muscles, and internal organs showed through torn and missing skin as though a flesh-eating or hemorrhagic virus ravaged the animal.

"Don't run, and keep moving slow, Elena," Boone hissed.

Nearing the road to safety, Elena clasped the cylinder of bear spray in her hand.

He raised the rifle and squeezed the trigger. The bullet entered the animal's eye and burned its way through its brain, exiting in a spray of black blood. He fired a second time but missed.

"You've killed it," she yelled, throwing up her arms.

"Get moving," Boone hissed.

In the tall grass, Ohto hunkered, crept toward the animal.

Adrenaline might keep that dying bastard from attacking until he kills me. I'll aim to hit center mass this time.

Through his sight, Boone centered between the jawbone and the legs. He chambered the round, inhaled, and held it.

Boone pulled the trigger. *Boom.* The explosion rebounded across the water, rousting a flock of mallards.

The bullet tore a ragged hole through the creature's chest. His bellow reverberated through the trees, and he fell on all fours.

ELENA — WATERING HOLE

Spots swam in front of Elena's eyes, and her hand pressed against her thumping heart. Bullets do nothing.

Unbidden, her goddess sight unlocked the Penumbra. Elena saw the true nature of things. Queasiness assaulted her. She struggled to close the way without success. *I better have enough juice for this.* Elena let the vision wash over her.

Blood leaked down the bear's face, mingling with his spittle as he glared at Boone. Elena's senses reached for him. She realized the monstrous bear felt no pain. They weren't a threat. They were nothing but insects buzzing around his head.

Huffing, he sauntered toward Boone.

Dark magic swirled over the monster's skin, and a black and maroon mist escaped from the holes in its body, spreading and dissipating.

Mediena protect us. That things not a Real-Time animal. It's a sorcerer's construct, and the working is unraveling.

A slurry of black blood oozed from a gaping hole at the center of the animal's chest. Yet, it stalked forward.

If the enchantment charges before Boone reloads, it will be on him. Elena feared she would pass out.

Hands flying, Boone pulled the bolt back, checked the chamber, and slid three cartridges into the magazine, one after the other.

Ohto, eyes wide, bared his sharp white teeth. He circled to the left behind the target. With a rapid volley of barking, he charged back and forth, drawing the creature's attention away from Boone.

The dog nipped at its legs and thighs, herding and distracting it so Boone could finish loading.

A massive paw with razor-sharp claws swatted at Ohto, who leapt away.

Boone took aim. A clean strike exploded in the kill zone between the neck and shoulder, blowing away another hunk of flesh. *Three kill shots, and it's still on its feet.*

A spout of dark magic erupted from the wound. *Metal might destabilize the construct, but it would take time.*

The monster turned on Ohto. The dog jumped back. Another swipe of its paw passed without connecting. Bobbing and weaving, Ohto pressed his assault until the bear's side faced the barrel of his master's rifle.

He would give his life to protect us. Gratitude and affection for the dog filled Elena.

The target was in his sights. Boone aimed and pulled the trigger.

Thump. It hit the animal's chest.

A long strand of enchantment broke free and tumbled away. This time, the monster reacted, recoiling and staggering.

Elena felt the bear's anger at being fooled and regret for missing the kill. His body spasmed. Elena knew he wouldn't lie down and offer his life to Boone. He would flee to its den. Fate would decide, hunt again or die and feed worms.

The creature halted the attack and bolted in the opposite direction. *Bang.* The rifle sounded again, but the creature didn't stop. The sound of crashing through the undergrowth receded until it was silent.

Boone lowered the rifle and reloaded. He shouldered it. He met Elena's eyes. Like a peal of thunder, the tension fractured.

Elena ran across the clearing and threw herself into Boone's arms.

Their lips pressed together, their bodies fused. Kisses, burning and wild, frantic hands moving. Passion neared a point where instinct overpowered reason. Boone pulled away.

"What the hell am I doing?" he said.

"What is it?" Elena said, her eyes dilated near black.

"No time for this." He touched her cheek. "It might circle back." Yearning filled his eyes. "We gotta get out of here, but don't think we've finished this conversation, either."

"You're right." She turned and glanced over her shoulder. "Oh, I have a great deal more to say on this topic." She sauntered down the logging road.

He admired her retreat.

"You coming?" she said, her eyes forward.

"Oh, boy, am I in trouble." Boone turned to Ohto and said, "Let's see if we can find you a cookie."

At the mention of the c-word, the dog scampered after Elena, tail wagging.

CHAPTER TWENTY-TWO

ELENA - THE WADDLE CREEK ROAD

Elena, Boone, and Ohto pulled themselves through the thicket and dropped into a ditch.

"The pickup point is about half a mile," Boone said. "Can you make it?" Boone took Elena's hand, helping her up the talus bank.

"I think so." Her dream-walk at the pond had weakened her, but this time, she'd recovered faster.

Clear-cut, rubble, skeletal roots and branches, lent a battlefield air to the downslope side of the road.

Yawning, Elena covered her mouth with the back of her hand.

"I could jog ahead, bring the truck back to get you." He smiled, studying the gravel roadbed.

Her lower lip pursed. She shook her head. "I'm grateful, Boone. You and Ohto saved our lives. Saved my life."

"It's nothing." The ghost of a grin showed at the corners of his mouth.

The dog, trotting between them, looked up at Elena.

"I could have been alone with that thing." Mirroring Boone's movement, Elena bowed her head, not meeting his eyes. The gravel crunched under their feet. "Okay, I'll say it. I was wrong, and you were right."

Boone nodded twice and grunted.

"Aren't you going to rub it in? Say I told you so?"

"Nope." He kept up the easy pace.

"Good." Playfully, she bumped his arm with her shoulder.

Boone chuckled.

Around the next bend, a WDFW truck sat by the side of the road. Buzzsaw snoring drifted through the open window.

"Our chauffeur." Boone raised his chin toward the truck.

Dan Sitton dozed with a green ball cap over his eyes.

Bam, bam, bam. Boone beat the tailgate with his palm.

"What?" said the vet, yawning and shaking himself awake. "Hey, about time you got here, cowboy." He exited the truck, then cocked his head when he examined their disheveled appearance. "What happened to you two?"

Boone and Elena shared a conspiratorial glance.

"We went off-trail," he said. "No big deal." Boone secured his rifle in the rack.

"The glorious outdoors, bugs, scratches, and all the usual stuff," Elena said. "Hello again, doctor."

"Hi, Professor Lukas. I see you are still with us." Dan said, grinning. "Anderson, I drove all the way out here and sat around for a blasted hour. Least you can do is tell me a fascinating story."

"It's a lengthy one, doc, but we don't have enough time right now."

"What's another moment or two? Spill, man."

"Okay, okay. Long story short, we tangled with the man-killer."

"The bear?" Eyes wide, Dan scratched his jaw.

Elena and Boone exchanged another look, rich with meaning.

"I guess you would call it that," she said.

"Not like any I have seen. It was over fourteen-feet-tall, standing on its hind legs."

"Where is it now?" Dan eyed the tree line.

"Off licking its wounds," Elena said.

"I hit it dead center three times and once in the head, and it kept coming."

"Still standing? How can that be?" Dan Sitton said.

"It was breathing last time we saw it." Elena leaned against the dusty dark green fender.

"The thing's dug in somewhere, bleeding out." Boone cleared his throat. "We're okay for now." He turned to Dan. "Come around the office tomorrow afternoon and I'll show you a carcass."

Elena removed her day pack.

Boone touched her shoulder and said, "Let me help you with that." He placed the bag in the truck bed.

"Thanks," she said.

"The professor's exhausted, and I want to get her home," Boone said. "We're tired and hungry now. I'll submit a full report tomorrow."

Sitton opened his mouth to argue but seemed to change his mind. "Okay, everybody aboard, the bus is leaving."

ELENA — FALL CREEK TRAILHEAD

The WDFW four-by-four bounced into the Fall Creek Trailhead parking lot, stopped, and the passenger door opened.

Boone and Ohto got out, with Elena following. Dan Sitton stayed in the cab. Elena walked uneasily across the lot to Boone's truck.

The doctor's truck idled while Boone leaned

through the driver's side window, deep in conversation with the vet.

Her hand grasped the door handle, but it held fast. "Damn, locked." She leaned against Boone's truck to wait.

The setting sun cast long shadows, and the thermometer dropped further. Night threatened.

Shivering, Elena wrapped her arms around herself. *I can't remember the last time I was so tired.* A lump formed in her throat. *How do I tell him the truth about what happened today?*

Ohto sat next to Elena. He pressed his warm body against her chilled one.

Sitton popped his truck into gear. Boone stepped away. The gravel crunched as the vet's vehicle moved forward.

Boone put his hands in his pockets. He watched the Ford drive away, then turned to join her.

He pressed the remote. *Click.* The lock released.

Elena wrenched the door open. "Up," she said. Ohto rocketed onto the seat. She clambered in beside him.

Without a word, Boone got behind the wheel and slid the key into the ignition, then slammed his fist against the dash.

"What happened?" Elena said, facing him.

"Dan said they're taking Mr Poole off life support," he said, his voice choked with emotion. "He'll be gone soon."

"Oh, no, that's sad."

"I could have done more." Boone lowered his chin and swallowed. "This is my fault."

"There was nothing you could do."

"I could have, damn it. I should have hunted that freak down the day we first met." His hand touched his mouth.

"The past can't be changed," Elena said.

His jaw set, and he breathed deep.

"What will you do?" she whispered.

"About the bear?" His eyes averted, he patted Ohto. "Find it and make sure it's dead."

The truck's metal frame contracted, ticking with the dropping temperature.

Elena shifted in her seat and inhaled. "Boone, that wasn't a bear."

"What's that supposed to mean?" Boone's voice was tired and irritated.

"Have you ever seen an Ursus like this one?"

"No, but…" he shook his head. "It's a diseased animal with extreme genetic abnormality, and that's all."

"That creature is a contagion, but not in a biological sense," Elena. "Its very existence violates nature."

"What the hell is that supposed to mean?" He closed his eyes. "We're tired, and I've had my fill of bizarre stuff today."

"It was a magical illusion," she continued. "My people call it a construct."

"A magical what?"

"Construct. A powerful mind created that imitation life using thought and intention. But it isn't natural, so the form is unstable."

"That is ridiculous," Boone said.

"I know it's hard to believe, but I've seen it done." Elena patted her chest with her hand. "A dark magician molds a form out of bone, dirt, and blood. He imbues his making with life. At first, it looks real, but it isn't, and it begins degrading right away."

"Like a mud puppet?" He pushed the idea away. "Jeez."

"Yes, a constructed lifeform has similarities with the legends of golems and zombies."

"I don't believe in those, or fairies, vampires, and monsters." His jaw clenched, and he grasped the wheel.

"Boone." Elena touched his arm, but he pulled away.

"This is such bullshit." Boone slapped his palms against the steering wheel and replied in a cold, even tone, "I don't want to hear any more."

"When you fought the creature, I saw the magic holding it together unravelling," she said.

His volume increased. "Professor, you tell me that your grandmother is a fortune teller. Okay, families are weird. Then your crow warns you there's danger. I'm not sure I believe in things like that, but I tried keeping an open mind. But this is too much."

He turned to face her, highlighted by the amber light of the setting sun.

"Get real, damn it. We saw a mutant bear today, a very sick one, but a real one." Boone pointed toward the forest. "I shot it three times in the head and chest, and now it's dead and rotting in a hole."

Chin lifted, Elena's nostrils flared. "Wake up, detective." Her voice was strident. "Whether you want to believe it or not, we both saw a creature that hasn't walked the earth in ten thousand years. Something you shot four times, and it didn't react. Did you see the bones and the organs showing through its skin, and the thick black blood? Did that look normal to you?"

"I don't care," he said, cutting off her words. "I've seen a lot of weird shit in my life as a cop in Montana and as a soldier in Afghanistan and Iraq. Reality is a dangerous, scary place, and I don't need the existence of magic to explain it." A mask of anger concealed his face.

Boone turned the key, and the engine started. "Professor, whatever it was or however it got here, it's dead. That's all I need to know."

Mediena's next vision hit Elena like a mallet. She buried her head in her hands and screamed.

LƏ'NÍ - THE BURROW

The burrow's entrance gaped like a maw. Animated by Lə'ní's gurgling and uneven breathing, the earthwork appeared alive.

Swaddled in darkness, he forgot his hunger for the kill. Even pain, his constant companion since waking, abandoned him. Only the cold and damp endured.

The fragrance of his blood mixed with the rich soil dominating his other senses. The copper tang brought what comfort was left to him. Time twisted, minutes passed like decades. His eternal spirit, holed up in the rotting body, longed to return to death and loosen its grip on life.

Droning insects buzzed around his head. He wanted to snatch them down but lacked the will. The drone crystallized into words of Lə'ní's maker.

"Lə'ní, my weapon, does your spirit inhabit the body I forged?" asked the voice in the darkness.

"The flesh is filled, but I am sorry, my Maker. I'm weak and have little left to serve you."

"Our ritual nears completion. Your third kill is dying, and the god of the hunt waits to accept the sacrifice."

"Are you near, my Maker? I cannot see you."

"Rest, Lə'ní. Soon, your service will be complete."

With effort, the huge creature stirred. "I will come to you."

"Stay, my Weapon, and when it's done, I'll unbind you from the pelt you wear. You'll shed it like a winter coat in the warmth of spring."

ELENA — FALL CREEK TRAILHEAD

Images of him crashed over Elena like a tsunami and tugged at her soul. She knew his name, Lə'ní. Pain impulses fired down her spinal column in rhythmic waves. Body rocking, she heard a faraway scream. It was hers.

"What's wrong? Talk to me?" Boone's voice came from miles away. He called her name again and again.

As the spasms receded, she struggled to speak. "I-I-I-I know who he is. I know where he is." she rasped.

"Who? What are you talking about?"

She opened the truck door, and she dropped to the ground, her legs buckling. "I have to find him before he's reborn or he'll never find rest."

Varnas landed on the hood of the pickup and spread his wings. He screeched.

"Elena, where the hell are you going?" He sprang out and ran after her. Grabbing her by the forearms, Boone lifted her to her feet. "Talk to me, damn it."

Elena shook him off and staggered toward the trail with Ohto at her heels. "Darkness binds his poor spirit, and I need to free him. Take me to him, Varnas."

The raven cocked his head, then took off into the forest.

"Stop. Where are you going?" Boone reached for his rifle but the rack was empty. His weapon was in the vet's truck on the way back to Olympia. He swore under his breath and sprinted after Elena.

"I've seen his lair. If you want to kill him, follow me," she yelled over her shoulder.

In darkness, they followed the corvid up the trail for a quarter of a mile until Varnas landed on a Douglas fir branch hanging over a deep ravine.

"Yes, I see the path." Elena scrambled down a muddy bank into the chasm. "It's not far," she shouted.

The bird launched off the branch and sailed ahead of her.

"This is crazy. Come back here." Boone slipped and stumbled as he followed.

Varnas perched on the limb of a cedar and cawed.

"In there?" Varnas spread his wings again and bobbed his head.

"Thank you, Varnas," she said.

The raven made a shrill alarm call, and he flew into the sky and away.

"Where is he going?" asked Boone.

"He's done all he can to help. Varnas' power weakens after dark. He needs to find a secure roost for the night."

"There is nothing here." Breathing heavily, Boone's cheeks blazed.

"His den is right in there," Elena pointed toward a hollow in the hillside. "We just need to find it." She strode forward. "There it is." Elena bent toward the entrance to the burrow. "Do you have a flashlight?"

Boone grasped her shoulders. "Get back. If a wounded animal is in there-"

"He *is* in there, but he won't harm us now." Elena pulled away, knelt, and held out her hand.

Approaching her, Ohto snuffled the leaves scattered over the forest floor. His snout wrinkled, and his lips furled.

Forgetting it was missing, Boone reached for his rifle. "Shit."

On her knees, Elena squinted into the hole and gestured Boone forward.

"Okay, okay." He squatted beside her, and the reek of decay washed over him. "Smells like he's in there all right." Boone's flashlight illuminated the cavity, and the animal opened his eyes, glowing deep red. "Oh, my God."

"His name is Lə'ní," Elena said, her voice sad. "His aspect is a construct, but his spirit is real."

Lə'ní's growl rumbled in the enclosed space.

"I'm sorry someone is using you, my friend. With the help of my lady Mediena, I'll release you from bondage so you can move on."

The creature raised his paw to strike. But shuddered and collapsed as the pain overwhelmed him. Lə'ní moaned, low and plaintive.

With her arms extended, Elena reached for power. Little of the goddess' reserves remained, but she had no choice but to help him. The forest creatures were her charges, even this monster.

The massive creature's eyes softened. He panted, each exhale wheezing.

"I'm here, and I will release you from bondage and send you to rest," she said.

Lə'ní lowered his head onto his paws, his body relaxed, and his soul reached out to her for release.

The wave of malevolent power hit, pushing Elena aside and snatching Lə'ní's spirit from her grasp.

"No, no!" she cried as she watched the dark magic slither over his body. Her heart broke.

The eternal in Lə'ní, his master's spirit knife, withdrew, and his unnatural form dematerialized.

CHAPTER TWENTY-THREE

GABBY - SKATELAND ROLLER RINK

J anie made a second splay-legged revolution of the roller rink, still hugging the wall to keep from falling. Gabby winced when her friend attempted a spin, barely avoiding a tumble. She beckoned Gabby to join her on the floor. She greeted the invitation with a single sharp shake.

"No," Gabby mouthed.

Jacob Brooks and a group of his friends snickered from the sidelines, but Gabby ignored them with a pointed lack of interest.

A head taller than his friends, Jacob jabbed an elbow into the ribs of the kid to his right. His head tilted in Janie's direction. The other boy, Keshawn from her French class, nodded and shot out onto the polished wooden floor, powering his way toward her friend.

Spreading his arms, heels inward and toes out, he transitioned into a smooth revolution in front of the girl, then pulled his arms and into a spin ending with an exaggerated *ta-dah* pose.

Janie clapped.

Keshawn's lips moved.

The girl laughed and nodded in reply.

Hip hop blasted through scratchy speakers. Keshawn executed a rhythmic grapevine. Janie grinned and performed a shaky imitation of the steps.

The boy's hand reached for Janie, and she took it.

"They look good together, don't they?"

Gabby jumped. Jacob Brooks smiled down at her. His voice changed last year, no longer reedy, but warm and deep. A sparse five o'clock shadow sprouted on his jaw.

"Wanna skate?" said Jacob, tossing his head and flipping back his long bangs.

"I don't think so." Gabby crossed her legs and turned her head away.

Jacob sprawled next to her on the raked benches. "I know you like me. You're always watching. You don't have to play hard to get."

"I'm not playing anything," she said. "I'm not a child."

"I agree with that." He winked. "Let's cut the foreplay and get out of here."

"I don't want to go anywhere. Besides, even if I did, I can't." She clasped her hands in her lap. "My boyfriend wouldn't like it."

"Ha, you're lying." Jacob leaned into Gabby. "If you had a boyfriend, I'd know it." His right leg jittered like a rabbit's nose.

"I do so." Her toes warmed, and the sensation worked its way up her body.

"Okay, where is he then?" His hand shading his eyes, Jacob scouted the room. "Not over there. Nope, not there, either."

"He doesn't go to our school."

"Right," he chuckled. "Okay, I'll play. What school does he go to?"

"Seth is in college," Gabby said, holding up her chin. "Yesterday, we talked on the phone for a whole hour, and it wasn't about kid junk." Now, even her ears blazed.

"What does he talk about?"

"Seth told me about the places he's traveled."

"Big damn deal. Everybody's family goes to Europe. So what?" Jacob sneered.

"He's been to a bunch of places like Africa and Thailand. He went to Rio in Brazil. That's in South America. There's this carnival there. They have floats, people dancing with no clothes on and everything. Like in New Orleans, where girls lift their tops and people throw beads to them."

"Oh, I get it now. There's one reason college boys waste time on little girls like you."

"And what's that?" Every cell in her body burned.

"To get in your pants," he hissed, eyes cold. "Has he?"

Smack. Gabby's palm connected with the boy's cheek, leaving a bright red handprint.

"Ow." Jacob's nostrils flared, and he covered the side of his face. "You bitch."

"You're an asshole." Leaping to her feet with tears flowing, Gabby darted from the rink.

ALICE - UNIVERSITY

When she packaged the express delivery, same day mail and rush order to the University of California, Davis Veterinary Genetics lab, Alice's hands trembled.

She'd kept a small sample. While she waited, she worked in her laboratory. By early evening, the UCD results landed in her inbox.

She searched the data for clues all night. By early morning, Alice formed an amazing theory - the specimen was from a chimera, and she had proof.

What a relief. Alice slipped a yellow Post-it on a page in the UCD report to mark her place.

Alice ran a yellow highlighter across a section on the page. It read:

"…the exemplars (saliva, epithelia, follicles) came from unrelated species.

"The saliva resembled an extinct Ursidae (bear), the hair tags a modern Polar bear, and skin cells a Castoroides (a prehistoric rodent)."

Heck, that sucker was eight feet long.

The old laptop chugged. Alice opened a document called Unknown_Sample.doc. It contained the results of her own experiments.

She typed.

"Exposed to sunlight, heat, moisture, and oxygen, Deoxyribonucleic acid degrades at a slow rate. Under optimum circumstance, DNA can remain intact for thousands of years.

"UCDVGL compared the specimen to various samples (Articus, Castoroidas and others)."

"Blah, blah, blah," Alice said. She paged down to the end of the document.

Her fingers hammered the keyboard. "Under strict laboratory conditions, the Capitol Forest DNA lost thirty-five percent greater integrity than a control group," she typed.

"The binding sites holding the double helix to-gether unraveled at a rapid rate. With no environ-mental changes, the speed of degradation escalated at five percent per hour."

Her hand over her mouth, Alice mouthed her words. "The unnatural forces holding the DNA to-gether can't resist natural forces. It is seeking an inert state." *Alice backspaced.* "Better leave that part out, too airy-fairy."

Play this one right and you can publish. Her fist pumped. "Take that, tenure committee."

She dialed Elena at 10:30 p.m. The phone rang four times.

Her breathing rapid, she blurted, "Hello, professor?"

The recording cut her short when it stated,

"You've reached Elena Lukas. I can't answer the phone right now. Please, leave a message at the tone, and I'll get back to you."

Beep.

"This is Alice from RSU. I have a fascinating story to tell. Please call me."

GABBY — ALLEY BEHIND SKATELAND

The fire exit resisted her attempt to force the door closed, so Gabby left it to shut on its own. She threw herself against the chain-link fence. Tears merged with her running nose, and she brushed them away with the back of her hand. "I hate my life," she said, gasping for air.

Her forehead leaned against the chain-links. Gabby's sobbing neared hysterics.

Mucky puddles dotted the loading area. Against the cinder block building, escaping trash surrounded dumpsters and recycle barrels. The oily stink of blacktop burned her nose.

The metal door burst open, hitting the wall.

"No stupid girl hits me." Jacob charged ahead.

"Stay away." Gabby's heart pumped at a furious rate. Beads of sweat formed on every surface of her body. *I'm burning alive.*

"If you're giving it away, maybe I'll have some, too." The boy grabbed Gabby by the shoulders, pushed her against the brick wall, and ground his lips against hers.

"No, no," she cried.

A voice spoke. *Gabija. You have my power, use it.*

"Leave me alone," she screamed. A wave of heat exploded out of Gabby's body. The surge tossed Jacob aside like a doll. He hit the dumpster and collapsed in the dirt.

Gabby ran.

REGANA — IN THE PENUMBRA

Regana pulled a purple pulsing misfortune away from the cluster of bright yellow strands of destiny. She pushed it in another direction and watched it float away. She couldn't prevent every catastrophe, but she could dissuade minor hardships and nuisances and target them toward those that could benefit from a lesson. She grasped a tiny peach string of luck. It wriggled like a trout in her hand and escaped. She laughed and watched as it streaked away, disappearing in a tangle of fates.

"So, you have ideas of your own, little one," Regana said in Lithuanian.

In the distance, lightning flashed for the second time.

"An auspicious day for us," she said.

The first flash occurred when Mediena sealed a thought bond with her pranašas. It was a weak binding but a start.

Regana sucked her teeth and grimaced. "That girl must turn to the mundane or make her ascent soon."

Another strike hit accompanied by an intense clap of thunder.

A grin crossed her elfin face. "Gabija walks the earth this day." Regana lowered her head and said, "Welcome, my sister. My granddaughter is powerful, and she will serve you well."

GABBY - THE ROAD HOME

What have I done? I killed him. Headlong, she rushed down the two-lane road, past fallow fields lined with broken fences.

A hot breeze like one off the desert at night played at her clothing and hair. *The boy is not dead,* the goddess said. *His pride won't reveal his shame.*

"Lady Gabija, goddess of home and hearth. Is it you?" She clasped the strap of her shoulder bag.

Yes, my priestess. You're weakened. Return to our hearth to replenish. The lady's voice faded.

"Where are you going? Come back. Don't leave me."

I must or I may harm you, the goddess said, her voice a crackle of fire. *You drew upon your own life force to channel my power. This was foolish but necessary. Be patient. Days will pass, but I will return.* As the lady withdrew, the faint nip returned to the spring air.

Gabby turned back toward Skateland. Janie's parents had dropped them off and would come to pick them up. But not for hours.

"I'm not going back in there." She considered her options. "It's only a couple miles to home," she said. "I can walk."

Gabby made good time, but after a mile, the magical hangover hit her hard, with pounding head and bone-aching fatigue.

A flash car slowed. "Want a ride, gorgeous?" A shaggy haired teen with a spray of acne across his face hung out the car.

"No." Gabby continued walking.

"Your loss, you stuck-up cow." Tires squealed when they peeled out.

All boys are children. They don't mature as fast as girls. Gabby trudged on, feet dragging. *Janie will be way pissed, but I don't care. She'll get over it.* "I would rather have no boyfriend and die a virgin," Gabby said.

"Hello, little one."

"Yikes," Gabby said.

Seth's smiling face greeted her. A wave of relief washed away any visions of white vans and stranger danger.

Standing tall with shoulders back, she cocked her head and with her best nonchalant voice said, "Oh, Seth, what are you doing here?"

"I was on my way to your house to meet with your sister."

Her heart sank. "Oh?"

"She called and asked me to pick her up for a late dinner. But I'm early. I'd hoped to spend more time with you. Talking."

Did he say what I thought he said. He wanted to talk to me. "Did you?"

"Yes, partridge, I do. Why don't you get in, and I'll give you a ride home? We can chat along the way." He opened the passenger side door of the red convertible.

"I can't. I want to go with you. I just can't." *Mama will put me on restriction until I'm thirty if I get in there with him.*

His brow knit, and he frowned. "Why not?"

He looks so sad. "It is hard to explain. My family insists on treating me like a child."

"I understand you, Gabby. You know you can talk to me." He looked into her eyes, radiating honesty.

"It's dumb and kind of embarrassing."

"Tell me, love." He oozed sincerity.

The truth flooded out. "I'm not allowed to ride with strangers." The moment she spoke the words, she regretted them. *Now, he will think I'm a child.* Gabby hung her head, and tears formed in her eyes.

Seth laughed. "Is that all?"

She sniffed and nodded.

"That's not a problem then because I'm not a stranger."

Gabby lifted her head and smiled, like the sun emerging from an eclipse. "Yes, we're friends." She slid through the open door onto the passenger seat.

"You look exhausted, my sweet friend. I know what you need, some refreshments. Have we time for a coffee?"

GABBY — COFFEE SHOP

They pulled into a lucky parking spot, right in front of the Batdorf & Bronson Coffee Roasters. This place was off the customary route to Swan House, but Gabby didn't care.

Seth opened her car door. "Thank you." She took his offered hand and stepped out onto the pavement. *It's like exiting Cinderella's carriage.* Gabby tried not to giggle.

"I'm delighted you're joining me for afternoon tea. But I don't want you in any trouble," Seth said. "What time should you be home?"

"Mama thinks I'm at Skateland and doesn't expect me home until after six o'clock."

They strolled down the sidewalk, and their hands bumped.

Just go for it. In a leap of courage, Gabby slid her hand in his. *Is anybody watching?* She glanced up and down the empty street.

Seth squeezed her hand back and didn't let go.

He's so handsome and sophisticated.

Seth dropped her hand and opened the door. Cool jazz escaped. He gestured for Gabby to enter.

She walked in B and B's feeling taller, thinner, and sexier.

Inside the coffee shop, marble-topped tables, mahogany booths, and overstuffed couches scattered over the pine board floor. A fireplace against the far wall blazed.

Most days, customers filled every seat. But today, a handful of students scoured oversized textbooks or typed on laptops.

"Let's sit over there." He touched her elbow, turning her toward a table in a corner of the room. His hand moved to the small of her back. He escorted her to the table.

Gabby reached for her chair back but stopped, with knitted brows.

Seth frowned. "Allow me." He pulled out her chair.

What am I supposed to do?

"Take a seat, my dear."

"Okay. Um, thanks." She sat with as much grace as she could muster.

"I'll order for us, shall I?"

"Ah sure. Should I wait here?" Her shoulders drooped.

"Make yourself comfortable, little one. I'll bring you a wonderful treat."

When he turned his back, Gabby pulled out her phone and texted, "Ull no bleev w@ Im doiN" *Janie's a fool for flirting with that stupid boy Keshawn. This'll show who's a child and who isn't.* Without waiting for a response, she typed, "DrinkN cofy W HIM."

Seth busied himself with their drinks at the condiment station.

She popped the phone back in her purse. Seth returned with the two cups and a plate of pastries on a small tray. He winked.

Seth positioned one cup in front of her. "Here is hot chocolate with extra whip for the young lady and espresso macchiato for the old man."

"Oh, don't say old. You're not old."

"All right, the older man." He winked again, and he placed the treats in the center of the table. "Sweets, sweet girl?"

Ornate frosted petit fours and flaky strawberry Napoleons reminded Gabby she was starving, not having eaten since breakfast.

"Oh, yes, please."

"I like a woman with an appetite. Not the ones who pretend they never eat."

Gabby intended to take the largest pastry but diverted her hand to the smallest instead. *Seth called me a woman.* Her cheeks warmed.

"Try that cocoa, my darling, and tell me what you think," he said.

She lifted the white ceramic mug to her mouth and took a sip. It was sweet and thick, and it slid down her throat. The sweetness hit her like a drug.

Seth, with the lightest touch, wiped the whipped cream mustache off her upper lip with the cloth napkin.

Gabby quivered at the thought of a more intimate touch. Her fingers lifted to her mouth, and she filled her lungs with the aroma of vanilla and dark chocolate. *And something else?*

"Did you like that?" he asked, his voice quiet. Seth massaged the top of her hand in a long slow motion.

"Yes," she whispered, her eyes locked on his hand.

His fingers paused midair a millimeter above the soft area between her index finger and her thumb. "Would you like more?" he asked.

Gabby's eyes opened wide. She opened her mouth but couldn't think of what to say.

He chuckled, low and carnal. "Chocolate? Don't you like the hot chocolate, mia cara?"

"Oh, uh, cocoa. Yes, I do." She giggled, picked up the heavy mug, and took a deep draught. The hot drink was intoxicating.

"Good girl. Now finish it?" He gestured to the cup.

She drank it all down in one long gulp. Setting down the cup with a *clank*, a big lopsided grin spread over her face.

"That is yummy hot chocolate, Seth." She covered her giggles with her hand.

"It is time for us to go now, dear one." He pulled out her chair. Gabby's gazed into his eyes. She grasped his arm to keep from listing.

"Where are we going?" she slurred. *I should go somewhere, but I don't know where.* "I feel funny."

He opened the car door and helped her into the passenger seat. "You feel good, don't you?" He buckled her seat belt.

"I think so." She fought to bring him into focus.

"Close your eyes and rest now."

"Okay." Gabby drifted off into a twilight sleep.

DAY FOUR

SATURDAY - 6 P.M. — MIDNIGHT

CHAPTER TWENTY-FOUR

MINA - SWAN HOUSE

A late afternoon sun crept toward the horizon as outside dogwood leaves and white flowers roiled in the wind.

This morning, Mina tripped over four cans of albacore tuna in the service elevator and found the two-foot-long pruning shears under fresh linen in the airing cupboard.

Later, while making her mother's lunch, she opened the silverware drawer, discovering an antique silver hairbrush tucked amongst the serving spoons.

She scoured the entire house. In the sitting room, she unearthed two odd pieces of costume jewelry, and on the dining room sideboard, a silver lighter with a skull and the motto, "Memento Mori," painted on it.

Mina stared at the random objects piled on her desk. She tapped her knuckles against her lips.

Neither Gabija nor anyone here would steal these things and hide them around the house. Mina lifted the rhinestone ear-clip, the height of fashion in 1955, and turned it over in her hands. *This doesn't belong to any recent guests.* She dropped the earring next to the rainbow plastic bead necklace with a unicorn pendant. "Why would anyone steal this useless rubbish?"

Eyes closed, she kneaded her forehead. *I can't think about this anymore. I must talk to Gabija before I search again.*

Mina glanced outside, surprised to discover the darkness. The desk clock informed her it was after seven in the evening. During her wild hunt, she'd lost track of time.

"Oh, my dear, she should have been home from the skating rink over an hour ago."

Picking up the desk phone's receiver, Mina dialed her adolescent daughter's mobile number. It went directly to voicemail. "This is Mama, please call me. Love you, sweetheart,"

Removing her cell from her sweater pocket, she sent a text to her youngest daughter. "Call home."

She waited. Her stomach fluttered. *Gabby lives with that phone attached to her hand. I can't believe she'd ignore my message.*

Mina paced the small office for fifteen minutes, the longest interval Gabby had ever resisted responding to a text.

Still no answer.

Brrring. Brring.

Mina dove for the telephone. "Hello, ah, Swan House Inn, may I help you?" She crossed her figurative fingers.

"My dear Mrs Lukas," said Tobias Stephens, clearing his throat. "I fear we must take our leave of you tomorrow morning at five, and we plan to take our breakfast on the road."

"Certainly, Mr Stephens."

"We will be out late this evening. But I would like to clear our accounts before we depart. Please, place our bill under the door of our room. I will have a bank draft prepared for you, and my good wife will deliver it before we leave in the morning."

"Will there be anything else?"

"No. That's all. Good evening, Mrs Lukas."

Without waiting for a response, Tobias Stephens hung up.

Filling time, Mina printed the invoice and ran it upstairs.

By the time she returned to her office, Mina's worry reached its threshold. *I can't wait around doing nothing.*

She picked her cell phone up off the desk and found her daughter's current best friend Janie's number from contacts. *This girl's nice enough and no sillier than the others.*

The first number was the family's landline. It rang three times before Janie's mother answered and put her on the phone.

"Hi," Janie said.

"This is Mrs Lukas, Gabby's mother. Is she there with you?"

"Ah, no-" the girl stammered.

"Do you know where she is?"

Janie paused. "Not for sure."

Mina leaned her chin on her left palm, holding the phone to her ear with her other hand. "It's getting late, she hasn't called home, and I'm worried. Janie, are you sure you can't tell me where she went?"

"I don't know right now."

She's still covering. Mina pushed back her rising panic, "Janie, Gabby isn't in trouble. I just need to find her. Where did you last see her?"

"Okay, we were like at Skateland talking to these cute guys, but Gabs didn't like them, so she totally bailed."

Mina's heartrate increased.

"Thank you for telling me the truth, Janie. What time did she, um, bail?" Mina picked up a ballpoint pen from the desk and doodled a random geometric pattern on the water bill's envelope.

"I didn't see her leave, but she texted around 5:30. So, it was a while before that."

"In her text, did she say where she was?" The pen was running out of ink. She pulled out the desk drawer and threw it back. Holding the phone in her clammy hand, fear rooted her to the spot.

"Some coffee place, I think," Janie said.

A long pause held until Mina broke it.

"Janie, it's late. It's dark. Gabby hasn't come home and isn't answering her phone. This is serious. I'm worried about her, and you *must* help me find her." Mina closed the desk drawer and tore the envelope into pieces.

"I don't know where she is, Mrs Lukas. I really don't. All I know is she was having coffee with some guy she met. I haven't seen him. She told me he's like a friend of her sister's, an older guy from the college."

"Thank you, Janie. If she contacts you, will you tell her to call home?" Mina swept up the pieces of paper into her hand and threw them into the waste basket at her feet.

"Yes, Mrs Lukas, I will."

Mina inserted the phone into the desk charger and watched the charge light blink.

Who could it be? Mina averted her eyes, her brows knitted. *Elena doesn't know any faculty or students yet.* She squeezed her eyes shut tight. *Where is Gabby?*

ELENA — ON THE ROAD

"We'll be home soon," Elena said. They passed a sign reading ten miles to Olympia. Boone didn't grunt a response. He hadn't spoken in an hour.

He can't handle my crazy world. That's all right, we part ways after tonight. Elena patted Ohto on the rump. *But I will miss you, boy.*

He whimpered, a sound so plaintive Elena feared she might cry.

Beethoven's "Ode to Joy," her mother's ring tone, filled in the empty spaces of the truck. "Sorry, it's my phone." Tempted to let the call roll to voicemail, Elena wrestled it from her pants pocket and answered.

"Hi, Mama. What's up?" She feigned a cheerful voice. "What?" Hand to her mouth, Elena bit the nail of her middle finger. "Where was she? Uh-huh. Okay. Okay." She licked her lips. "Missing? For how long?"

Boone tensed and glanced to her. "Is something wrong?"

"Yes," she mouthed.

Mina told her everything.

"Try to stay calm, Mama. I'll be there soon. Well, soon as we can. No. Nah-uh. I don't have any idea who Gab's friend meant. Did you call any other girls? Okay. Okay. I love you, too, Mama. I'll be home soon."

Staring forward, Elena held the phone between her palms.

"Problems at home?" Boone's hand gripped the stick and down shifted.

"It's nothing."

"Come on, tell me. I can help," he said. "I'm a wildlife cop, remember?"

Elena faced him. The headlights of passing cars illuminated her face. Tears formed in her eyes. "My baby sister is missing. We think it might be a stranger abduction."

GABBY — ON THE ROAD

This quarter in film class, Mrs Daniels taught them about montage. Gabby learned it meant a whole lot of pictures or music spliced together into a single scene. At the time, she still wasn't certain what it meant, but she got it correct in the quiz.

"I'm in the middle of one right now," Gabby mumbled. Her face in a mirror, two bright eyes coming closer, a mumbling chant, one image after the other.

"Cut. Print it," she said, giggling.

A red light turned green.

"I'm so tired."

"Sleep." He sounded angry.

"I can't, I have something important to do." She fought to stay at the surface.

A flash - a vision of Capitol Dome alight.

"Pretty," Gabby said, reaching toward the window. "Wait, my house is that way." She pointed, but someone pushed her hand into her lap. *Say something.* "What was I saying?"

In her personal montage, the face of a man whizzed by. *Who is that?* She yawned without covering her mouth. *Oh, yeah, it's him.* "What's your name?"

The man petted her hair and said something, but she couldn't understand. *I like this hair petting part.*

But for the streetlights passing overhead, it was full dark. As they sped past, she counted. "One, two, thr - three." Gabby's eyes closed, but her eyelids glowed red as each light passed overhead, each illumination occurring farther apart.

The music reminded her of a lullaby. *Wasn't I supposed to be somewhere?*

"That isn't important," *the music sang.* "Sleep- Sleep-"

"You're at home in bed having a dream."

Gabby curled against the seat.

"Sleep, sleep-"

"But I-I wanna wake up," she said. Gabby's body flopped with each step. "This is all wrong." Tears fell. "I want my mother."

Gabby fought to stay awake, but sleep won.

BOONE — SWAN HOUSE

Elena tore off her jacket, bolted up the steps, and burst through the front door. Her coat landed on the bench in the entry hall where she threw it. "Mama, where are you?"

"I'm here." Mina's hands shook.

Elena reached out and held them. "We will find her, Mama. I'll check with the college and see if they have any ideas." She disappeared down the hall toward the office.

Boone, with Ohto at his side, loitered in the entryway, observing the scene.

"Is that you, detective Anderson?"

"Yes," Boone said, stepping into the parlor. "The professor told me your daughter's missing. I called in an AMBER alert, and the authorities are looking for her."

"Thank you." Mina touched his arm, her eyes glistening. "I'm grateful to you, Detective Anderson."

"Call me Boone, Mrs Lukas."

"Thank you, Boone." She pointed to herself saying, "Mina."

He offered a reassuring smile.

"I reported her missing, but the police said I had to wait for a few more hours," Mina said. "They think she's with friends and lost track of time." Mina wrung her hands. "But something is wrong. I can sense it."

"We'll find her." The muscles in Boone's jaw tensed. "It's difficult but try not to worry."

Elena emerged with a business card in her hand. "I left a message with Alice at the college. Perhaps she can identify our mystery man."

Boone sat on a burgundy overstuffed couch. "Mina, sit down and tell me what your daughter's friends told you."

Ohto prepared to leap up next to Boone. "Don't even think about it," he said. "Lay down."

The dog circled and positioned himself on the rug. His ears swiveled following the conversation.

"I spoke to three more friends." Mina sat in the wingback chair by the fireplace. "They said the same thing." She templed her hands. "A few days ago, Gabby met someone new, but she's secretive about him. It isn't anyone from their high school. But she hinted he's from the college where her sister works. That's all."

"Have you searched her room?" Elena asked.

"No, but I guess we must," Mina said.

CHAPTER TWENTY-FIVE

ELENA - SWAN HOUSE

After completing their unsuccessful search, Mina, Elena and Boone gathered in the sitting room.

"Are the police looking for her?" asked Elena.

"The alert's out," Boone said. "All we can do is wait."

"We have to do something." A hint of panic surfaced in Mina's words.

"I've got a detective friend with the Olympia Police Department I can call," Boone said. "See if he can throw his weight around."

The cheerful ring of Elena's cell phone mocked the seriousness of their vigil.

She snatched it out of her pocket and checked the display. Her heart and shoulders sank.

"Who is it?" Mina leaned in to see the phone.

"It's the college." Elena accepted the call and put the phone against her ear.

"Hello, Alice, thanks for returning my call, and forgive me for not getting back to you on the DNA results. Today's been crazy."

"It's exciting but can wait. What do you need?"

"This is a real long shot, but I'm wondering if my younger sister has been on campus looking for me?"

"No one's asked for you. There aren't many folks around. Summer students won't come back for another week or two. But it is more like a week and five days-"

Elena cut her off. "That is all right, Alice. She's fifteen and missing, so we are looking into every possibility."

"Maybe I've seen her around campus, what does she look like?

By the tiled fireplace, Elena sat straight-backed in the rigid wooden chair. "She is a high school freshman and looks it. She is five foot six inches and weighs around one hundred and twenty-five pounds. Her hair is copper colored, straight, and hangs below her shoulders. She has blue-green eyes, and a telephone held to her nose."

"That could be my niece, but with short blonde hair. And she is shorter and weighs more. Come to think of it, they don't look alike at all except for the cell phone part. All the time texting, right? That kid will have carpal tunnel syndrome before she is out of high school. I have told her mother-"

"Have you seen anyone like that, Alice?" she shifted in the uncomfortable chair.

"Copper hair, blue eyes... This might be easier if I had a picture."

"Nevermind, Alice. I don't want to take the time to email you a picture. I appreciate your help but-"

"You don't have to send anywhere. You can just hand it to me. I'm standing on your porch."

Elena darted to the door.

Alice stood on the welcome mat, dressed in an emerald green shirt with "All Hail the Mighty Geoducks" printed on it.

Eyes averted, she continued to speak into the phone, "I was at Ralph's, well, not at exactly. I pulled into the parking lot when your call came in. I planned to get some chocolate because they have the best selection, and sometimes, I get a powerful craving for it. Not the too sweet American, but the European kind. Chocolate doesn't have to from there, just made the same-" Alice lifted her head. "Oh, hello."

"How did you know where I lived?" Elena shook her head. "Nevermind. Come in." She ushered the woman into the sitting room where the others waited. "Mama, this is my friend from the college. Could you get her a picture of Gabby?"

"Hi," said Alice.

"Hello," Mina said. "Excuse me while I fetch a picture." She left the room on her task.

Elena turned to Boone and said, "This is Sergeant Anderson from the Fish and Game Department, you worked on his DNA sample. He's providing his law enforcement expertise."

"We've spoken a few times," Alice smiled. "Nice to meet in person."

Boone extended his hand. "Thanks for your help on the case."

"Boone, what do you suggest we do now? I'm at a loss." Elena crossed to the carved marble mantlepiece. "Should we drive her route while my mother makes more calls?"

"It wouldn't hurt," he answered.

Elena turned to her colleague. "If you have the time, could you circle our neighborhood? After you've seen the picture, of course."

"Or, um-" said Alice

Boone faced Elena and said over the top of Alice's response, "We could check in with the state patrol again, but I'm not sure what more that would do."

"Or, ah-" Alice raised her hand.

Boone continued, "I'll call my buddy on the force to check for any similar incidents in the area."

They looked at each other, sad and serious.

"Or you could track her cell phone?"

All three heads snapped in Alice's direction. Her broad smile beamed back.

SETH — THE CAPITAL FOREST

The red sports car shot down an unlit forest road, kicking up gravel. With the city lights far behind, a million stars blazed in an obsidian black sky. The full moon, broken free from the horizon, peeked through the trees.

Their sharp turnoff was unmarked. But Seth knew the way and took the corner at speed, the wheels never losing contact with the pavement. The convertible bounced along the dirt road until it reached a dead-end and came to an abrupt stop.

Seth Capello glowered at the drugged girl. "So much power wasted. Don't worry, love, I will put you to better use."

She whimpered.

He leaned over, inhaling deep. *If I consume her life-force, I could maintain this form for four or five years. So tempting.* He lifted a hank of her red hair. *That's a short-term solution.* His nose wrinkled, and he dropped the strand. "Transformed, she'll make a beautiful and potent ally. We will hunt together for a millennium."

Gabby awoke and mumbled, "Am I home now?" She attempted to move but only managed a single twitch. *"Where are we?"* she slurred.

The car door opened, and he dragged her out, wrapped his arms around her waist, and with a rough jerk, threw Gabby over his shoulder.

She opened her eyes and tried to focus on his face. "Who? Are? I…" she mumbled.

"Go back to sleep," he barked.

Seth packed her through the woods to his ritual site and flung her aside like a sack of fertilizer.

Gabby tumbled into a pile of dirty rags. Her body sprawled limp as a dead animal.

He prodded her with his foot, and she didn't move. "Good," he said and removed the box cutter from his pocket.

A glittery pink logo and script emblazoned Gabby's oversized black sweatshirt. He cut it and the rest of her outer clothing off and flung them aside.

When the girl was trussed and ready, he removed his clothing. One by one, he carefully folded and stacked each item on a fallen log.

Nude, his muscled flesh glowed in the moonlight as he stretched. He strode to the girl, snatched up a blanket and small drum.

The ritual site was sizable. Two concentric circles of stones surrounded a fire pit. In the center, a log cabin configuration of willow branches protected a red-cedar teepee of kindling bound in twine.

He spread the blanket on the ground near an enormous willow basket. Sitting cross-legged, he positioned the drum between his knees. He thumped against the head of the drum and swayed in counterpoint to the beat.

Before long, the surrounding air vibrated, blurring his image like a lens, achieving and losing focus. His voice droned in a forgotten language, a guttural buzz peppered with clacks and wheezes. The song grew in volume and strength. He flung the drum aside, but the pulsing continued, rising from the bedrock.

He took up the basket and admired the contents. Gathered at precise times of day and season: fur, powdered otter skin, earthen pigments, and ground plants and flowers filled the clay pots in the basket. He selected a vessel, and color by color, drew a complex mandala of shapes and symbols. He continued the intonation, never ceasing until his song reached its climax and his mystical yantra diagram was complete.

The man leapt to his feet, arms outstretched to the sky.

"Full formed, I sprang from this soil before the time of men and beasts," he chanted. "I am this place, I am the Takakush. I call upon you, the divine spirit of pursuit. Accept the prey hunted in your name."

A violent air current swept through the clearing, and a spark ignited the stack of tinder. The glow brightened until, with a *whoosh*, the tent of twigs burst into flame.

Seth's — the Takakush's — body quivered and spasmed. A vulpine smile contorted his once handsome face, and he threw back his head.

A scream, like a cougar, cut through the trees. It came again and again. A wave of ebony fur sprang from his skin, covering his mutating body. His legs and arms elongated, and his nails lengthened into talons.

Gone was the educator, the man, and in his place hunkered the Takakush, the hunter.

ELENA — SWAN HOUSE

"Track her cell phone, how can we do that?" In the doorway, Mina froze with the framed picture of her youngest daughter in her hands.

"There are lots of ways, some legal and some not so," Alice said. "I'm not a hacker, but I have skills."

"I don't see how," Boone said.

Alice continued, "Legal methods require you to install some software on the phone you own or have someone accept a text on the phone you want to track. Too late for that now." Alice pushed her bangs out of her eyes. "But some brands of phones have tracking software installed already, and many cell phone providers have services that allow parents to track their children from a computer with internet access.

"It is easiest on the newer phones that have GPS."

Her hands rubbed together, and she licked her lips. "There are loads of privacy concerns and a million court cases against the government using it to track people. The American's Civil Liberties Union is in the middle of-" She rolled her eyes to the ceiling. "I guess we don't have time to talk about this right now."

"You're a lifesaver, Alice. This is a magnificent idea." Elena smiled at her friend. "Can you work with my mother to locate my sister's phone?"

"Okie dokie. Sure thing," Alice beamed.

"Boone, if you are still willing, we can get out there and drive her route. See if we can find any clues."

"All right, professor. I'm ready when you are." Boone slapped his thigh, calling Ohto.

"Does this work for you, Mama?" She threw her arms around Mina and pulled her close.

"I'm so glad you're here, honey." Mina broke the embrace first. "Don't worry, Alice and I will find her phone." Mina patted her daughter's hand, and in a quiet voice said, "And I will speak to your grandmother, see if she has any thoughts."

"Call us when you find something." Elena headed to the door. "You ready to hit the trail, cowboy?"

Boone, his smile wry, said, "Whatever you say, professor."

Ohto ran out ahead of Elena and Boone, but he pulled up short on the front walk. The hackles on his back raised, and he growled.

A large black cat perched about ten feet up a flowering cherry tree.

"Ohto, leave it." Boone dashed to the dog and grabbed his collar. "We don't have time for this, big guy. We have work to do." Ohto was reluctant to leave his quarry, but when he heard the word, "work," he looked up.

Boone let go of the harness. "Come on."

Elena opened the passenger side door. "Here, Ohto."

The dog loped to the truck. He vaulted inside.

Stepping up onto the running board, Elena slipped inside the cab and put on her seat belt.

Boone turned the key. The truck engine roared.

"We'll find your sister," he said.

"I hope so, Boone."

Despite the city street, the ride wasn't smooth. They passed Ralph's Market. The parking was full of shoppers.

"Can we head out toward the roller rink?" Elena leaned her forehead against the glass. In her eyes, every woman or girl they passed was Gabby. As she assessed each one, Elena's hopes rose and fell.

Two miles out, Elena's phone trilled to life.

"Mama?"

"No, it's Alice. We signed up on your carrier's website and located her phone. She isn't moving, or at least the phone is staying in one place."

"Where is she?" Elena asked. "They found her," she mouthed to Boone.

"She is about seven miles west of here. Looks like it's a massive wilderness area called the Ca—"

Elena completed the sentence, "Capitol Forest, dammit."

"I know the place, professor," Boone said, attempting to lighten the mood.

"I'll send GPS coordinates to your phone."

"Thanks, Alice, I can't tell you what your help means to my family. Can you tell my mother I'll call when we find Gabija?"

"Don't worry. I'll stay with her," Alice said. "Good luck."

"Thanks, goodbye."

"We better swing by my office, so I can pick up a weapon," Boone said.

Elena nodded. "I hope we don't need it."

Boone gunned the engine. They sped off into the dark.

GABBY - THE CAPITAL FOREST

A drumbeat pulsed through Gabby. She followed each blow like a bread crumb to consciousness until, at last, she opened her eyes.

Long gaunt trees hunkered around a clearing. At the center, a designed circle bounded a raging wood fire.

P-pop. P-pop. Embers escaped the flames, falling into the pit or drifting away with the wisps of smoke. Phantom shadows danced in the yellow light.

A harsh and guttural voice chanted.

Gabby attempted to stand, but zip-ties bound her hands and feet. Teeth chattering, she shivered. Her jeans and sweatshirt gone, only a thin muslin smock covered her panties and cami.

"What is going on? Where am I?" Awake now, anger pushed aside Gabby's fear. She struggled, battling against the bindings. "Let me go, or you'll be in massive trouble."

The song continued without pause.

She struggled against her bounds. "Let me loose, or I'll scream." Gabby let out the loudest, longest scream she'd ever produced.

Nothing.

Gabby's tear-streaked face blazed. "Help me. Help me," she screamed until her voice cracked, and she could only gasp for breath.

The drums ended, and the wind through the trees hushed her.

"No one can help you," the singer near the fire hissed. "There's no one here to listen, or care."

The incantations began once more.

CHAPTER TWENTY-SIX

GABBY - FOREST

Gabby struggled against her bounds but, so far, all she'd accomplished was rubbing her wrists raw and making them bleed.

Her cheeks hot and nose running, she sobbed, "Why are you doing this? Why won't you let me go?"

A figure, robed in a dark blanket, squatted by the fire. "You will be silent."

"I want to go home. Let me go," she cried. "Please, I'm begging you."

Gabby's captor rose, strode over, and backhanded her across the mouth.

She cried out, leaned away, and covered her head with her arm.

A blanket covered his body, and he'd pulled it over his head like a hood. A stylized animal mask obscured his face. Wooden and painted in bright primary colors, a snarling mouth displayed long sharp teeth.

"Let me go." Her voice shook. *Don't show fear. Be brave. Be brave.* "Who are you? Why am I tied up?"

"Very well, I will tell you." He squatted on the balls of his feet. "I am Takakush. At the beginning of time, this land bound my kind to it. We roamed this coast from here to the far north."

"I want to go home." A quick shallow breath escaped between each word.

"Your people think they can come to my territory and give me no offerings." He reached into a bag hanging at his waist and removed a small pot. "We tolerated the old ones. They showed respect. They told stories, sang songs, and carved our images. We took the offerings. But not your people. You are camp robber jays - thieves. Arrogant. Selfish. Careless."

"I don't understand?" Gabby struggled to free herself. "Ow. You're hurting me."

"You've hurt us, too. Every time your people butchered the great cedars and poured your waste into the rivers, lakes and sea, the land cried and died, taking one of my kind with it. I might be the last, and I've held the form of a man so long I barely remember who I am."

"What do you want from me? Why won't you let me go?" A sheen of sweat formed on her forehead, and her entire body trembled.

"It's simple. You have power." His finger dipped into the pot. A dark ointment covered it. "At first, I intended to draw your sister away and watch her blood and power flow. But then I found you." He knelt and painted figures on her face with the ointment. "I could have lured you to the river and drown you as a blood sacrifice. But I am not cruel, and nature must return to balance."

The ointment smelled strong and rancid. Her eyes burned. "No. Please."

"So, I have stolen you." He laughed and returned the ointment to his bag. "No one has tried a transformation in two hundred years." From a rawhide envelope, he poured yellow powder into his open hand. "I'm honoring you, fool, despite the insults of your

people. I will transform you. You will join my family."
He inhaled and blew.

It splattered on her face. All went dark.

MINA — SWAN HOUSE

"Mother, are you awake?" Mina cracked open Regana's door. The room was dark but for a nightlight by her shrine. "I brought you soup and a cup of hot tea."

The old woman coughed, and the bedside lamp blazed. Its light filling the dark bedroom.

"I wondered when you would come to me, daughter." Regana hadn't changed into her night dress but lay under the covers. The pendant at her neckline glowed darkly.

"I'm glad you're awake, Mother." Mina pushed the door open with her shoulder. "Something horrible has happened. Someone kidnaped Gabija and-"

Regana coughed again. "This I know." Her tired face forced a smile. "And I know your fear."

"I snatched a boy from the god of death," Mina said. "Now, I fear he took my child to punish me."

"Pfft." The old woman shook her head. "Not him. I would sense *him*. This is very dark and unknown to me."

"Did you see this coming?" Mina stepped inside, leaving the door ajar.

Regana pushed herself up on her elbow. "My deivė warn evil come, I watched, but I no see it."

Mina carried the tray over and placed it next to her mother on the quilted bedspread. "That's strange. I didn't sense him, either. Perhaps her abductor isn't a regular man but a magic wielder who can mask his power somehow."

"It no man. It monster, ancient and wily."

"Why would it want to take my daughter?" Mina

fluffed up the pillows and helped her mother sit up and lean back.

Regana patted her cheek saying, "*Ačiū dura.*"

"Prašome, Mother." She placed the tray on Regana's lap. "Will you eat something?"

Her hand shaking, the old woman lifted the soup spoon to her mouth and slurped. The aroma of homemade chicken noodle soup wafted from the bowl. The old lady smacked her lips, then tucked into her meal with enthusiasm.

Patient, Mina waited for her mother to finish. She asked again, "Motina, why did this creature take her?"

"What?" Regana lifted the cup with both hands and sipped her tea.

"Mother." Mina took a deep breath. "Why did it take your granddaughter?"

Thump. The cup slipped from Regana's hands but didn't spill. "The girl deivė power shine like a… like švyturys."

"I don't understand." Emotion choked Mina's voice.

"Gabija draw wolf to her light." Regana's hand beckoned. "Gabija is beehive of our sister, Austeja, and *he* is bear." She pushed the cup away. "It not eat her magija." Shaking her head, she corrected herself. "Her magic. I tired, this English. Jis nori ją transformuoti ir paversti ją meiluže.." She spoke the words at light speed.

"Mother, slow down, I don't remember most of these words." Mina furrowed her brow.

"Jūs pamiršote senus papročius," Regana mumbled and frowned as her eyes drifted closed. "You lost old way. Not good."

For a moment, she feared Regana had fallen asleep or retreated into the Penumbra. "Mother?" Mina touched her shoulder. "Are you all right?"

Shaking her head, she continued, "It scourge, not our line. It is Žemės vergas."

"A Genus Loci?" Mina asked, frowning. "A spirit protecting a place?"

Regana grunted in the affirmation.

"I think I understand now. We didn't sense it because it *belongs* here, and *we* are the foreign magic." Mina pushed the mug toward her mother. "Will it hurt her?"

"No, I think." She shook her head and put her withered hand over the cup. "Žemės vergas love her."

Bong. The wall clock chimed ten more times.

"All we can do now is wait," Mina said, checking her watch.

"I go see possibles, and I weave," Regana chuckled. "Leave me."

"Thank you, Mother." Mina picked up the tray and turned toward the door.

"Mediena and warrior maybe retrieve her, but who she be?" Her mother's laughter faded into a light snore.

Mina spun back. "What do you mean?"

Pale and wane, Regana lay flat on her back. Her hair spread across the pillow. But for the slight rising and falling of her chest, her body remained still. Regana's youthful smile revealed she wandered the Penumbra.

BOONE — ON THE ROAD

The truck sped down the one lane dirt road so fast that, every time they hit a bump or dip in the road, Elena flew off the seat. To steady herself, she gripped the strap above the door.

"You all right over there?" Boone asked.

"My backside is almost as sore as Gabby's will be when I find her."

Boone chuckled. "We should be close now."

This was a well-practiced exercise. The dog knew what to do. They'd circled the clearing, Ohto going right, and Boone left. The dog would hide and wait until Boone broke cover and charged.

An empty clearing, with an unattended fire burning low at its center. On the far side, a pile of blankets. No sign of the girl or her kidnapper.

At the nine o'clock position, Boone watched in silence. His patience paid off, a slight movement beneath the layers of cloth.

They began the silent sweep, and Boone completed his circle until he reached the blankets. Still hidden he whispered, "Miss Lukas, are you there?"

A low moan. The fabric moved again.

"I'm Detective Anderson from the Washington Department of Fish and Wildlife. Your mother and your sister sent me to find you."

Looking around the clearing and seeing no one, Boone broke cover and crept over, and Ohto joined him.

"Miss Lukas?" He pulled back the covers.

Beneath, he found a girl-sized cocoon, covered in a thick coat of crusty slime.

CHAPTER TWENTY-SEVEN

ELENA - THE CAPITOL FOREST

The only radio station Elena could find played in the cab. She'd hoped for a news report but located a country station, which faded in and out. Elena switched off the music. "It's only draining the battery," she muttered.

The full moon was high enough to fill the world with a cool blue radiance. She waited in the dark. Unease crept up on her like the cold.

The underbrush rustled.

"Boone's coming back." Elena's pulse quickened. *Has he found her?*

The undergrowth parted, and a two-point buck stepped onto the road. His nostrils flared. He searched for danger. Finding none, the black-tail browsed. Velvet covered his new antlers. He was magnificent.

Elena opened herself to the forest. From the Penumbra, she watched summer pass, and his horns dried and fell away in winter. In four years, he'd wear an impressive rack and sire many healthy fawns.

Elena wandered through his past, present, and future. When she returned to Real-Time, she was awake, fatigued, but smiling.

The buck's head lifted, a tuft of grass hanging from the corner of his mouth. Every muscle taut, he held still, his ears rotating.

Crack. A broken branch. Elena flinched.

The deer bounded into the forest.

In the truck, Elena held her breath and waited. Nothing arrived.

I can't wait alone in the dark all night. Her teeth chattered. *My God, it seems like he left a decade ago.*

How long has it been? She checked her mobile phone. Boone disappeared over an hour ago. *That's a long time.*

"Don't sit here, use the time," Elena sighed. "There's nothing to tell Mama, so that's out." She set her phone on the dash and studied the roadster. "Maybe her kidnapper left clues in the car. There might even be a registration in the glove compartment."

Elena slipped out the truck. Her down coat almost held the chilly spring air at bay. She hurried over to the other vehicle.

Elena went to the driver's side first. She flipped down the sun visor, checked the door pocket and under the seat. Nothing. Moving to the passenger's side, Elena leaned and opened the glove compartment. A folded sheaf of paper fluttered to the floor. "Come back here, you sucker." Raising to her toes, she stretched and reached for it. Her fingers touched the paper and-

A woman screamed.

Elena froze.

"What was that?" *An owl's screech or fox mating call?*

Another scream, longer and louder.

Her heartbeat stuttered. "That's not an animal. It's a woman," she said. "Gabby. Is that you?" she yelled.

Motionless and holding her breath, she waited for a response.

The unknown woman cried out again.

Every nerve grated. *That's Gabija, I know it.*

Rushing back, Elena snatched her phone and dialed Boone's number.

It rang - once, twice, three times.

"Answer your phone, damn it." Her words escaped in a wail.

Beep. The screen went black.

"What the hell?" Elena tried rebooting, but nothing happened. The battery was dead.

"Where's the darn charger?" She dug into the depths of the daypack. *Nothing.* Elena executed a frantic search of the cab: the glove compartment, center console, and under both seats. No charger.

Another scream. It was her name. Louder and from her right, not far.

"I can't leave, I gave my word." Elena grasped her head in her hands. *That's my baby sister. Frightened and hurt.* Elena rocked in her seat.

"No," Gabby screeched. "Help me."

There IS no choice. She tumbled out, leaving the door open. "I'm coming, baby," she shouted.

Without thinking, Elena dashed into the darkness, armed with determination and a five-inch flashlight.

TAKAKUSH — THE CAPITOL FOREST

From the forest, he watched Elena. When she crossed to his car, he knew it was time. *She's desperate and making mistakes.*

He called, and she responded.

The sister's fooled by my decoy call. Joy filled him. *Follow me into the forest, and I'll lead you to the water.*

For thousands of years, his kind used two ruses to trick men. First, appear as an attractive stranger like he'd done with the girl. That always worked. But he liked the other ploy better: imitate a woman's screams or a baby's cry, luring the prey into his trap.

Stupid. Foolish. Blind. He chuckled. *They always follow the cries of their young and vulnerable. So easy to kill when they're lost, isolated, and frightened.* His arms swung as he walked. *I'll draw her to the water's edge, hold her down, and gorge on her power until she joins her maker.*

Takakush licked his chops and screamed like a woman.

BOONE - THE CAPITOL FOREST

"What the hell is covering her skin?" Boone attempted to assess her condition. "Is it a disease? Is it contagious?"

I can't leave her here. Boone searched through the pile until he found a dirty blanket and wrapped her encrusted body in it. He tried not to touch the cocoon.

"Someone brought her here," Boone scanned the tree line. "Where'd they go?"

Gabby moaned, her body twisting inside her prison.

"We've got to get you to the hospital," Boone said. "I'll carry you." He lifted the shell into his arms.

Boone hiked down the darkened trail. Avoiding risk to the girl, each step was measured and cautious.

The return trip seemed shorter. Moments later, Boone and Ohto found their way back to the road.

"Elena, I found her." He raised his voice.

No movement.

"Elena?" His heartbeat raced. *She's on the seat, asleep.*

Holding Gabby in his arms, Boone rushed to the pickup. The cab was empty.

"Elena." *Where the hell are you?* His jaw tensed and he clenched his teeth.

Boone lifted Gabby's chrysalis into the truck bed.

"Don't worry, Miss Lukas," he said. "Rest. I'll be back."

Gabby didn't respond.

He scanned the perimeter, but the woman wasn't in the immediate area. *Damn, I asked you to stay here.*

Boone returned to the girl and looked for a place to check her pulse. The cocoon was hard now, but an outline of a figure was visible through the translucence. The flashlight's beam reached the girl inside, and she shifted.

"Hello," he said. "Are you all right in there?"

She twitched.

"Miss Lukas, lie still. I need to find your sister. Everything will be all right." *I hope.*

"Ohto, where is Elena?" he called. "Find her."

Karelians aren't natural scent-hounds, but Ohto was trained to track shotgun wads, wild animals, and lost people. Hearing his master, the dog's ears perked. He sniffed the area around the truck until he alerted. He'd found the scent.

"Okay, big guy," he said. "Let's go find our girl."

Ohto barked, dancing in place.

"Find her," he commanded.

Head down, nose to the ground, Otto ran.

"You better be alive, Elena, or I will kill you," muttered Boone as he took off after his dog.

ELENA - SUMMIT LAKE

"It's like chasing a frigging phantom," Elena said. One moment, she was far behind, then close, yet always out of reach.

To gain her bearing, Elena considered the stars, local topology, and surrounding flora. *I think I know where I am.*

She rushed through the trees until she smelled the earthy musk of decaying plants. Elena pushed through the bushes to discover she stood on the shore of Summit Lake.

The full moon reflected in the inky water, smooth as a slab of onyx.

A voice, like the wind, whispered, "Help. I'm lost."

Frantic, Elena's gaze scoured the shoreline.

Twenty yards down, Gabby, her missing sister, stood up to her waist in the lake. Her wet hair hung in long snaggles, partially covering her pale face. "Help me, Elena," she screamed.

Elena waded in. "Stay there, honey. I'm coming."

The cold leeched the warmth from her body and she sank deeper into the muck. When it reached her knees, Elena wondered if she could keep going. "I must," she said.

The water was up to Gabby's chin.

Elena's sodden clothing threatened to drag her under the surface.

"Elena," her sister screamed and slipped below the water.

Where did she go? "Oh, no, no-" Splashing, forcing her legs through the mud, the cold water pulling at her limbs, she struggled to reach the girl.

Elena dove beneath the water and opened her eyes. Surrounded in turbid midnight blue, she recognized movement, but nothing distinct. *Too dark to see.*

Her hair tugged. Elena jerked away, untangling it. Her head spun. *You're running low on air,* warned her tightening chest. *Oh, my God, I've lost the direction to the surface.* Her stomach rolled.

Rays of wavering moonlight penetrated the navy waters and above her head shone the underside reflection of the moon.

That way is up. She swam to it.

Elena broke through, caught a breath, and dove again.

Engulfed in the cobalt darkness, something brushed Elena's leg. *A fish?* She shivered and kicked her feet. Diving straight down, she touched the muddy bottom. *I'll never find her.* She rose.

Gasping, treading water, Elena caught a breath. She circled, seeking any sign of her sister. The darkness hid the bank. She knew it was far. A couple side-strokes drew her nearer, but it was still too deep to stand.

That must have been Gabby. She hyperventilated. *Why can't I find her?* Elena's muscles cramped, and rage filled her. *She is hiding from me, thinks it's a game. Wait, why am I so angry, and why aren't I cold anymore? Oh, no.*

"Hypothermia," she said, choking back water.

Hands grabbed Elena's ankles and pulled her down. No time to fill her lungs.

Arms flailing, she struggled, but her body continued descending. The death grip holding her never slacked. Deeper and deeper. Elena reached for her power, but she was too weak, and it slipped through her fingers.

Pain assaulted Elena, and her pounding head threatened to explode. As her brain consumed the last molecule of oxygen, the CO_2 in her bloodstream demanded, "Breathe."

Elena sucked water into her airway, filling her lungs. Her heart began beating irregularly, and her vision dimmed.

The forest goddess' power flowed away, and her body joined the night.

BOONE - SUMMIT LAKE

Trusting Ohto's lead, Boone followed Elena's trail. Someone gasped, and the water splashed. Boone halted.

"Elena," he called. Her name returned to him.

At the lake's edge, the calm flat surface reflected

the moon. Boone panned the shoreline and surface of the water with his flashlight.

"Elena."

She didn't answer.

Ohto charged up and down the shore, then stopped and barked at a log floating in the water. Boone focused the light on it.

Elena floated face down in Summit Lake.

"Come," he called. "Ohto, down. Stay."

Ohto whined, then complied.

Dropping the flashlight, Boone stripped off his jacket, flak vest, and rifle. Two long strides and he dove in. He reached her in three strokes. Boone threw his arm over her body and towed her to shore.

In the shallow water, he stood, and with one sweep, lifted her. Although the muck pulled at him, he strode toward the water's edge. Arriving at the bank, Boone put Elena on the grass and covered her with his dry coat.

"Stay with me, Elena," Boone said, checking her breathing and pulse. Nothing.

After clearing her airway, he flipped her on her back, tilted her head, and pinched her nose shut. His mouth on hers. Boone offered his breath twice and started chest compressions. His hands below her breastbone, he pushed down two inches. The cartilage in Elena's sternum cracked.

That's the spot. Boone continued the cycle. Thirty compressions and two breaths. Thirty compressions and two breaths.

Elena, you can't die. "Come on, baby, breathe," Boone whispered and felt for her pulse.

Thump th-thump. There it was, her heartbeat - faint but present.

"Thank God." Boone took a deep breath, closed his eyes. He continued the life-giving rhythm until a choking Elena pushed him back. She rolled to her side and hacked her lungs clear.

"Where is Gabby?" Elena gasped, and tried to sit. "Where is my sister?"

"I found her, she's safe in my truck." Boone helped Elena into his jacket. "Do me a favor, please. Lie down and just breathe for-"

The butt of the rifle struck the back of Boone's skull, and he never finished his sentence.

Gabby — the Truck-bed

Grandmother Regana stood over Gabby, speaking rapid Lithuanian.

"This is a weird dream." Gabby knew Elena's hunk had saved her, carried her out of the woods, and she was in his truck.

"What are you doing out here, Grammy?"

Her grandmother replied in her native language.

"Important? Urgent?" Gabby said. "I don't understand what you're saying?"

Frowning, the old woman stomped her foot.

"You're a pretty irritating delusion, Nana." Gabby rolled on her side. "Go away. I'm tired. I need to sleep."

Regana placed her hand on Gabby's forehead, and her thundering voice filled the girl's mind. "You take journey, Gabija. At the end, you lost."

"I don't feel so good. Take me home, Nana, please?" she said.

"I not help, not in his place." Regana wrinkled her nose and *tsked*. "Warrior and Mediena return. Say come home to me." She shook her index finger at Gabby. "Now, stay awake, this no simple. You fight."

Regana faded back into the Penumbra until no image remained.

BOONE — SUMMIT LAKE

Boone tumbled forward into the shallows but remained conscious.

Splash. His attacker threw the rifle out of reach.

The creature scooped up a kitten weak Elena and headed into the lake.

With a terrifying roar, Ohto lunged. Elena's assailant swatted him away like an irritating insect. The dog cried out in pain when he hit the ground.

Boone struggled to his feet and threw his body at them. Elena dropped into the water. His tormentor mule kicked him. Boone flew backwards, and the attacker fell on him. It squeezed the detective's throat.

A self-satisfied smile distorted its inhuman face. Sharp canines glinted in the moonlight.

Boone tried to push his attacker away, but he was getting weaker. A black vortex appeared, and stars circled before his eyes. Boone realized he'd soon reach his end.

The stranger let out an inhuman howl, released its grip, and a spray of blood covered Boone's face. Another scream, and the beast fell to the side into the water.

Over Boone stood Elena, holding Regana's copper knife.

DAY FIVE

SUNDAY

CHAPTER TWENTY-EIGHT

MINA - SWAN HOUSE

Shades of rose crept from the horizon. Wrapped in a knitted afghan, Mina sat on the porch swing. She'd been there all night.

At two this morning, Elena called. They'd found Gabby. This news brought little release. Her young daughter was hurt, and Elena couldn't explain. Mina waited.

The WDFW truck roared up the driveway.

Mina reached the vehicle before the engine died. She leaned into the truck bed, and her mouth dropped open. "Oh, my goddess," Mina wailed. "What is wrong with her?" She placed her hand on the hard shell.

"We don't know, Mama. I'm sorry, but we found her this way." Slamming the passenger door, Elena darted to her mother's side. "Boone, we need to get her downstairs."

"Are you sure? Shouldn't we take her to the hospital?" He left Ohto in the car and joined them.

"There is nothing the doctors can do. We have to get her to Grandmother," she said.

Boone offered a grim nod, leaned in, and lifted Gabby's chrysalis out as though it was made of glass.

Keys jangling, Mina darted ahead and unlocked the front door.

"Bring her this way." Elena ushered him to the ancient cage service elevator. She crowded in and pushed the button for the family quarters. The barred gate rattled closed, and moments later, their journey was complete.

The door opened. Bathed in firelight, Regana waited. Bronze embroidery on her dark velvet dress complimented the ornate head-dress and copper jewelry.

"*Gerai, gerai. Sekit mane debar.* Come now." Regana hobbled to the sheet-covered kitchen table. "Here." Regana pointed her long, crooked finger.

Boone lowered the girl. Mina removed a second sheet from the counter and, with Elena's help, covered the cocoon.

Regana moved to the head of the table and extended her hand to the others. "*Pasirengti ritualas mano vaikai.*"

Mina and Elena bowed from the waist and went about gathering the required items.

"What are you doing?" asked Boone, rubbing his forearm.

"Preparing for the ritual of restoration." Elena ran her hand through her hair. She smiled.

Mina removed four rough bee's wax candles from a drawer and placed them in small silver candle holders. "Boone, would you place these candles around Gabby's prison, like a cross?"

"I guess?" Awkwardly, he did as he was told, then asked, "Is that right?"

"Shush," Regana told Boone.

"I can-" He took a step to the stair.

"Warrior, be there." The old woman's eyes burned with anger and power and pointed to a place at the foot of the table.

"Yes, ma'am." He took another step toward the exit.

Fire burned at the hearth. Mina ignited a long taper in its flame. Mumbling under her breath, she lit the candles as Elena placed crystals, bundles of herbs and other small objects at each cardinal point.

"I should leave." Boone edged toward the stairwell.

"Warrior, stay but quiet," Regana said. She reached out her hands to the other women. "Come now."

Without a word, Boone took his place around the table.

Mina and Elena took their places across the table from one another. They each took one of Regana's hands and created the ritual circle by placing the other on the husk covering the girl.

"Aš esu Ragana, tamsios nakties šmėkla ilgo kelio pabaigoje. Gražink mūsų vaiką," she said. Her demanding voice filled the room with power.

Regana nodded to Mina.

"I am Žemyna, the rich and vital earth," she said. "I am the eternal nurturing mother, and I demand you leave my girl and return her to me. Leave this place, *now*."

Somehow Boone sensed power building in the room. *This is crazy. Words, candles, and a handful of rocks can't change anything.*

"You, now," Mina said. "Speak the words."

Elena cleared her throat, and after a brief pause, she said, "I am. I am."

"You must speak it," her mother pleaded.

"I am! Mediena, the virgin forest is my domain."

Although a tentative start, her declaration became strong and commanding. "I am the eternal hunt. I live in the claws and fangs of the predator and the divine blood sacrifice of the prey. I demand you leave this girl and *leave this place*."

Beneath their feet, a rumbling tremor built. The quake grew in intensity until the dishes in the cupboards rattled and the hanging light fixtures swayed.

Boone leaned forward and placed his palms on the tabletop to keep from falling.

The shell imprisoning Gabby vibrated and pulsed.

A fissure, thin as spider silk, formed, then another fracture, and another, until crazing covered the pod.

The buzzing reached a crescendo, and as if shot by a rifle, the chrysalis shattered. Shards flew in all directions.

Three generations of women stood around the girl on a table. The ritual finished.

Gabby opened her eyes. "Mama? Oh, Mama," she whispered, her throat raspy.

"Can you sit up, dear?"

"I think so."

The girl managed to make it to her feet. With her mother's help, Gabby got off the table and let Mina lead her away to rest.

Boone stared at Elena. "What the hell was all that?"

She raised her head to meet his gaze. "The world is larger than you've imagined." She shook her head. "And it'll never be the same."

"But-"

Elena cut him off, saying, "We'll talk more. Now, you need to clean up, eat, and then sleep."

MINA — SWAN HOUSE - LATER

"I've got a full house," Mina smiled. "The first of many, I hope."

At ten the previous night, the Stephens' returned to the inn and retired to the Odette suite. Alice waited with her until Boone and Elena called. It was very late, so Mina shuffled her off to the Wild Swan gigantic bed.

After the restoration, Elena and her detective retired to separate corners to clean up. Her daughter went to the carriage house, and it was the Black Swan guest room for him.

Downstairs, Regana watched over Gabby.

Mina trudged up the basement stairs. She longed to rest, but soon, her real guests would check out. *I've got to give them a good send off. The inn needs that good review.*

As she reached the main floor pantry, Mina heard Tobias Stephens descending the stairway.

"Mrs Lukas," he called.

"I'm here, Mr Stephens." She met him in the dining room. "Did you have a pleasant night?"

"Satisfactory." He handed her the key. "Mrs Stephens is loading our vehicle and will be in to settle the bill momentarily. Good day, Mrs Lukas." Stephens gave Mina a tidy nod, about faced, and strode out.

Mina sighed and returned to the sanctuary of her small office. In her comfortable office chair, she balanced on the edge of a dream.

A knock on the frame of the open office door woke her. There stood a smiling Cecily Stephens.

"Mrs Stephens, I hope you found your visit satisfactory as well?"

The woman bent her head and held out a check.

"Thank you, and we hope to see you again soon," Mina said and took it from her extended hand.

With a brisk nod, Cecily gave Mina an engraved envelope, then walked away.

Mina followed her to the front door. The little round woman paused on the porch. She opened her mouth.

A single word, like the croak of a bull frog. "Thanks."

Mina watched as Mrs Stephens opened the car door for her waiting husband, moved to the driver's side, and crawled inside.

"Goodbye and thanks for coming," Mina called as they drove down the drive.

When they were out of sight, Mina opened the envelope, removed the letter, and read it aloud.

"Congratulations, theshrewdtraveler.com awards Swan House a four-star rating."

Smiling, Mina folded the letter and put it in her pocket.

BOONE — THE BLACK SWAN

Snoring Ohto curled on a fuzzy rug by the four-poster bed.

Shower fresh, Boone admired his newest cuts and bruises in the mirror. "A few of these might join the permanent scar collection." He snorted.

Boone picked up his uniform pants. He sponged the dirt off with a washcloth.

When he gave up, Boone slipped into his trousers. The torn and bloody work shirt hung on the chair where he'd tossed it. He hesitated, then shook his head. "I'll put that filthy thing on last."

Sitting on the edge of the bed, he slipped into his boots.

A quiet knock.

"Come in," he said, standing.

"I thought you might need a clean shirt," Elena pushed open the door.

Boone met her in the center of the room. "Are you a fortune teller, too?" he asked, smirking.

"No, my grandmother has the franchise on that one."

Boone took the faded denim work shirt. "About today?" he began.

Holding out her palm, she said, "Boone, my life, my world is... complicated. You're not ready to hear about it now, and I'm not ready to try to tell you. Give it a few days, okay?"

"I guess," Boone said, his reluctance apparent. "But–"

"Where we're from there is a proverb: 'let us turn this page down for now,'" she quoted. "Finish cleaning up, and perhaps my mother will cook you a scrumptious breakfast."

He turned to the bathroom. Elena recognized the familiar scars marring his muscled back. Her heart fluttering, she hurried from the room. Ohto galloped after her.

MINA, ELENA AND BOONE — ENTRY HALL

Boone descended the stairs to the foyer. Mina and Elena, deep in conversation, hushed when they saw him.

"Thank you for your hospitality, Mrs Lukas."

"Boone, I can never thank you enough for helping us find my daughter." Mina's voice held all her warmth for the young detective. "Come. You must let me make you breakfast at least."

"There's no need for you to feed me, and honestly, I don't have the time. I have an avalanche of 'after reports' to file."

"A rain check then?"

"Certainly," Boone smiled. "I hope Gabby will be well soon. Goodbye." Boone turned to Elena. "I will talk to you later."

"I look forward to it." Elena covered her smile with her hand.

Boone turned the knob and pulled the French doors open. Ohto pushed him out of the way and escaped, snarling and barking.

All three raced out behind the dog.

Ohto chased a big black cat down the walkway.

"Leave it. Leave it," Boone shouted.

With a burst of speed, the dog grasped the cat by the neck, and they rolled end over end.

As they tumbled, the cat changed shape. Its black fur transformed into green scales, and wings sprouted from his back. The tom disappeared, and in its place, a small dragon hissed and spat.

"What the hell?" Boone said.

Shocked, Ohto lost his grip on the creature's neck, and it flew into a tree at the corner of the yard.

"What is it, Mama?" asked Elena.

"Oh my, it's an Aitvaras," Mina said. "I haven't seen one in-" She glanced at Boone and cleared her throat. "A very long time."

"They're from the old country, aren't they?" Elena stepped to the banister.

The dog growled and circled the tree, his attention never leaving the creature.

"They're common in the Balkans. I've never heard of one here." Her hands clasped together. "This explains a lot, you know. The old folks say the Aitvaras bring good fortune by ill means. Most boons, stolen from neighbors, lead to misunderstanding and violence."

The dragon flapped its wings and screeched.

"How do we get rid of it?" Elena asked.

"I'm not sure we can. There's no doubt it's a trickster, but they're household guardian spirits, too. This creature appeared to Gabija and might become her pranašas. It makes sense. Varnas came to you around your fourteenth birthday."

"What should we do now? Invite it to stay?"

Mina placed her hand over her mouth and sighed. She addressed the dragon with a bow. "Aitvaras, you're welcome in our home. Bring us happiness, wealth, and abundance. Harm no one."

High in the branches, he bowed his head, and with a flare of light, transformed into a glossy black rooster with a tail of fire.

The morning sun cleared the horizon, and Trouble threw back his head and crowed.

"The neighbors will love that," Mina said. "Children, I am off to bed."

"Kuk-ko-kie-kuu," crowed the Aitvaras.

She shook her finger at the bird. "And you, no more stealing." She blew them a kiss and retreated inside Swan House.

Boone shook his head. He came to stand beside Elena. "Things keep getting weirder and weirder around here." He placed his hand on hers. "My lady, unless you need me to slay yon dragon, I'll be off, too."

"Boone, I don't think we-" A pained look crossed her face.

"Then we won't." Boone pulled her into his arms and kissed her. His hand slid to the small of her back, and he pulled her body into his. Passion boiled under a veneer of gentleness and threatened to break free.

Their lips and bodies parted, eyes locking. The barriers between them dropped. Boone inhaled and caught the aroma of pine and mountain wildflowers. Sunlight, escaping the heavy clouds, lightened. *I could lose myself right here.* "I've got to go," he whispered, his voice husky.

"I know," Elena smiled. "Bye."

Heading to the truck, Boone snapped his fingers. "Come on, old man."

"*Woof, woof, woof.*" Ohto ignored him and stood with his front paws on the tree trunk, stretching and jumping toward the bird.

"Get over here. Leave the whatsit alone, and let's go home."

Ohto dropped to all fours and hung his head. He sauntered to the open truck door.

"Up," Boone commanded.

The dog jumped, settling on the passenger seat.

Boone slipped behind the wheel, then whispered, "Maybe you'll catch it next time." He patted Ohto's hindquarters, and the dog's tail wagged.

The engine roared to life. He drove down the driveway, and Boone watched Elena in the rearview mirror.

The End.

MISSING PROFESSOR'S CAR FOUND ABANDONED

Olympia, Wash. (AP) — Authorities have located the vehicle belonging to a missing Rainforest University instructor.

Professor Seth Capello, a popular member of the anthropology faculty, was reported missing when he failed to appear at the beginning of Summer Quarter.

Hikers found the missing man's vintage Alfa Romeo Spider a few miles off Summit Lake Shore Road. A search of the surrounding area produced no clues to Capello's whereabouts.

Anyone with information should contact the sheriff's office at 360-555-2500, reference case number 22F08616.

GENUS MAGIC

BOOK TWO

COLONY COLLAPSE
PREVIEW

E mily Brown watched a yellow raft shoot the rapids and disappear under the bridge. *Funny. I bet it's not that cold in that water.* Elbows on the railing, she held her head in her hands.

If you lean far enough you can find out.

This was the third time today that quiet voice in her head urged her to take reckless action. On the way home from school, he urged her to dart out into traffic, and later reminded that her sharp objects cut flesh the same as paper.

It's the strangest thing. Until this morning, Emily never thought of harming herself. Now, a spider perched on her shoulder and whispered in her ear. *Ssssp ssp spus.*

I wonder if mother will buy a new dress to bury me in or use my old prom dress. She made a face. A white dress is best, but a bridal gown is better. Tons of net and lace, frothy like the river.

Emily rose to her tiptoes and leaned over the railing until her upper body extended into the canyon, and her arms reached out to embrace the river.

"Rock forward," hissed the spider in her mind. "Farther, farther. In a moment, it's over."

"Yes," whispered Emily.

"Do you choose this fate?" the spider asked.

"This is my idea. It is what I want, and soon, it will be me and the silence. I take my destiny in my own hands."

"You. Hey, kid. What are you doing? Get down from there." A man's feet beat against the pavement. He rushed toward her.

"Don't listen to him," the spider hissed. "He is nothing. Can you feel the river calling you?"

"I hear it," the girl said. "It's singing a lullaby." Her feet lifted from the ground.

Sinister black clouds crowded overhead, and raindrops pattered on the pavement. *Splat.* Then another. *Splat. Splat.*

"Get down." The man gasped for breath as his feet pounded the pavement.

A rumble of thunder preceded a torrent of raindrops, soaking the girl's light summer clothing and her would-be rescuer's uniform.

Emily Amanda Brown slipped over the lip of the barrier. Pointing her toes and arching her back, she plummeted into the Skokomish River.

Officer Mendoza collided with the barrier. He grasped for the woman but was a moment too late. She slid from his grasp as he felt the velvet of her skin.

"Shit," he spat. Breathing heavily, he croaked into the radio, "Conservation Officer Mendoza, four-one-three, at High Steel Bridge. There's been another jumper. Female, mid-teens to early twenties, wearing a flowered blouse and jeans." He leaned over the edge, scanning the water. "Low probability of survival. We need a recovery team. STAT."

The radio crackled, and after a brief pause, said, "Sergeant Anderson will coordinate the response. He's on his way and will meet you below the bridge."

"Acknowledged, Dispatch."

"Any note or ID?" asked the woman on the radio.

"Nope. I'll check the parking lot, see if I can locate her vehicle. It'll take a while. We got a lot of hikers out here today, so I'm not optimistic. If I can't find an owner, I'll call in license plate numbers until I find her. Mendoza out."

The dispatcher responded, but he'd stopped listening.

Beads of water rolled down the young officer's broad face and into his eyes. He blotted his forehead with his sleeve and scanned the area, then searched for a note in the jumper's belongings.

Nothing.

A wave of sorrow crashed over officer Mendoza. Recovering drowning victims was the only part of the job he disliked. Young people with a bright future and happy life ahead of them shouldn't get drunk and fall overboard or dive off bridges due to broken hearts or melancholy.

An image of his first love filled his mind.

She stood you up at the junior prom. You wore those thick glasses, an ill-fitting tux, and a cereal bowl haircut. Held that stupid corsage in your hand in front of the high school gymnasium all evening. Everyone laughed at you.

She flipped back that beautiful long blonde hair. "Did you really believe I would go anywhere with a loser like you?" She laughed and laughed.

"She was right," whispered the spider. "You are a loser. You let that girl jump. She needed you, and you let her down."

Coming to Amazon in 2021

You can support partnerships like Ohto and Boone to protect wildlife and wild places.

Contribute to:

The Washington Department of Fish and Wildlife's Karelian Bear Dog program, a budget-neutral state program, 100% funded by private donation. Support the mission of these hardworking dogs.

To learn more, go to: **https://wdfw.wa.gov/about/enforcement/KBD**

The Wind River Bear Institute's Sponsor a K-9 Program. WRBI's mission is to reduce human-caused bear mortality through training and education.

To learn more, go to:
http://beardogs.org/about-us/#ourdogs

Working Dogs for Conservation, trains conservation detection dogs and puts them to work protecting wildlife and wild places.

To learn more, go to:
https://wd4c.org

Or, contact your local state, provincial or governmental conservation organization. And ask if they

have a wildlife K-9 program and how you can contribute.

*This book's author and publisher are not affiliated with
these or any other organizations and not compensated for
mentioning them in this book.*

ABOUT THE AUTHOR

Raine Reiter is an emerging author of northwest gothic and paranormal suspense. Takakush is Raine's first book in the Genus Magica Series. Colony Collapse - Genus Magica Book 2 is set for release in 2021.

A fourth generation Washingtonian, Raines wanders the wilds of the Olympic Peninsula with her silly dog, Luke.

Follow Raine on Facebook, Twitter, Pinterest and www.twanohpress.com.

CPSIA information can be obtained at www.ICGtesting.com
Printed in the USA
BVHW040104260121
598620BV00004B/11

9 781735 685007